# LITTLE UGLY TRUTHS

LACHLAN PARK TRILOGY

## CASSIDY COLE

Cover Design: Cassidy Cole

Editing & Proofreading: Lunar Rose

Print ISBN: 979-8-9914281-2-5

Ebook ISBN: 979-8-9914281-3-2

# ALSO BY CASSIDY COLE

**Lindenvale Brothers Series**

*The House on Lindenvale Hill*

**Lachlan Park Trilogy**

*Little Ugly Truths*

*For my husband,*
*my greatest muse and the love of my life.*

*For those who find beauty in broken things.*
*Some things are worth saving.*
*And in return, they might save you.*

# AUTHOR NOTE & CONTENT WARNING

Dear Reader,

*Little Ugly Truths* is the first book in the Lachlan Park Trilogy, and it does end on a cliffhanger.

This book explores dark and potentially triggering themes, including extreme violence, captivity, explicit sexual situations, knife play, descriptions of domestic violence, descriptions of blood play, alcohol, emotional manipulation (off page), trauma, and more. Please visit www.cassidycoleauthor.com for the full list of trigger warnings.

If any of these may be triggering for you, please take them into consideration before choosing to read this book.

**Your well-being and mental health come first.**

XOXO,
Cassidy

# ONE | KATE

If you asked me a year ago what I thought my life would look like, I wouldn't have guessed I'd be saying, "Please keep your hands, arms, legs, and feet inside the ride at all times," to a young teenage couple already lip-locked and tongue-heavy in a ride cart.

It may be protocol to relay the information for safety purposes, but to them, and most people who stand in that line, I'm invisible. Which is ironic considering that's precisely what I'm going for. However, their blatant neglect of me doesn't make me feel any better either.

This reality is far from the life I envisioned. The life I worked for. But I only have myself to blame for ending up here, working at a goddamn amusement park on the coast of Maine.

It's less than ideal, but it's safe.

Secluded.

Under the radar.

It may be one of those small tourist towns that lure in families for a quiet vacation every summer, but it's the first place I landed where I didn't feel like the air was tangling around my neck like a noose. Maybe I had run far enough to snap the tether that had me in a constant state of paranoia despite the distance I created.

All the other places I stopped before Lachlan Harbor—and there were many—I cautiously scanned and analyzed my surroundings. Examined every person's face and frame. Inspected the shadows. Peered over my shoulder for any evidence of the parasite that had somehow embedded a piece of itself in my bones, paralyzing me from the inside out with a fear I've never been able to escape.

The fear may be muted now to a dull, distant hum that stirs more in my dreams, but it doesn't entirely dissipate the feeling that eyes are following my every move.

It's my imagination. It has to be.

That, or I've been doing this so long that I'm starting to have a psychotic break.

As I said, I never thought I'd end up working at a place like this, and maybe that's part of my problem.

Lachlan Park sits at the edge of town, tucked into the forest's edge and along the rocky shoreline. It's a short walk to the harbor where commercial fishing boats bring their shipments in and out. The air is always bursting with the scent of fried food, yet it carries a familiar tang of sweat that clings to your nose. Then, the briny sea air off the coastal waters, which stretches out for miles, stirs the potent combination into a uniquely unforgettable scent that somehow permeates all of Lachlan Harbor, as if the park is its very essence.

For now, it's my haven.

A loud pop splits through my daze, making me jolt. I turn around to see Nicole, my coworker, chewing on her gum obnoxiously like she always does this time of day. It's a sign she's bored. Somehow, I hold my eyes back from rolling like they want to.

Her head slants slightly in deliberation, her features pulled together in that way that tells me she's scheming. "Hey, Kate. I bet you ten bucks that they'll keep making out when they hit the backward track." Nicole blows another pink bubble, sinking her teeth into it before she follows it up with a wicked smile. "Or should we make it fifteen?" Her focus drops from me to the camera footage of the ride, displayed on the monitors in front of her.

Now my eyes roll.

That's an hour of my pay. No, thank you.

I'm not in a position to be throwing away money like that when I can barely afford my studio. I shouldn't entertain her. However, I have a keen talent for reading people and have been working here long enough to understand the behaviors of our guests.

I really shouldn't...

Yet, I have a high probability of walking out fifteen dollars richer.

And when I say *working here long enough*, I mean four months.

Which may not seem like a lot, but to me it is.

I watch the track carry the young couple's mine cart into the cave entrance. The dark tunnel swallows them whole, taking them to the belly of the ride.

I contemplate for a second before giving in. "Let's make it fifteen, and cleanup duty. Because I bet you that in the next five minutes, one of them is going to get motion sickness."

Nicole narrows her eyes, regarding me. It only takes a moment before she excitedly claps her hands together. "You're on. I had my fair share of make-out sessions back in the day. I would come here on dates whenever I could get away from my parents. So, I should know that they are bound to keep this up the entire ride."

Back in the day? It was more like a few weeks ago, since she literally just turned eighteen.

I swallow the groan wanting to escape my chest.

Yep, this is my life now. A twenty-four-year-old runaway who traded a full-time nursing job with a steady paycheck, benefits, and a 401(k) for a position working the haunted mine ride at an amusement park that has been here since the 1930s. Of course, it's been updated with new rides, booths, and restaurants since then, but there are some stains and scars from the past that years can't erase.

So, for now, I'll remind myself that working this minimum wage job with a bunch of teenagers is less painful than the hell I endured before I was shaken out of the poisonous fog that kept me submissive and voiceless for far too long.

I guess I can't forget about Vincent, the mid-to-late sixties cleaner whose tattoos and permanent scowl are older than any of us.

Not that I've carried on any conversations with the man or watched him clean, for that matter. There's an aura about him that chills my skin and keeps me on high alert when he's nearby. I know it's rude, but I usually rush away when I see him. However, our paths often cross, especially after my evening shifts when he's starting his.

Sure, there are all the other employees at Lachlan Park, but this is the job they hired me for. I *should* be friendly, but I don't enjoy spending more time here than is absolutely necessary. To further my case, that would mean wandering around to all the other booths and rides, or engaging in small talk after staff meetings.

Plus, this place could be temporary, and making friends seems pointless.

I'm not foolish enough to hope that this could eventually be my home.

As long as I'm running, nowhere is.

At least not in the way the Pacific Northwest was.

I traded one coast for another, hoping that it might feel similar, though it's a whole country away.

Lachlan Harbor is approximately an hour's drive from Portland, Maine, which is why it is a popular summer destination for Maine residents who want to escape without being too far from home. For being a place where tourists flood, it still feels quaint and quiet, giving you enough space to breathe and not feel like a sardine jammed in a tin can.

I lived in Portland, Oregon, before, but I'm starting to realize that even though it lacks the rugged mountains and babbling creeks of the West Coast, I might be turning into a small-town girl—and not just because it means fewer people to train my eye on and observe, like everyone is out to hurt me.

There was just something about it when I stepped off the bus. A comfort in the air settled in my lungs, giving me my first real breath, along with clarity that had eluded me everywhere else. It felt like the ideal place to barely penetrate the ground with some roots and plant myself in a place that appears off the map.

Nicole slaps a hand over her mouth, bursting into a fit of giggles. "The headless miner just popped out. It scared him so bad that he could've bitten her tongue off!"

Spinning around, I ignore her, helping a mom and her young daughter onto an empty cart that slows beside the loading platform. The mom gives me a kind, thankful smile that has warmth circulating through my veins, despite the cave-like interior. Imitation stone walls enclose the space, stalactites and stalagmites lifting from the floor and dropping from the ceiling to enhance the illusion. Whoever created this place went to great lengths to marble an opaque, gold-looking substance into the rock, using lights behind to make it appear as if it were shining. The soft, themed music accompanies the soothing crackle of water trickling down into a pool of water on the other side of the track from the loading area.

I used to love the musty smell of damp earth, but now I've grown so accustomed to it that it no longer hits me as strongly as it once did.

The excitement is palpable in her tone as she watches the security footage. "*Oooh, we're coming up on the backwards track.*"

This part of the ride is a guest favorite. It's where the surround sound and projection on the rock wall make it look like there's a cave in. Then the cart shoots backward to give more thrill to the experience.

I give the mom and daughter the same spiel as always and send them on their way, right before Nicole curses under her breath behind me from the control panel.

My smile is instant. I'm fifteen dollars richer and have one less mess to clean today.

Nicole makes her annoyance with me clear as day when she groans so loudly that it nearly echoes off the faux cavernous walls.

And since the line is all caught up for now, I walk over to her. "Who was it?"

"It was her—she threw up over the side. Dammit!" She anxiously pulls her fingers through her long, bleached blonde hair. "How did you know she was going to do that?"

Maybe it's because I'm an eavesdropper and overheard her telling her boyfriend while they were waiting in line that she felt nauseous after the rollercoaster. The brief time I studied her, I noticed her pale features and the way she had her arms wrapped around her stomach before I loaded them into their cart. Motion blended with distraction never bodes well for most people, especially when the queasiness is already stirring below the surface.

Being perceptive has its perks.

I wish I could have learned to sharpen my awareness in a different way, rather than from a man who trained my ears as much as my body.

But I don't tell her how I knew she would get sick on the ride. Instead, I shrug and mutter, "Just a lucky guess."

Now that I'm right, it means I don't have to stay an extra twenty minutes and clean up the mess. And as if my replacement heard me talking about him, Jeremy waltzes out of the employee area and joins us to take over the next part of the shift.

He stops beside Nicole, peering at her face with an inquisitive expression twisting his mouth. "What's your problem?"

Her side-eye glower could burn him alive. It's so terrifying that I contemplate stepping back. She pushes herself out of the chair to a standing position, smoothing out the dark gray overalls dusted with permanent dirt stains. We are required to wear them as part of our uniform to "sell" the ride more effectively. "I've got a mess to go clean up."

"You lost a bet again?" he snickers, looking a little too amused. The three of us partner on shifts the most, so he knows how much Nicole enjoys making our workdays a little more interesting.

Most of the time, it backfires—on her.

She slaps his bicep. "Shut up." Her weighted sigh has me suppressing my grin. "I'll be back in a few minutes."

His mouth quirks. "Don't let the ghosts get you."

I blow out a breath, containing a hint of a chuckle. "You guys are ridiculous. Those ghosts aren't even that scary." Unless you're terrified of plastic mechanical mannequins lit up with a projector.

Jeremy's brows draw together, but there's mischief hidden between the creases and flickering in his eyes. "I'm not talking about *those.*"

I tuck a loose strand of dark blonde hair behind my ear,

folding my arms over my chest. "Ha. Ha. Nice try. You forget that I'm older than you and less gullible."

Jeremy and Nicole hold my gaze, both with smiles on their faces that should be playful but seem eerie under the circumstances.

Jeremy's manic laugh sends chills down my spine. "You don't know the real story about Lachlan Park, do you?"

# TWO | KATE

I'm not gullible.

I'm not.

But I also believe in gut instincts, and mine is one hundred percent telling me that they aren't bull shitting me. Jeremy's words toxically churn in my stomach.

*"You don't know the real story about Lachlan Park, do you?"*

I stare at Jeremy curiously, waiting for him to divulge the information that's sitting eagerly on his tongue as he studies my expression.

I'm not scared of a little ghost story.

There's only one thing that terrifies me, and I'm hoping he's thousands of miles away and not tracking my scent like a shark trailing its prey's blood drifting through dark waters.

We work at an amusement park. Which I assume means that since this place is over ninety years old, there were some deaths back in the day from poorly constructed rides, and those unfortunate souls haunt the park.

That's what I expect him to say.

What I'm not anticipating coming out of his mouth is, "Have you ever heard of The Evisceration Cellar?"

Evisceration...as in the harvesting and removal of organs?

The low thrumming of my heartbeat fills my ears, competing with the awful music we have on repeat for the ride. My chest rises and falls a little heavier now. Why am I breathing faster?

I gulp down the unanticipated nerves prickling my throat. "No."

The smirk on Nicole's face irritates me more than it should. I'm going to be extremely pissed off if they are messing with me. I'm the most recent hire to work with them; there was bound to be some joking and humiliation at some point. If this is light hazing, I damn well don't appreciate it.

My already fragile psyche doesn't have the capacity to deal with this, too.

Nicole's petite frame can't conceal her excitement. She's bouncing with eagerness. "Have you ever stopped to listen after you close down the ride and turn off the audio at the end of your shift?"

My eyes bounce between them inquisitively.

"Like really listen," Jeremy adds for extra measure. "Sometimes you can hear muted screams that seep through walls."

"This is an amusement park," I remind them, annoyed. "People scream on rides all the time."

He shakes his head leisurely in a way that appears mechanical. "They're faint. More like roars from pain and torture. They can be almost unrecognizable unless you know what you're listening for—"

"Get on with it already!" My sudden outburst makes him grin wider.

"Okay, okay. I didn't learn about it until my second summer working here. Do you at least know about the massacres?"

God. So much for getting out of here on time.

I should leave. I really should.

I may regret it later, but instead, I shake my head.

Nicole is listening as intently as I am, though I know she already knows where this is going.

"Wow, you know nothing," he sighs, running a hand over his jaw in exasperation. If it's that much of a hassle to tell me, then he should just let me go home. But for some reason, my feet are firmly planted on the concrete floor, and I'm a little more interested in this story than I wish I were. "Guess it's not surprising since you haven't been working here long. Three massacres happened in the park."

That catches me off guard. Three? It seems excessive, considering this park is still as popular as it is.

"One in the 1950s, another in the 1980s, and the most recent one was about five years ago. The one that happened five years ago was the biggest. Twelve people were shot in the middle of the night, where the old rollercoaster was at the edge of the park before it was rebuilt. The other murders before that were one or two people in the middle of the night when the park was closed." He inhales, shaking his head like he's trying to add to the horrifying factor of this story.

That's what this is—a story.

Jeremy continues. "There are rumors that someone witnessed what happened during the massacre five years ago. They watched as their bloody bodies were dragged off through the night to one of the nearby buildings. The incident was reported to local authorities, but by the time they arrived, the park was spotless. Not a trace of blood left behind."

Nicole joins in now, "The next day, multiple workers came forward saying they heard disturbing screams coming from somewhere nearby. But when they checked it out, the sounds weren't coming from anywhere around them. It wasn't until they listened more closely and followed the noises that they realized it was coming from the air vents. They were being tortured."

My brows pull together. Despite my best effort, my voice shakes. "They?"

"Some of those people were still alive when someone dragged them off," Jeremy clarifies.

The gears in my head are running on overdrive. I swear, Jeremy and Nicole are waiting for the moment when they finally burn out and smoke starts billowing out of my ears before they yell, "Just kidding!"

But they don't. I analyze their body language, and the seriousness there is unsettling.

The pieces start clicking into place. "You said people call it The Evisceration Cellar." My face contorts into disgust. "Is there a conspiracy theory that they were removing the organs of those people who were shot?"

Jeremy's lips twitch as he nods.

I blow out a raspberry. "You guys are so full of shit."

His hands rise in front of him, palms facing me as if I offended him. "Hey, I didn't come up with the story."

"There's no way that someone is doing that under the park. Or *was* doing that." My argument feels weak somehow.

*But people can be disguised as monsters, Kate.*

*Don't forget that and let your guard down.*

I don't want to believe it.

It's preposterous.

Eccentric and immoral in ways that knot my own organs into balls I'll never untangle, just pondering the visuals of it all.

And I was a nurse.

My stomach can handle a lot, but this is another level that will make me physically ill if I think too much about it, since exposure to a blade while being cognizant is something I'm familiar with and wish I weren't.

I can tell myself that it's implausible all I want to. Still, it doesn't calm the hungry, curious part that wants to dive deeper into the theory—the history of a place that appears joyful on the surface but may be concealing something darker beneath.

"It's said that they are still trapped under the park and that you can hear their souls crying out for help if you listen closely enough. I've heard them." I don't like the way Jeremy says that arrogantly, like he should win a trophy for having the ears of a damn bat.

"That's it?" I say. "That's the story?"

"Mostly." Nicole picks at her pink, neon nail polish, a tell-tale sign she's procrastinating because she doesn't want to clean the floor. It's not my fault she wanted to make a bet and lost. "But some people still think there's a secret floor underneath the park that is being used for organ trafficking for the black market."

A giggle bubbles out of my throat. Yeah. Sure. I move toward the door that Jeremy came out of, which leads to the break room at the back of the large building we share with a few other restaurants and storefronts. "All right, I've had enough of this."

"We're not joking with you, Kate. It's true," she pushes. "You should ask Vincent about it the next time you see him. He's been here longer than any of us and was working here in the 80s, and when those twelve people were shot and disappeared five years ago."

My nose wrinkles. Nothing against Vincent, but he's ominous. My pulse accelerates whenever I see him for some reason, and I'm not sure why. Sure, I have exchanged some one-word greetings with the man, but there's something off about him that puts me on edge and makes me want to avoid elongating my interactions.

"You've talked to him about it?" I ask.

Nicole's shudder is a little exaggerated if you ask me. "Hell no. He gives me the creeps."

She's not wrong. Those hard, gunmetal eyes set under

bushy brows contain a world of stories that I'm not sure I want to hear. Most people avoid him for a reason, and I just suspect I should, too. But it doesn't stop me from giving him a gentle wave when I'm leaving after my shift, and he comes to clean. I'm not a total bitch.

"Thanks for the remarkably believable ghost story," I deadpan, pointing at the door, "but I think I'm going to head out." I cluck my tongue. "I'll see you guys tomorrow."

I register their whispering voices behind my back as I push past the door and walk to the break room to gather my things from my locker.

When I enter the small space, it's still. Quiet compared to the thoughts creating discord in my head.

I won't entertain the idea.

That thought lasts about two seconds before I inhale a deep breath. My eyes flutter closed, my ears adjusting to sense every sound that reaches me.

I tell myself it's not true.

However, it still doesn't stop me from wondering if a world exists beneath my shoes. A hidden place harboring an evil that will fuel my already bone-chilling nightmares the moment sleep drags me under.

# THREE | PRESTON

The pounding of my fists against the bag is controlled. Precise. Impeccably matching the drumming of my pulse in my ears.

It satisfies me knowing that, although there may be a goddamn war raging in my head, I can keep myself collected under pressure. Nothing makes a man more vulnerable than disregarding your boundaries to submit to your rage. Allowing your anger to take control causes you to lose sight of your objective, and I can't afford to slip into those depths. If I do, I'll never pull myself out.

It took me years the last time.

The rage poisoned me.

Altered my being until I shifted into a monster that crawled out of my flesh with the determination to gnash and tear a vile man apart with my teeth. I wanted to relish in what it would feel like to rip his organs through his esophagus and make a noose out of his intestines to rob him of breath.

That vision of him blanked my vision and weakened my resolve to be patient.

But over the years, I've learned that revenge isn't impulsive.

It's planned.

Executed with as much precision as my fists smashing into the bag in time with my dead, but somehow still beating heart.

The truth is brutal. Patient or not, nothing I do will bring *them* back.

It wouldn't fill our home with laughter. It wouldn't inject the lightheartedness back into the bones of our estate that instantly decayed and rotted the moment they were taken from us.

My father and I both died the moment our eyes locked on that box sitting outside our estate's main gate.

When my father picked it up, a wordless conversation flowed between us in the form of my father's exhale. Somehow, we both knew. We've held enough body parts to recognize that the weight is unmatched. Not even the styrofoam box, concealed behind cardboard, could erase the metallic stench and hint of cigar that stained the floral spring air.

When we finally got our wits together enough to open it, it was the first time that the sight of human organs made me release the acid searing my stomach. For days. Until I was the shell of a man wishing that bastard would've had the balls to carve my father and me instead, since we were the ones he wanted.

At least, that's what we thought.

His war was with us. Not them.

But that would've been too kind.

And Luciano Giovanni has never been known for having an ounce of compassion.

He rose to our level.

Wanted to play our game to destroy us and claim what's ours in retribution for a sin that isn't ours to bear.

The Megalley Syndicate is bound by blood, related or not. Once you pledge your loyalty, there is no escape but death. If it takes blood to get in, blood is the cost to get out.

What we do means nothing if our family isn't by our side. And the only reason my father and I are still breathing is to carry out the plan we've so carefully crafted. To keep the heart of our operation still beating, even if we wish ours weren't, because we failed to protect the two things more precious to us than our narcotic, illegal weapons, and money laundering operations.

Our silence for the last five years hasn't been because we've given up.

Oh no.

Our strike will be violent. Bloody.

When I was younger, my mother would stroke my cheek with her fingers and speak words of admiration, telling me how proud she was that, though I was born to rule a dark world, I still had compassion.

Not a hint of that man remains.

The only thing that might give me peace at the end of this is smashing my fist through Luciano's chest cavity to feel the final beats of his heart cease in my hand. I might even use it like a stress ball as the healing process of losing my mother and sister finally starts after years of observing. Surveillance. Carefully collecting any information that can give us an edge to end this once and for all and take out the leader of the Calco Cartel. The don of the Italian Mafia, whose borders are slowly leaking across the southern states and near our territory.

Carter's voice barely registers through the hammering pulsing through the gym. "I thought you'd be in here."

I fight through the distraction, sinking my naked fists into the synthetic leather of the boxing bag, soaking up my aggression. The late morning light beats down through the wall of windows facing the gardens that stretch out beyond, before it meets the rocky beach of the Atlantic Ocean. My hot, sweaty skin and muscles are burning from the relentless heat of the sun. Beads of sweat trickle down the valley between my pecs and along the ridges of my spine, further drenching the waistband of my gym shorts.

I observe my best friend, my right-hand man, break through the threshold of the gym in the reflection of the mirrors in front of me. He moves further into the room, watching my movements with an attentive gaze.

I'm twenty-nine. He may be three years older than I am, but we've been inseparable since my father saved him when he was twenty and gave him a job. A home.

He pulls his fingers through his ruffled black hair, cropped short on the sides, then tucks his hands into the pockets of his slacks. "Rowan and Cathal touched base. The shipment is thirty minutes out from the marina."

I place my hands on my hips to rest, the inferno in my lungs raging. My breath is rapid as I meet his dark eyes in the mirror. "They're late. They were supposed to arrive two days ago. They know how I fucking feel about punctuality." One of the reasons I'm taking out my anger this way is to tame my inner beast that's hungry to plant my fists through some facial bone the moment I see Rowan and Cathal to prove my point.

He swipes a tattooed hand over his nape and shrugs. "They said they had to reroute due to a tropical storm."

I turn slowly, narrowing my eyes. "For their sake, I hope we have the AIS data to back that up and validate their course."

Carter notices the water bottle on the floor and bends down, grasping it before he tosses it to me. "Consider it done. I'll head to the marina now."

I uncap the bottle, taking a long swig to quench my thirst, heaving a sigh. "Thanks. But don't touch anything until I get there."

It's not Carter's fault. He just happens to be here to witness my frustration with the situation that's had me on edge since we lost contact with one of our commercial lobster boats. A boat that was bringing back one of the several narcotic shipments we receive throughout the month, which arrives straight to the docks of our harbor.

Lately, I haven't been a very trusting person. This is the third month in a row where several bags of our fentanyl and cocaine have gone "missing." Though they may be small amounts that might slip past someone who is unobservant, I am not one of those people.

Neither is Arden, my father.

We're thorough.

We're also not naive enough to think they are low-balling us with the amount we are paying our cartel partner in Mexico.

There's something else transpiring, we're just not sure what it is yet.

However, if anything is missing from this new shipment, corrective actions will need to be taken. And both Rowan and Cathal might find themselves at my mercy. My blood sizzles in exhilaration just thinking about it. It's been a while since I've taken such violent measures. It may be on a few men in my mob, but this world isn't for the faint of heart. If we ask questions, they should be answered promptly, and that applies to everyone. If not, we use our favorite methods to get people to talk.

Even if it's our own people.

Carter's eyes roam the floor before he glances back up at me. I can already see a question flickering in his gaze before he opens his mouth. "I know I've been taking a lot of time off, but I was wondering if next month I can take a week and a half to head back to Chicago."

Gulping down the rest of the bottle, I place the cap on and toss it into the small trash can against the wall. "What is it now?"

I can tell from the way his mouth twists to the side that he's being cautious about saying too much. He knows by now the topics that send me into a depression spiral. I'm right when he says, "My little sister is getting married." I swallow, briefly thinking how my sister will never see that day, but I push that thought far back to the recesses of my mind. "Her fiancé is an asshole, but I need to be there to support her. My parents would be pissed if I missed it. They already think my tech job," he puts in air quotes, "takes me from them enough."

I reach for my towel on the nearby bench, clearing away the thick glaze of sweat on the slopes of my neck. "I get it. Just be back in time for the security briefing." Arden wants to review some new protocols, since none of the recent deliveries are matching up with our agreement. "It doesn't seem like it's a coincidence anymore that small parts of our shipments aren't arriving."

He sharply nods in agreement. "Wouldn't miss it."

A few beats of silence pass between us before I clear my throat. "Your sister's fiancé may be an asshole, but I hope you enjoy every minute of it. I'll never get to experience that."

Something passes over his eyes, and I try to dissect the expression. It's not pity. He knows I fucking hate pity. It's more like sympathy combined with something else I can't place. After all, I didn't just lose my sister; he lost a friend.

Carter was there for me every step of the way when it was confirmed that Tayla and my mom, Lynn, were never going to be returned to us. Their heartbeats ceased before we could negotiate or fight to get them back—and God knows we would have burned the world for them. But the ruthless wind rose instantly and never gave us the chance to strike the match.

Between the moment they were abducted and the morning we got that box, Luciano hadn't even kept them alive for more than eight hours. We knew that thanks to the photos in the box containing time stamps and brutal images of their murders as they lay bloody and lifeless on an unknown concrete floor, side by side.

I choke down the bile burning my throat. "I'm going to shower, and then I'll meet you at the marina."

He presses his lips in a line and says, "I'll head there now," leaving me alone in the gym.

Pacing over to the floor-to-ceiling windows, I glare out over the expanse of the yard till it meets the maze and garden before it drops off to the rocky beach below. On the right side, through the towering fences, watch towers, and a half-mile expanse of forest that creeps down the hillside, lies the edge of Lachlan Park. Usually, the impeccably mowed crisscrossed lines that meet the ten-foot-tall security fence would give me some sense of comfort, but it doesn't come.

Until three months ago, our only worry was vengeance. Now, with small parts of our product vanishing, I can't help but feel as if it's going to deter us from our mission to take down Luciano. Our operations come first, no matter how difficult that is to swallow. My chest can only support a few feelings at a time.

Retaliation.

Resolve.

Too many distractions will make me a half-asser, and nothing irritates me more.

I'm just hoping there won't be any more.

# FOUR | KATE

It's been three days since I sat there listening to a haunting story that I shouldn't believe. Exhaustion is rotting me from the inside out. No matter how many cups of coffee I consume, it won't dissolve the dark circles under my eyes or the constant yawning that is starting to become a nuisance.

Doesn't stop me from guzzling the drink as if it will randomly decide to start boosting my system as it should. At this point, my caffeine intake should give me an overdose.

I lift the paper coffee cup to my lips from Bloom & Baked, a local coffee shop on the other side of the boardwalk from Lachlan Park that sits on the bay. I take another drink of my vanilla oat milk latte, as the soft ocean breeze floats off the water and brushes through my hair that has far too many tangles for this time of day.

There was only a sliver of a second when I thought about getting ready, then changed my mind. After all, it's my day off, and enjoying my coffee with my journal by the water sounds like a peaceful way to spend my late morning. Besides the slight waves to my hair from my shift yesterday, there isn't an ounce of makeup on my face. Not that I wear much anyway, but it's nice not to have a care in the world when you're trying to remain a ghost in it anyway.

The chatter of birds blends with the soft waves caressing the marina's dock. The occasional horn from a boat cuts through the vibrant blue sky, dusted with those light wispy clouds that remind me of the cotton candy machines at the park when they heat up just enough to melt and spin the sugar as it wraps around the wand. Light. Fluffy. And in a way, magical.

Boats sail across the expanse of deep blue, with those subtle and gentle waves that only this time of morning can accomplish. It's the calm before the afternoon wind picks up, creating white-capped waves that fold repeatedly, stirring up the surface.

The warm light bathes my skin, making my lips tilt upward to greet the sun that energizes me more than the caffeine that runs through my veins.

My feet pad across the dock, gently swaying with the water. I'm not quite sure what convinced me to decide on the marina today. Still, as I walk farther out into the water with boats on either side of me, the end of the dock provides a perfect display of a sailboat against the backdrop of water against the horizon. I'm drawn to it, and there just so happens to be two beige lounging chairs propped at the end with a small matching coffee table positioned between.

The only thing keeping me from them is the fence I come toe-to-toe with, separating one part of the dock from the other. The massive red-and-white restricted sign should deter me, make me turn around, and find a different spot. But I want that one at the edge of the dock with a chair that my ass is aching for.

Okay, my ass is fine, I'm just trying to justify all the reasons I should cross this barrier.

Plus, there are only three massive fishing boats flanking the sides. They aren't the expensive yachts and sailboats like the other ones I passed to get to this point.

And there's nobody even using those chairs.

They are alone, longing for someone to appreciate them. I want to give them the attention they deserve.

My eyes fall to the keyless combination lock.

If they were genuinely trying to keep people from this section of the dock, they would make it harder to access. But since the fence only spans from one side of the dock to the other, there is a straightforward way of getting around. I move to the part of the gate that juts out a foot over the water. I crouch down, maneuvering my hand through the vertical bars to place my coffee safely on the other side.

I reposition my cross-body bag to ensure it's secure around me before I grasp the bars and step vertically across until I'm hanging over the water. Swinging a leg around the last bar at the edge of the fence, I work my way around to the other side and shuffle my feet across the horizontal bar at the bottom with cautious steps. It's not long before I hop back onto the dock on the private side.

Crouching down, I pick up my coffee and take a sip, satisfied with my ninja-like abilities to defy security.

When I first started walking across the dock, the air was greeted by the sound of lapping water. Now, as I approach the very end of the marina that stretches out into the harbor, aggravated voices carry with the soft hum of the ocean. The first fishing boat I pass has two men on deck, one middle-aged with a graying beard and old tattoos spreading across his leathery, sun-damaged skin. He's wearing grimy black overalls over an army green t-shirt.

The other man with him could not be more opposite. He's young, with jet-black hair that's effortlessly tousled, and built like one of those nude statues people ogle in Italy. Not that I've ever been to Europe or can see what those expensive slacks and his gray button-down are hiding, but I've got a pretty good idea by how the shirt stretches across those muscular arms. He irritably motions to the man, giving me a flash of his inked hands.

Their heated voices carry, making it obvious they're arguing —and equally obvious that I'm somewhere I shouldn't be. Head lowered, I quicken my pace, but not before overhearing a part of their conversation.

"I don't know what to fucking tell you," the older man snarls. "We had to dodge the storm. That's why we lost connection and why we're late. I don't appreciate you making accusations that could have me hung up by my fucking balls."

The younger man responds, his voice husky and laced with disdain. "Doesn't matter. Boss needs to validate your story. It's protocol, and you know that. I suggest you tell him what he wants to know. You know what will happen if you don't."

The older man curses, spitting something in a language I don't understand.

My head shoots upward to glance at the two of them in surprise, before the younger one interrupts. "Now leave me," he growls. The side of the boat obscures my view as he adjusts the strap of whatever he's carrying on his shoulder. "I don't need him hanging both of us by our balls for wasting even more damn time."

Lowering my gaze, I hustle past the other two fishing boats to the end of the dock. It's not long before I plop down onto the chair and close my eyes to feel the salt air kiss my face.

After a few minutes, I peek my head around the chair to scan behind me, watching as the handsome man who was on the boat struts back down the dock toward the parking lot with a large duffel bag. God, that ass in those slacks. He's not the first man I've admired that way. For some reason, the gene pool is strong in Lachlan Harbor, as the men here are built much like the security guards at the park.

Turning back around, thankful he didn't see me when

getting off the boat, I blow out a breath of relief. Usually, I'd walk the beach and settle on a boulder that's secluded, giving me the moment of peace I need to forget about the brutality of the world for just a little while. A few heartbeats of stillness to provide me with the reset I need when I feel helpless and tired.

God, I am so tired.

Tired of running.

Tired of living but not thriving.

Tired of feeling weak and helpless.

Inhaling and exhaling long, steady breaths, I allow my body to sink and relax into the chair. I remove my crossbody and reach in to take out my journal and pen, ready to clear my mind onto paper. The first three quarters of the book are scrawled with entries from over the last year. My week in Idaho, my few weeks in Montana, moving my way across the states in my Subaru Crosstrek until I landed in Wyoming, thinking it might be remote and far enough to settle down for a little while.

It wasn't.

I was there for two months working as a waitress at a diner before I got a knock at my motel door. I thought I was being safe, traveling and staying in places that would accept cash, since I had closed my bank accounts and canceled all the cards in my name. I destroyed my phone. I thought I was untraceable. But I didn't realize just how far Xander's obsession could go.

I thought indulging in his fascination with role play was just a kink—a way to elevate our sex life. I was too late when his true psychotic nature started to show, and I realized he viewed *everything* as a game.

To this day, I still don't know how he found me. I assume it was the laptop I had thought was perfectly safe to bring along. And at three in the morning, I squeezed out the bathroom window and left everything behind, except my wallet.

And I mean everything.

My keys. My car. My faith that maybe his fixation would

end if he took what he wanted one last time. But what he wanted left the hotel sheets drenched in crimson.

It should've ended with his blood seeping through the threads instead. Not mine.

I reach up to the spot below my ear, lightly dragging my fingers down over the impostor that decorates my skin. Just like always, it awakens the ones on my stomach, like the blade released a web that threaded through my body and connected all my scars.

A raspy throat clears behind me, solidifying my body. "Everyone always thinks rats are such intelligent creatures. I think they're cunning little pests that always find themselves in places they shouldn't."

# FIVE | KATE

It takes me a second to pick up my jaw off the dock while that bewildering comment somehow boils my blood. Irritated, I peer over my shoulder, thankful I'm sitting.

One look at this man, and I know he possesses the raw power to drop me to my knees. From a single look.

Excuse me while I wipe the drool off my chin.

His light brown hair is swept lightly away from his face. His cropped beard on his cut jawline is the same light walnut color, contrasting with his soft, tanned skin, which makes him appear to be in his late twenties, perhaps thirties. As I take in the sight of him, there are faint lines carved into his face that convey the kind of exhaustion I feel.

The attractive stranger's dark aviator sunglasses keep me from seeing his eyes. His massive frame is clad in an impeccable navy-blue suit. Paired with a white button-down and tie, he seamlessly blends with the blue sky and water. A gold watch adorns his wrist, where the tattoos glide under and onto his fingers.

I realize I'm taking him in a little too long. When my eyes flit back up to his, hidden behind those glasses, his slanted head makes me think he's taking me in, too. Yet I'm not sure what is going on in his head, considering his scowl is blinding. He's pissed.

My nose wrinkles. It's hot out here. Why is he in a damn suit?

Also, now that I'm thinking about it, why are so many of the men in Lachlan Harbor decked out in ink? Is that a requirement to live here? Even security at the park is branded from head to toe in tattoos that stretch over nearly every muscle. Not that I'm complaining.

They are always nice to look at.

He's been sucking the oxygen out of my lungs, so my voice comes a little airier than I expect. "Did you just compare me to a rat?"

His gaze washes over my body, leaving a searing heat in his wake that I try to ignore. The authority this man is commanding is enough to squash me right here, like an ant beneath his leather brown dress shoes.

I thought his tone was already hard, but when his mouth parts, it drops another octave. "You're trespassing. Did you miss that big fucking sign that says restricted on your way in?"

His voice glides over my skin like smooth honey. Holy hell. At first, I was so frazzled I didn't hear the Irish accent slipping through. My core isn't the only part of my body responding to his presence—he has the kind of deep tenor that makes anything he says sound filthy.

My brows furrow. "And what makes you think I'm trespassing?" I counter.

A muscle in his jaw twitches. "You want to try that again? I highly suggest you answer my question. I'm not a very trusting man."

Good grief. What an ass.

My eyes land on one of the boats, navy and white, with thick poles that stretch into the sky. Large, cage-like boxes are stacked on top of each other on the deck. The name "Carpus Diem" is written in cursive on the side in large white letters. I assume it's wordplay, since it should be "Carpe Diem." Creative, though I'm not sure what Carpus means.

I point at the vessel. "That's my boat."

A single dark brow raises, his thick arms folding over his chest. "That's your boat?"

"Yep." He hums, the sound low and disapproving in his throat at my answer. "What, a woman can't own a fishing boat?" His eyes might be hidden behind his aviators, but I can feel them fixed on me. I wave a dismissive hand. "It was a long morning out on the water, so if you don't mind leaving me alone to decompress, that would be great."

His head tilts, the sunlight hitting his tanned skin so perfectly that it reveals the thick cords in his neck. The kind of tendons that my tongue would love to trace.

"And what were you out there catching, *on the water*?" His cynical tone grates against my nerves.

"Fish," I deadpan, like it's obvious.

He's dressed in a blue suit that appears tailor-made to hug his huge, strapping frame. I'm hoping that means he's as clue-less as I am about fishing.

He drags a hand over the cropped beard peppering his jaw. "Interesting, because last I checked, that's my boat."

My heart stutters. My discomfort with this situation slithers up my throat, lingering there. A reminder that lies always have a way of catching up with you. Some sooner than later.

Shit.

I was banking on him owning one of the other two. It was a one in three chance, so I guess the odds weren't in my favor. At least I tried. But also, this is a smaller town, and all the fish-ermen are bound to know each other.

"Well then," I blow out a breath, snapping my journal

closed and placing it in my bag beside the chair. I zip it up, stand, and grab my coffee cup.

His unrelenting scrutiny feels hooked to every part of my body. Despite my long floral skirt with a slit that shows my long legs and white tank top that feels like it enhances my smaller breasts and curves, he has the kind of eyes that feel like they are stripping me bare, with the way his head tilts downward to sweep his gaze from my head to my toes. I'd say the heat pouring over me is from the sun, but that would be a lie. I may not be able to see his eyes, but he's handsome in ways that blur everything around him like he was meant to be a focal point.

I fill the awkward silence, somehow adding to its discomfort. "That's funny, mine looks identical. Same name and everything."

His mouth almost lifts, but it disappears just as quickly. It's hard to tell against his cynical expression. "How ironic."

"I should go find my boat." I step to move past him, jumping in shock when his large hand gently grasps my forearm to hold me still.

He lowers his head, and for some reason, I wish I could see his eyes instead of my disheveled appearance staring back at me. I'm so flushed that it's noticeable in the reflection, which means he undoubtedly knows my lies are painting my cheeks —a physical red flag.

"Curiosity can be a double-edged sword, darling. You should be careful and consider the consequences the next time you find yourself drawn somewhere you aren't supposed to be."

I swallow, my eyes flitting between his, wondering if they're blue like the water surrounding us or if they're green, like the stage where new growth on a plant matures into the dark green color that is warm and inviting, unlike his presence.

But I'll never find out.

He releases my arm, nodding toward the fence. "How did you get in here anyway?" I withhold my answer and quickly get the sense my silence vexes him when he grumbles, "And it's a lobster boat."

I stroll toward the gate, walking backward as he watches me create the much-needed distance between us.

My hand touches my temple, giving him a salute. It will probably piss him off more since he's already in a dickish mood. "Have a good day, Captain."

Without another word, I turn around and exit out the gate the usual way since the other side is the only one with the keyless combination. I'm not sure why I like the idea of his head swimming with all the ways I could've possibly gotten in here. It's not that hard.

The weight of his attention hangs over me like a thick fog. He's so attentive and observant that it's nearly suffocating.

The fence clicks shut behind me, and I force myself to slow my steps the rest of the way toward the parking lot to appear like I'm unfrazzled instead of running away like I want to. I don't know what it is about that man, but I feel like I should.

# SIX | KATE

Reaching into my locker, I feel instant relief when I see the white envelope with my past two weeks' pay. I grasp onto it, tucking it into my purse.

I may have never imagined myself working at an amusement park, but I'm grateful for this job. That Lachlan Park gives me the ability to remain hidden in a world where someone's information is sickeningly accessible to anyone. That I can keep myself from creating those thin threads across cyberspace that could lead Xander to me.

When I asked my hiring manager if I could be paid in cash, they didn't even blink. Getting the woman who owns my house to accept cash for my monthly rent without leaving any digital trail was a different story. I got those narrowed eyes that made me feel like I was going to crawl out of my skin and word vomit the shit show that is my life all over her lap when I was signing my contract.

I was desperate.

So, instead, I asked, "Do you have daughters?"

Sindy observed me skeptically and nodded. "I have two."

My soft, anxious smile was accompanied by an exhale. "If they were in trouble and running from someone dangerous, wouldn't you want them to find a safe place?"

That got her attention.

Perhaps she recognized the fear in my eyes or the shallow breaths that floated between us, revealing my anxiety over using any digital form of payment that would require a bank account. Sindy's hand reached out to grasp mine out of instinct. My eyes started watering thinking of my mother, who I knew was worried sick about me.

My landlord gave in, and I nearly doubled over, crying in appreciation that I wouldn't have to keep temporarily living in shitty motels that were as menacing and disturbing as the situation I had found myself in—running from an ex whose tenacity is as potent as his psychotic nature.

Sometimes I wonder if ending our relationship earlier would've saved my conscience, protected my body—or if ending it when the first signs of fear that poisoned my gut would've tempted the monster to emerge and play even before I recognized the red flags for what they were.

But it's no use in wondering when this is my reality.

People always say to get out of a toxic relationship before it's too late. But sometimes, at the beginning, it's unrecognizable. Little moments that are a grain of sand, adding to the bag attached to your feet, meant to slowly drag you under until getting out seems impossible.

The scars of my three years with Xander run deeper than colorless, risen skin, and my fractured soul feels like it's been tossed into a wood chipper one too many times. Even if I was able to put the pieces back together, there are some slivers and shards I'm sure I'll never get back.

Xander and I had started as strangers at a blood drive when I was attending nursing school in Oregon. Something about catching the attention of an older man as a fresh twenty-year-old was confidence-boosting. He didn't just pierce my skin with a needle when I was giving blood; he burrowed deep, hypnotizing me with a blindness that made me as obsessed with him as he was with me. It wasn't until the comfort with each other started to settle that his true nature began to seep through ordinary moments.

A month after we started dating, I handed over my virginity. That first time wasn't gentle. It didn't make butterflies swoop in my stomach with gentle wings or make the emotion of contentment fog my head and tighten my chest in those beautiful ways like it should.

It was rough.

Hard in a way that, at first, I got no pleasure from.

But the following praises that spilled from his mouth at how well I was doing in response to the mix of pain and pleasure he was giving me somehow made me validate his actions as being normal. That he was a man with experience, and therefore, since I had none, I needed to be everything he needed. Now, I can't get off without the euphoria blending with a mixture of pain.

Believe me when I say I wish I could. Even when I stir my own pleasure, my fingertips twist my nipples to haul me closer to the brink. And when I shatter, the guilt that follows is like that one grain of sand in the bag tied to my ankles that I can't fight anymore. It lugs me to the depths, leaving a lingering self-loathing that never truly vanishes.

He trained my body.

It wasn't until the blade came out to play and he'd drag his fingers through my blood that I realized how truly unhinged he was.

Often, I wonder if I'll ever find the shelter that my heart craves. The peace that never feels within reach when I'm constantly looking over my shoulder.

Healing is difficult when your demons aren't dead.

Maybe that's why I wanted to run yesterday when that jaw-dropping and panty-wetting god on the dock knocked me off center with his aura alone.

The vibes radiating off him weren't good ones, but I couldn't ignore the way his presence branded my memory.

A man who dresses like that isn't meant to be forgotten.

I shut my locker and turn around, taking in the minimal break room: nothing more than a small, round, wooden table with four matching chairs in the center, and a small kitchenette against the wall with a fridge. On the other wall is a door that leads to a little cleaning closet.

This room is small and confined with no windows, so whenever I'm on my lunch break, I usually settle onto one of the outdoor picnic tables near the food court section of the park. Today, my brain craved silence. The ride may have a repeating song every day, but so does every other area on the property. It may be a soundtrack, but I still know every instrumental and gleeful song on that list.

I press my back against the lockers, closing my eyes for a brief second to reset. When they pop open, I gasp. Before, the closet was closed. Now, the door is propped open with a body lurking in the shadows on the other side. Vincent's face is void of any expression as it usually is, the hardness in his wrinkled features and narrow eyes making a lump form in my throat. Faded tattoos have bled across his muscular, age-marked skin, making the ink on his neck difficult to distinguish. I can recognize it as a script; however, I'm unsure what language it is.

He's standing in the doorway, in dark gray pants and a button-down that looks like a solid-color flannel, the closet completely dark behind him. An ominous void that infuses an extra dose of unease into my veins. I am just about to finish my lunch break and have been enjoying my sandwich alone for thirty minutes, which means he's been enclosed in that small space the entire time I've been in the break room.

I can't help myself. "How long have you been in there?"

His eyes hold mine. "Doesn't matter."

It's supposed to be a dismissal, but I ignore it. Noisily, I push harder. "I've been in here for thirty minutes. Which means you've been hanging out in there—alone." I eye the light switch on the outside of the closet. "In the dark." I fold my arms over my chest to cover the unexpected gooseflesh that peppers my skin in response to his callous presence.

He moves out of the small closet, shutting the door behind him. "If I were you, I'd return to work and mind your own business, girl."

His advancing steps have me backing toward the exit. I almost don't want to move and hold my ground since he has no authority to tell me what to do, but I think better of it and escape the room, hastily walking back to finish the last part of my shift.

A slow, antagonizing four hours later, I rest my chin on my hand, my arm propped up on the control panel table as I watch the four video blocks on each of the three screens roll by and switch to other views. A family unloads off the cart, the father pushing his two young kids through the exit gate in front of me as Jeremy ushers two teenage girls onto the cart next, who were at the back of the evening rush line.

Through the large, open, garage-like doors, with rope weaving through to navigate the line, rosy pink and dusty orange pastels paint the seascape over the carousel across from the haunted mine building. Its vibrant, rainbow-flickering lights pierce the oncoming darkness, looking like something out of a fairy tale.

When the cart disappears through the cave entrance with the two teenage girls, Jeremy hops onto the top of the rotating turnstile, which lets guests pass after they scan their tickets. He folds his arms over his chest, looking like he's ready to be done with this day as much as I am.

"Hey." Jeremy looks up at me, curiously waiting for me to continue. "Have you ever seen Vincent hanging out in the cleaning closet by himself...in the dark?"

His bushy brows knit together at my question. "I mean, I saw him come out of there once with a duffel bag. It was strange, but then I thought that maybe he was changing or something."

"Changing in the closet?" I say it out loud, more so to process it myself, since we have access to staff bathrooms and showers in several parts of the park.

He shrugs. "I guess. Why?"

I purse my lips, shaking my head. "Never mind."

"Yeah, he's fucking strange. Doesn't really talk to anyone, and I've worked here for the last several summers."

"If he's so unapproachable, then why did you tell me to ask him about those massacres that happened in the park?"

"Because Nicole and I are curious but have never wanted to ask." His lips tilt upward. "We thought maybe you would."

My eyes roll. Not happening when he clearly told me to mind my own business when I asked him what he was doing in the closet. "Forget it—"

"Hey!" a feminine voice screeches.

The two teenage girls hop off the ride at rapid speed, the brunette with a crop top and cut-off shorts damn near tripping over the open gap where the cart meets the landing. It happens far more often than it should.

"You need to stop the ride," she huffs out frantically, bracing her hands on the counter of the control panel. "I was taking a video, and I dropped my phone, and it went under the tracks!" she rushes out in one breath.

Jeremy briefly flashes me an annoyed expression as a few more people weave their way through the ropes. He gestures them onto the ride.

I shrug, meeting her uptight stare. "It's protocol that I can't stop the ride unless someone is in immediate danger or there are mechanical issues. Emergencies," I clarify.

She thins her eyes into tiny slits. "This is an emergency."

Is it though?

I purse my lips, trying to refrain from laughing. "Sorry, I don't know what to tell you." If I had a dollar for every time someone has dropped their phone out of the cart, the pay for this job might actually make it worth it. It's a pain in the ass.

Her unrelenting eyes stay steady on mine.

"What part of the ride did you lose it?" I sigh.

"Right after we went under the curtain waterfall that turns into rivers on both sides."

Of course it was. Why did it have to be the part of the ride that is the hardest to access?

I force the sweetest tone I can muster. "I won't be able to get it until after we close later tonight. If you want, you can pick it up tomorrow at the main gate."

She processes that for a moment and grips the edge of the counter in a frustrated manner that has me gritting my teeth. "Fine, I'll come back tomorrow." She turns to her friend, and they start to walk off, but not before I hear something that sounds like "bitch," muttered under her breath.

It's not the bitch part that aggravates me; I've worked with my fair share of personalities when I was a nurse at the hospital. It's the fact that some people expect us to drop everything when there is an issue, when we aren't the ones calling the shots. I have to follow protocol. I also prefer to keep my limbs and don't want to be reaching around to find a phone among the rotating track and belts that are constantly moving from the time we start in the morning till we close at ten.

My wave is obnoxiously over-the-top, my sarcasm palpable. "Thanks for riding with us. Please do come again."

When those two teenage girls left, a chain reaction of unfortunate events ensued. The rest of my shift was hell. A kid dropped his slushy on the platform before getting on the ride, splattering the concrete with red. It looked like a sweet, sticky massacre. I mopped it up, but the sugar is clinging to the bottom of my shoes, leaving a cracking sound whenever I walk.

Then a poor little boy was scared shitless when the headless miner popped out and peed all over the seat and the floor of the cart. In that case, I had to momentarily pause the ride to quickly deal with the mess, which meant that a few boys were paused long enough that they started splashing each other with water along the small river that flows through. Jeremy scolded them, threatening to get them kicked out of the park if they didn't keep their hands inside the ride.

I'm not a stranger to human bodily fluids or cleaning up other people's messes, but it's like that teenage girl put a curse on me and screwed with the entire rest of my day.

Little witch.

The dank scent of water and dust clings to the particles in the air as I walk down the dark, empty hallway to the closest door that leads to the part of the ride where the girl's phone should be. I open and step through the door, relishing in the sweet sound of silence in the cave-like atmosphere. Well, it's not entirely silent. The rushing water is still flowing in gentle rapids along the sides of the ride, adding to the underground effect, but the repetitive music has stopped.

I cross the small rock bridge over the water with stalagmites standing in towers on either side, leading from the door toward the tracks. Shuffling along the ledge, elevated above the floor where the track is built, I peer down, trying not to miss the device hidden among the trash that litters the floor. No wonder Vincent is always silently grouchy. I would hate it too if I had to make my living cleaning this up every night.

Just because we have a trash can on the platform before people get on the ride doesn't mean that they use it.

Assholes.

The waterfall is up ahead, creating a curtain-like effect around another cave opening that mists the riders below. It quickly became my favorite part of the ride since they made me do it several times when I was first hired.

The whirr of water intensifies the closer I get; the kind of rush that makes you pick up your voice to talk to someone standing right next to you. I crouch and hop down from the rocky ledge, lowering myself beside the elevated track with a narrow walkway on each side for maintenance. My eyes flit over the ground, but I still don't see it.

"Dammit. Where are you?" I whine. "I want to go home."

It's almost eleven, and I'm completely over this day.

When I'm under the waterfall curtain, water mists my body. I shiver, but it's not from the cold water peppering my skin. My eyes land on one of those thick metal grates with openings in the floor, partially hidden under the track. The kind that makes you cautious of your things when you walk over them through the streets, because if something were to fall in there, you'd never get it back.

My heart sinks into my gut.

No way in hell.

My skin prickles with keen awareness, knowing exactly where that girl's phone ended up. Bringing my toes to the edge of the metal, I glare down.

I expect to see darkness—a void of nothingness that makes you wonder what lurks beneath.

This isn't that.

My breath solidifies into something heavy in my lungs at the soft yellow light emanating from the tunnel. The phone is at the bottom, at least one story down, face up on a concrete floor. Somehow, it's mocking me for disbelieving in something so preposterous.

The story they told me about Lachlan Park blasts back at me like the rushing water on either side, hitting me at once with a force that should have me turning and walking away. But I find myself glued to the spot, a twinge of belief stirring behind my ribs, knowing that the violent world existing below my shoes might not be a fantasy after all.

# SEVEN | KATE

There's not much in life I've been terrified of. Sure, when I was younger, I had those typical fears most children navigate—monsters under the bed, vegetables, things that exist in the dark that I can't see, but I know damn well they can see me.

All of those seemed trivial compared to the one that's been hunting me since he got one taste. As if pieces of my flesh are lingering between his teeth, rousing a hunger that has sent him into an unhinged spiral. As if he finds sick satisfaction in playing with his food before he's decided he's had enough and devours me whole.

I never understood what genuine fear felt like until Xander pressed the tip of the blade to my skin.

A blade that was all play.

Until it wasn't.

It was that first draw of hot crimson slipping down the side of my belly where being scared took on an entirely new meaning. When my heart, which had always been safely tucked behind my ribcage, bounced so violently that it threatened to crack bones and impale itself, before I got so deep that I would never resurface from the damage.

That sensation has never entirely dispelled since I fled Oregon. Somewhere along the way, over time, I became desensitized to it. The lurching ache in my chest may have dulled, but it didn't stop churning the motors in my feet as I crossed state lines. Until the temporary feeling of safety settled in enough to let me momentarily rest my soul before the claustrophobia of wondering if he was close had me beginning again.

Starting again.

And again.

The concrete floor digs into my knees through the overly thick fabric of my uniform overalls. The light draft from below, pushing through the metal grate, brushes over my face, creating a shockwave of chills that textures my skin from my head to my toes.

I don't know when I lowered to my hands and knees. Maybe it was the shock that pulled me down. However, being on the ground is doing nothing to calm the way my heart painfully bursts in a chaotic rhythm in my tightened chest. My fingers grip the cool metal, like I'll fall through if I don't hold on with every ounce of strength my body can produce, while my brain tries to process what this tunnel could possibly lead to. It's the same beating, gnashing, feeling I was hit in the gut with every time I came to the ugly realization that Xander's sexual appetite was shifting into something violent.

Dangerous.

Growingly lethal.

The reality is that I need to get this girl's phone. So, what's the probability that their theories were correct, and it's a secret underworld where demonic people harvest organs?

A more likely explanation is that the tunnels were placed under Lachlan Park when it was first built, allowing staff to access their posts easily.

*It's like Disneyland, Kate.*

My eye roll at myself exaggerates the headache forming near my temple.

I doubt I'll see someone in a Pooh costume scurrying by to clear my reservations and dark thoughts running berserk in my head. A more realistic version would be Libby Lobster running by to start their daily shift at the fountain in the center of the park.

But it's nearly eleven, and I don't think there will be many people walking around this time of night. The only workers left now are the cleaners. And me, because I've clearly had a miserable day that keeps testing my patience.

The logical thing would be to locate Vincent and ask him about the tunnel.

My brain freezes on that notion.

That thought ignites a fuse, the spark coursing through my muscles. I jolt upright, nearly hitting my skull on the metal track looming above me. My earlier interaction with him in the break room stirs in my mind like wet paint until each stroke blends seamlessly and creates a bigger picture.

What if Vincent wasn't hanging out in the dark closet all that time that I was on break?

If there's an underground tunnel system, there must be different access points, some clearly marked and some not. An easy way for them to navigate the park without all the foot traffic and visitors.

*Maybe it is like Disneyland.*

I stand up, hopping over the ledge and back onto the faux rocky surface leading to the exit as if I'm attached to a cable that's dragging me through the building without my consent. I don't want to be curious, but I can't help myself. It's not long before I'm staring at the metal door to the closet in the break room.

Remember when I mentioned fears as a child? Isn't it a

common one to be frightened of something loitering in the closet?

That explains why I'm staring at the barrier between me and the small room of cleaning supplies like it will burst open, and a massive beast with fangs will pop out and sink its deadly claws into my flesh and render me helpless. Truthfully, I might have the same reaction if Vincent is lurking on the other side.

My trembling hand lifts to rest on the door handle, slowly turning the knob to open it toward me. As I suspected, it's dark, hitting me with that musty smell containing a hint of chemicals that permeates the air. I step through the threshold, peering around at the small space, maybe eight by eight feet. Extra paper towels, bleach, and other various cleaning products haphazardly line the floor-to-ceiling shelves, and per usual, there's a mop bucket positioned in front of them in one of the far back corners.

You would think that if someone were spending time in here, there would be a chair or a stool. Maybe even one of those old-school metal buckets to place upside down and sit on. But no. There is nothing of the sort.

Jeremy's words stick like glue at the forefront of my mind.

*"I saw him come out of there once with a duffel bag. It was strange, but then, I thought that maybe he was changing or something."*

It only further solidifies my suspicions about Vincent.

I swallow, ambling further into the small space. My eyes roam over the shelves, flitting over all the things that are usually ignored and disregarded by anyone who isn't a cleaner. My eyes drop to the concrete floor that matches the rest of the building—cold and gray with scuff marks and other mysterious markings that signal years of wear and tear. It's simple things like this that remind me that even the most solid things aren't entirely untouchable.

It's not until my eyes land on a faint, unusual curvature

marking on the floor that my pulse throbs in my ears. A gentle bend scuffed into the pavement. It's only because I'm scanning the floor with laser-focused eyes that I notice; otherwise, I would've never registered it.

One cautious step at a time, I approach the back shelves, knowing part of it must swing out. Peering at the wall between all the items chaotically placed around, I barely notice the crack behind. If there is anything that I have learned from movies, it is that there is always a secret lever or something that opens the door.

My heart wildly pounds in my chest, reminding me that it is very much alive and not in agreement with my body enslaved to the thoughts in my head. There aren't many times when I have an out-of-body experience, but this is one of those. I feel like I'm floating, my mind hazy as my body works absentmindedly despite the static circulating in my brain from overdrive.

Somehow, I don't realize what I'm doing when I start picking up every product like a crazed person looking for something they misplaced. I touch bleach bottles, move cannisters, and boxes of unlabeled products. I push aside cleaning supplies and random, unnecessary items that appear out of place.

God, this is so stupid.

I'm sleep-deprived from my nightmares and just need to go home. It's not my fault that the girl couldn't follow simple directions and keep her hands inside the cart. Her losing her phone is her own damn fault.

I release a tired breath laced with annoyance that I let myself believe that maybe there's more to Lachlan Park than I thought. Turning on my heels, I face the open doorway, my attention drawn to a mounted glass frame in the concrete box they call a closet. The frame contains information for workplace safety; the same one they have displayed in various places around staff areas. But it's the tilt of the framed poster drilled into the wall that has me gravitating toward it like I'm a magnet, unable to resist the pull as it clings to my curiosity.

My hair stands on end, my fingers trembling as I tilt it on its axis so it's horizontal instead of vertical as it should be. My eyes widen as I take in the small cutout in the wall, which houses a black button.

That's it. Nothing else.

You'd think that if they didn't want anyone touching it, there would be some sign—a warning. That's what I tell myself anyway as my trembling fingers lift and press the button. The silent groan emanating behind me prompts me to turn around, shivering as a breath of cool air drifts up the dark stairs that descend below.

Every step toward the secret door is in slow motion compared to the frantic beating behind my ribs. I take the first few steps down, my skin slowly adjusting to the increasing chill. My body is taut and vibrating, pushing my heart in my throat as the door clicks shut behind me.

My skin may be freezing, but it doesn't extinguish the heat licking every nerve ending as I warily take one step at a time. A heat that explodes into a chaos of liquid wildfire when the horrifying roar of a man cuts through the tunnels.

# EIGHT | PRESTON

I skillfully twirl the knife, the handle slipping and weaving through my fingers like smooth water I'm gracefully controlling.

I've done it enough times since my father gifted it to me at eighteen that it doesn't take an ounce of my concentration.

It looks intimidating as hell before it leads to one of two things: sheathing it back against my hip, where it always stays, along with my Glock, or it finds itself lodged into someone's chest cavity.

Or that sensitive part of muscle behind their kneecaps that attaches to the back of their thighs.

Or that delicate tendon in the back of their ankles that connects their foot to their calf.

There are too many fun ways to torture someone that fill my chest with a repulsively sweet satisfaction. It may be a twisted fascination, but my personal favorite is when I can feel the vibration of my blade grazing bone through my palm.

Depends on what kind of mood I'm in.

But I favor the latter before I remove their organs and

dispose of them like they're nothing but useless trash that has plagued this earth.

It's a Megalley thing.

A way of life drilled into my DNA before I even understood death. Our mark on the world was imprinted on me long before I learned how to ride a bike.

Sympathy doesn't run in our bloodline when it comes to someone fucking with our operations.

My eyes are locked on dull green ones that falter enough to shred any last remaining speck of trust I had in this man who has only ever defied me. Rowan knows I'll be the boss one day when my father, Arden, is torn from the only life he has ever known. Yet it doesn't stop the challenge that flickers in his lifeless eyes whenever he reports to me.

Which is most of the damn time, since I monitor the routes for our contraband and illegal weapons shipments.

The fucking nerve of this man has snapped my sanity, and now he has found himself at my mercy.

Too bad for him, I don't have much of a fucking heart to let his beat another moment. He's made a fool out of me one too many times, and in return, I'm making a mess out of him. There's a red splatter across the floor resembling a Pollock painting, tossed across a gray canvas, beneath the metal chair that keeps him restrained.

Powerless.

Defenseless.

When a month ticks by and he doesn't return home, I'll send word to his wife that he died at sea during one of our usual *lobster runs*. Navigating rough waters and unrelenting storms is a way of life for fishermen on the Atlantic Coast. Not that she'd probably mind. This bastard runs through wives like they're tissues. Nothing more than bodies to own and dip his dick into.

Not sure what happens to them once he decides to move

on, but I've got a pretty good guess if he's as drunk and ill-tempered as he is in the field working for the Megalley Syndicate. If he's like this here, I can only wonder what he's like at home when bottles of liquor are more easily accessible.

The blade I'm still twirling flashes in the overhead fluorescent lights, shimmering silver and red from the sheen of blood. I stop spinning the knife and grip the handle, lowering to his level to rip the duct tape off his mouth, taking with it salt and pepper strands of hair from his full beard. He flashes his teeth, his enraged growl thundering through the room. His once bright crimson bodily fluids seeping through his grimy jeans and t-shirt are a deep scarlet now from the break I'm taking, hoping his current pain will push the truth off his tongue.

Instead, his lip lifts in a sneer, revealing those yellow and decaying teeth that have resulted from years of smoking and alcoholism. A lifestyle choice that has the acrid smell of smoke seeping through his pores. It combines with the pungent scent of his sweat, overriding the musty odor of the concrete room we use for interrogation. And torturing if we aren't getting the information we seek.

It wouldn't astonish me if his insides are ash.

*I wonder what his lungs look like.*

My blade vibrates in my hands, curious to find out.

His Irish accent is potent. "It's not my fucking problem that you've got your head up your ass and aren't receiving full shipments. This never happened when Arden was fully in charge."

I'm not sure why my father decided to bring this fucker along when he decided to move us permanently to the estate in Lachlan Harbor instead of bouncing around from one estate overseas to the one here like we usually did.

I was fourteen when we began spending most of our time in the States after expanding our borders further. We still go home to Ireland a few times a year to visit my grandparents and check in, but not as often as we used to. Our operations are large enough and well-maintained that we have personnel stationed there to run everything while we're here.

Ireland is easy.

The States, on the other hand, are full of big, flesh-eating fish that we swam alongside in the dark for a long time when the Megalley Syndicate first started way back before my father was born.

Now we are among them.

Rowan's condescending laugh has me clenching my jaw hard enough to shatter my teeth. "Boss's biggest mistake has been splitting his empire with a fucking child—"

Similar to the crack of lightning zapping a tree on a mountaintop, my knife glides through the side of his beer belly like a warm stick of butter. A spitting roar cracks through the room, his body thrashing around in the chair that his arms and legs are bound to.

It's fucking music to my ears.

A lullaby that I will soon silence.

This is why Lachlan Park was built.

A façade to hide our real business.

The narcotics and weapons we smuggle in and out.

The money laundering.

Our various clubs and estates around the East Coast.

A front my family created and rules, while the rest of the universe is oblivious.

While themed music from the rides and the cheers and joyful screams of guests drift down from above, they mask the vile noises that originate from underneath. Masking the kinds of shouts and cries that a human can make before their lungs deflate for a final time and they become nothing but flesh and bones.

Sometimes I scare even myself, knowing the things that I'm capable of.

We are magicians, carefully conducting our tricks behind

closed doors, so what takes place on the outside is the reputation we earn. Lachlan Harbor and Lachlan Park are what we are known by to ordinary people. If only they knew what a few rollercoasters, lobster boats, and vibrant shops on a scenic stretch could hide.

Rowan's breath is ragged as he sucks in air through gritted teeth.

Fresh and dried blood paints my hands and gray suit jacket as I crouch down, getting eye level with the man. My tone is dangerous. Deadly. "I viewed the navigation route. I'm going to ask again, and I highly suggest you tell me what I want to hear if you want me to let you keep your pathetic life another day. Why did you make an unplanned stop in New York?"

His rotted mouth opens, giving me a whiff of his vile breath. "It was for a quick fuck! A man has needs that need to be fulfilled."

*Fulfilled by his wife.*

I arch a brow. "You disregarded my orders for pussy? What would your wife say about that?"

"Tight, young pussy. You can only use a toy so many times before it breaks, and you have to buy another one."

Acid bubbles in my stomach.

"And when you were off fucking, who was guarding the boat? *My* product? Was it Cathal?"

His posture stiffens.

*Interesting.*

His focus rapidly shifts from my eyes to the wall, where a window offers a view of the room from one of the hundreds of maze-like hallways, winding underground through the park. I've memorized every single one—where they go, what rooms they navigate to, doors that lead to the secret exits that nobody knows exist besides members.

It's only him and me.

There's nobody here to save him, because like the men we have patrolling these hallways, they listen to me.

"Help!" That one word spewed from his mouth causes my brows to furrow in surprise. "Help me!"

Who is he calling for?

I turn my head, prepared for him to be at that level of excruciating pain where he's hallucinating and reaching full-blown hysterics. But what I find blasts me in the chest to knock the air from my lungs.

A young woman stands on the other side, as solid as a statue in one of our uniforms. Even through the tint and the glare from the fluorescent lights in the room, her features paint a memory in my mind. A memory of a crisp, sunny morning when I discovered a stranger relaxing at the end of our private dock like they had a death wish.

I was prepared to drag their ass off until long, wavy locks of hair that appeared like liquid gold stopped me on the spot. Then, she turned—a gorgeous woman brighter than the sun that licked my skin despite the lies that spewed from her mouth like wildfire.

Now, her eyes are blown so wide that they could burst from any more pressure and splatter the glass. Those puffy blush lips I stared at for far too long the other day, part in shock.

Well, shit.

This hasn't happened since we increased security ten years ago after another worker had found their way down here. Another time in my life I'd rather forget entirely, but can't when it secured my place in hell as if I wasn't already going there to begin with.

And it's a major problem she's here, considering my knife is lodged in the side of Rowan's stomach, and I look like a psychopathic murderer with his blood coating my hands.

Which I am.

Time stands still as we stare at each other. One heartbeat passes. Then two.

And by the third, before I can get a full breath and comprehend what's happening, she takes off into a dead sprint.

*Fuck. Fuck. Fuck!*

I stand and retract my knife from his stomach, listening to his pitiful grunts before smearing his blood across my pants. I'll just buy another suit.

As I always do when carnage soils it.

You'd think I'd be running after her, considering the state she found me torturing this man who doesn't deserve to be labeled a victim. For some reason, behind the irritation clouding my vision, the thought of hunting her down through the maze of concrete sends an odd thrill that bolts through my body like a drug.

Darkness thrums in my veins.

I point a crimson finger at Rowan. "When I get back, you'd better tell me what I want to know, or this knife will find your heart. Or your throat. Or the back of your skull. I haven't quite decided how I want to end you yet. It all comes down to your cooperation." *If you don't bleed out before then.*

I straighten my suit jacket and huff out an irritated groan before marching across the room in only a few strides. One of the perks of being massive, from years of torturing my body in the gym and my 6'4 frame, is that I cover more ground taking normal steps.

When I reach the metal door, I open it and step into the hallway, slamming it behind me, hoping the sound reverberating off the walls sparks an extra sense of terrified urgency in her steps.

Reaching into my suit pants pocket, I take out my phone and click on Brody's contact, our head of security for the Megalley Syndicate. We pride ourselves on keeping our operations locked and impenetrable, but with a fucking huge empire and the amount of security systems we have, things are bound to slip through our fingers.

*Pretty, curious things.*

Doesn't happen often, but when it does, it's solved by a metal chain and a permanent vacation to the bottom of the ocean—perks of being on the coast. Most people are terrified of the monsters that lurk beneath the surface, but they forget that more dangerous ones breathe the same air.

I place the phone against my ear. As always, it rings once before he responds in greeting with a firm, "Boss."

"I'm in the West Wing. Someone slipped through our fingers. I need a location—now."

The unmistakable rapid clicking of a keyboard is heard over his voice. "Rowan?"

I wish. That would be easier to handle than this clusterfuck I'm about to find myself in.

The spark of exhilaration that punches me in the gut surprises me. I don't let it show. "More like a rat."

"Am I supposed to know what that means—" His following, "Oh shit," tells me he's found what I'm looking for. He chuckles. "She's headed for the South Wing."

I start moving, hustling through the hallway. My pace can't be described as a run or a walk. Somewhere in between because I can't ignore the flash of anticipation in my chest, knowing that this might be the most exciting chase I've had.

"Stay on the line. Let me know when I'm getting close. She's in the uniform overalls for the haunted mine ride. Can you get a good enough read on her face to—"

As if he were reading my thoughts, he says, "Her name is Kate Hannaford."

*Kate.*

Her name ricochets, penetrating so deeply that the other details fade to the background when he says, "Age twenty-four. We employed her four months ago." He hums low in his throat.

"Apparently, we pay her paycheck in cash. Odd request for a pretty thing like her."

The hairs on my neck gravitate toward the cement ceiling. The gears rotating in my head screech to a halt, nearly bringing me to a complete stop. "Did you say four months?"

"Yep." A few clicks in the background indicate that he is switching between views. "Take a right and then a left." I do as he says, and it's not long before the soft patter of footsteps echoes through the concrete maze. "If you take another right and then a left, she'll run into you."

"Put it on my reminders to bring this up at our next security briefing. We can't have shit like this happening. And I want any information you can pull up about this girl."

That stops him short. He knows it's his job, and I can practically feel the rush of air escaping him in panic, slipping through the phone. "But this never happens."

"Then what would you call this fucking situation?" I grit out, damn well knowing he's right.

And it just so happens to be the same girl I scolded about finding herself in places she shouldn't be while I tried to divert my attention from the swells of her breasts that almost evaporated the warning on my tongue. Her pink mouth drew my focus next, as I contemplated how much more color I could inject into her lips while they stretched to fit my cock.

Jesus Christ.

This is the exact distraction I can't afford. Doesn't matter if I've been sex deprived for years and my dick is craving something warmer than my hand.

Just like that day I saw her, suspicion blooms behind my ribs. This time, it's piercing—a bell knocking on the inside of my skull and ringing like an alarm. It didn't happen just once, when a shipment came in with missing contraband. Somehow, she also found herself in the walls of our empire.

*Bad little rat.*

"And under no circumstances," my tone harsh with no room for argument, "does Arden hear about this."

Brody releases a grunt of understanding. I take another turn, and he says, "She's headed your way." With that, the phone goes dead, and I tuck it back in my pocket.

My fingers tighten around the handle of the knife. My skin buzzes, my blood alight with fervor as I close in on Kate, as if I'm an eagle ready to snatch the scampering rodent with my talons.

The corner of this hallway, dimly lit by sconces, is just ahead. The patter of frantic footsteps swells, every sharp tap of her shoes ricocheting through the hallway and the pulse in my neck like a pinball machine.

When her small body sprints around the corner and crashes into mine, I fight the smile that wants to appear at the way my body mass knocks her backward. When she glances up at me, Kate's eyes are blazing with fear. Looking at her now, knowing her name feels dangerous. It does something to my chest.

This is why they say not to name an animal, or you'll get attached to it.

Can't have that happening.

"I should've believed them," she whimpers. " I-I only have one kidney," Kate stammers, breathlessly. She moves backward on instinct. I don't waste any time closing the distance. "And my heart, it has that weird thing where it murmurs, so it's not perfect, and I'm sure you don't want it."

*The fuck.*

Tears drop from her bottom lashes onto her pigmented cheeks. While I'm trying to piece together her rambling that's confusing the ever-loving shit out of me, she keeps talking, my attention locking on those flush, rosy lips she can't stop licking from the nervousness that is overtaking her.

Her bottom lip quivers, and I have this odd inclination to

stop it with my teeth. "I know kidneys are valuable, and you'd make more money out of someone who has all the organs you need. Please don't take mine," she hiccups, placing her sleeve over that distracting mouth.

What the fuck is she talking about?

She wraps her arms around her waist, as if it will give her some comfort. Unfortunately, I don't think anything can bring her comfort for what I'm about to put her through.

My mouth parts to ease the thoughts running rampant in her head about her organs, but I think better of it. Maybe it's better if she's petrified. I need her to talk. To find out why she was on the dock that day when the shipment arrived, and how the hell she ended up in the tunnels.

My eyes are lethal, locking onto her green ones—green like the leaves that climb the stone walls in the garden, accented by the magenta flowers my mother once loved. So many emotions flash across her face that she finally registers my state—my bloody, gruesome state. She slaps a hand over her mouth, her breath breaking into a wheeze as every drop of color drains from her skin.

"Oh my God. Whose blood is that? Who's that man?"

I reach out and snag her forearm, her warmth seeping into my cold fingers. "For now, be happy it isn't yours—and it won't be if you obey me."

She sucks in an audible breath, and my lips twitch before I bite back the sadistic grin threatening to surface.

I'm amused by the flash of terror that graces those big green eyes as she stares down at my stained hands that are on her. Touching her. The hands of an unsympathetic man, dragging her to a room where her night is about to get a whole lot worse.

# NINE | KATE

I'm fully clothed, but it doesn't help the icy metal of the chair from biting into my skin. My body is trembling profusely from the chill blanketing my body in this enclosed concrete room, tainted with the metallic stench of blood and piss threading through the particles in the air.

Bile lingers in my throat, threatening to be another bodily fluid splashed all over the floor.

I should run and sprint for the door, but my fight or flight instincts are paralyzed by the gruesome scene filling my vision. Somehow, it's just as restricting as the zip ties that secure the dead man to the chair across from me. He's in front of a wall and a table of unknown devices, guns, knives, and other torturous things that will add fuel to the nightmares I'm already plagued with if I somehow make it out with my life.

Which is looking slim, considering the handsome man who caught me on the dock is pacing back and forth enough to wear holes in his designer shoes. Yet his strides are controlled as he twirls a knife in his bloody fingers like it's a typical night.

For him, it probably is.

As I said, I should run. But he said if I obey him, my blood won't blend with the scarlet already caked on his hands.

Oh, God.

Why am I considering that this psychopath will let me live after I saw him plunge his knife into the side of this poor man's stomach? It was foolish to pray that the window I was observing through was one-sided.

Chances are, he's going to kill me anyway, and my heart or single kidney is going to end up in some stranger who doesn't give a damn about my life that was perfectly intact when it was taken from me.

Images of my family flash before my eyes. My beautiful, loving parents and sister, Natalie, who have done everything to help me escape the horrific situation I found myself in when it was obvious that law enforcement couldn't be bothered. I guess that's what happens when you live in the biggest city in the state, and there are more pressing matters to deal with than a boyfriend carving her girlfriend like a turkey at Thanksgiving. Restraining order or not, it hasn't mattered. Not even proof of the scars lacerating my stomach could entice them to take action.

"We don't have enough evidence to press charges," they said.

Bull. Fucking. Shit.

Running away was the last resort. Sometimes it still feels like I'm watching my life with an imaginary bag of popcorn and a glass of wine while I try to yell at myself about how stupid I am that I didn't do something when I first saw the signs.

Every day is another day my family could be in danger for maintaining silence about my whereabouts. But it's become clear that Xander's hunt for me scratches his urge for entertainment. He hasn't contacted them yet, but that doesn't mean he won't.

What happens when I've evaded him so long that my family becomes the only place left to look for answers?

To find me?

The last time I contacted them was over six months ago. I rummage through my mental boxes, trying to remember if I even said those three words to them that I've said absentmindedly so many times.

*I love you.*

Words that usually come so naturally, but it's not until something like this happens that I realize how much weight they hold.

I should've said it more—intertwined more meaning and love into them the way they deserve.

He pauses, walking toward me to brace his hands on the arms of the chair, caging me in. He peers into my glazed eyes that are still shedding tears. There clearly isn't an ounce of compassion in those entrancing bourbon eyes that burn with a fire that could scorch anyone who draws near.

They're a warning.

"Is he...dead?" I force the words out shakily as they slice through the eerily silent room.

He tilts his head, studying me with a stare that makes me feel like a microbe under his scope. "His pain is so excruciating that he is in and out of consciousness. He didn't answer my questions." His stern tone adds extra force to that last comment.

My poor heart shudders behind my ribs. "I come from a medical background. It would be a miracle if he survives those, even if he does answer you."

Deadpan, he says, "I'm not planning on letting him live, darling."

*No. No. No!* Is this what might await me?

My hands shake, so I clasp them in my lap tightly. "And if I do...answer your questions, you'll let me live?"

His head wobbles side to side. "Not sure yet. You've put me in quite the predicament." A tremor racks through my body, and his lips tilt just slightly enough that my body doesn't seem to agree with my head about how we feel about this man.

He's alluring in the worst way.

"But I can promise you that this will go a lot easier if you tell me what I want to know. Starting with why you were on my dock the other day," he tsks. The tendons in his hands strain as he grips the arms of the chair forcefully.

He's so close, we're breathing the same air.

Even over the metallic stench of carnage permeating the space, his masculine and smoky scent glides into my lungs as they rapidly inflate and deflate.

I think I'm about to hyperventilate.

My heart is on overdrive, and my body can't keep up. My own body might finish me off before he does, like a baby bird that can easily succumb to stress alone.

If I'm going to die, I'm not sure which way is worse.

The lump lodged in my throat stays even when I swallow roughly. "I wanted to enjoy my coffee in peace. I didn't think it would be that big of a deal."

One hand clutches the knife. The other is drumming on the arm of the chair with bloody fingers. "A sign that says *restricted* isn't a suggestion. Not very good at following directions, are we? Which brings me to my next question. How did you get down here, *Kate*?"

His use of my name has my blood coursing through my veins like cement. My name slipping off his tongue is like a bucket of ice water poured over exposed skin, but it also has an unexpected current of warmth penetrating somewhere unreachable. My teeth are damn near close to chattering from the terrified adrenaline and cold atmosphere that is trying to drown me.

"How do you know my na—"

Before I can finish the question, he lifts the knife and positions the tip at my knee.

It's probably the wrong time to release sarcasm, but I squeal, "There wasn't a restricted sign on the door."

His jaw jumps, his eyes narrowing. I sharply inhale, remaining completely still as he digs the tip of the blade into the fabric of my gray work overalls above my knee cap. Tears pour over my bottom lashes heavily now, leaving searing trails in their wake before falling to my chest. I only had a little bit of mascara on, but I'm betting it's swiped all over my cheeks like modern art.

My chaotic, ragged pants drift between us, but he doesn't let up or let me distract him. He starts slicing upward at a controlled pace, not at all deterred by the hysteria slowly taking over my body.

"A girl lost her phone on the ride, and it went down a grate. When I looked down, I saw the tunnel. Finding the secret door in the closet was just dumb luck." I don't think I've ever talked so fast, but my damn life is on the line here.

His condescending laugh doesn't waver his attentiveness as he continues cutting my pant leg open to expose my skin to him.

"Dumb luck? I'm not a naive man, darling. Give me more credit than that. All our entrances are hidden. Secure. Which means you were looking for them, whether you like to admit it or not."

He picks up his speed, and the rush of cold air that glides across my thigh has my eyes dropping to see the slit he's cut in my pants. As he gets closer to the dip where my hip meets my thigh, blackness starts seeping into the corners of my vision. Hard, crippling panic creeps up my throat like the long legs of spiders tapping on the inside of my esophagus.

The blade isn't making contact with my leg, but I swear I

can feel the cold touch of the metal hovering just above my flesh.

Flashbacks slaughter my vision, my body pressed below Xander's as he thrusts in and out while the tip of the knife slides effortlessly through my skin. I was too young to understand blood play. I guess it shouldn't have come as a shock, considering he was the phlebotomist who drew my blood at the drive where we met. His passion for his job was evident. In fact, his love for his career was one of the things that drew me to him. But his position was a cover to conceal his true obsession, and I didn't realize it until it was too late.

My tear-stricken face is uncomfortably hot.

His movements pause, drawing me back to the present. "Two times! I've caught you trespassing twice. Why is that?"

"This is all just a coincidence," I sob. "I swear."

He removes the blade, and although I should be filling my lungs with a breath of relief, I don't.

He points the tip of the knife toward me, and it's the first time I notice the sheen of blood on the blade glimmering in the fluorescent lights. "I don't believe in coincidences. I believe things are done with intention, even when we aren't aware of it. This is the second time I've found you lurking where you aren't supposed to, and there are far too many connections between complications with my operations and your *coincidental* whereabouts."

"I have no idea what you're talking about."

"No?"

I shake my head, sinking my teeth into my lower lip. The salty taste of tears coats my taste buds.

He leans over my fragile frame, lifts the hand holding the hunting knife featuring carved designs on the blade, and drags the blunt end of the cool metal along my neck. His eyes latch onto the three-inch scar below my earlobe, but that doesn't stop him from gliding the blade over the risen, ugly skin.

I choke back the cry that wants to release, my body trembling so much that I would be the reason if it pierces through my skin.

His control in this situation is frightening.

"Do you still have the same answer?" he murmurs. "Or do we need to release some of the blood that's rushing to your head so you can think straighter?"

Holy shit.

How can something so beautiful be so lethal?

Everything about him is hypnotic. The way those bourbon eyes remind me of melted caramel on a fall day. The way his broad shoulders stretch the material of his impeccable suit. The way the dark ink embedded in his skin peeks through the glaze of red on his hands and beneath the collar of his button-down. He is strikingly and dangerously handsome.

His other hand, calloused and hard, moves to cup my neck to hold me still. They are the hands of a man who inflicts pain and cruelty on whoever crosses him.

I happen to be a bystander who got caught in the crossfire.

"Do it," I challenge. "You'll have innocent blood on your hands." I'm doubting it would be the first time. "But once you realize you are wrong about me, I don't think it would put a dent in your sympathy, which clearly doesn't exist. You'd be doing me a favor anyway."

Those balls of fire in his eyes bounce between mine; I assume they are carefully dissecting my words. He *would* be doing me a favor. I'm so fucking exhausted from running. I may still have a family, but what does it matter since I can't see them anyway?

His eyes narrow, analyzing mine before he releases my nape and takes a step back. "You don't even know me, Miss Hannaford."

Somehow, collecting a little bit of strength, I lean over, pinning him in place as we stand off. "Likewise, Captain."

He twirls the knife again, entrancing me with the soft and precise movements of the blade spinning in the light. "What am I supposed to do with you?" There's a subtle hint of teasing blended with his sigh. Barely, but it's there, enough to loosen the imaginary shackles imprisoning me in place.

"Let me go."

"No can do, darling. I don't trust you. But I won't hurt you. Not yet anyway."

"I just watched you stab a man. You think *I* trust *you*?" I toss back at him.

He grips the knife's handle to stop its movements, slicing through the air. Our eyes dance, his jaw tensing. Several heartbeats pass before he rakes a hand over that cropped beard. I wonder what it would feel like between my—

*Not the time, Kate.*

He props his hands on his hips. "Are you prepared to do whatever it takes to prove that this is a coincidence?"

My heart patters obnoxiously. "Depends."

"One month."

My eyes lift to the ceiling in confusion. Huh?

When they settle on him again, his face is twisted into a scowl. "If you want to escape with your life, I need you under surveillance for one month."

I wipe my hands over my eye sockets. This must be a dream. There's no way he's suggesting what I think he is. When I put my hands down, he's standing closer, all brooding with his thick arms folded across his chest.

A nervous, post-crying laugh bubbles out of me. "Yeah, that's not going to happen. I have a job."

"I'll take care of it."

Deadpan, I can't hide my disbelief. "Will you now?" His firm nod doesn't instill any confidence in me. "No. I'm not going to let you hold me hostage for something I didn't do."

"You've got two options, Kate." He presses the tip of his

blade against his pointer finger, rotating the knife. I watch in fascination, wondering if he'll draw his own blood. "One, you end up with this knife silencing your heart before we toss you to the bottom of the ocean during our next lobster run." What the hell kind of lobster business is this guy running, where he murders people when he doesn't get answers? "Two, you come with me for a month and leave with your life if you're not related to this clusterfuck I'm dealing with. I need to be certain you aren't tied to whoever is fucking with my family's business."

Realization starts to dawn on me. Between this psychopath covered in blood and the suffocating concrete walls, I almost forgot where I am. He sheathes his knife, drawing my attention to the Glock attached to his hip. It's as if he knew the knife would petrify me more.

"You said 'family's business'." The lump in my throat expands as I try to ignore the other weapon. "Who is your family?"

Out of all the things I thought might kill me today, it isn't him saying, "I'm Preston Lachlan."

# TEN | PRESTON

"**A**s in Lachlan Park." It isn't a question; she's saying it out loud to process. Those bright eyes tinged with red from crying, swirl with questions as she gazes ahead, absentmindedly.

She's even beautiful when she cries. I'm not sure why the thought of that pisses me the fuck off.

"Lachlan Harbor," she mutters to herself. Her eyes widen, slicing to mine. "Your family founded this town?"

What I don't tell her is that technically, my full name is Preston Lachlan Megalley.

I shrug nonchalantly. "Something like that."

Those expanded eyes tell me she knows I'm heir to Lachlan Harbor. But the detail I leave out is that the responsibility is also tied to being the future boss of the Megalley Syndicate.

Ever since I was sixteen, the weight of my future as being the boss of the Irish mafia has slowly been added to rest on my shoulders. My dad has conditioned me to take on this responsibility because Arden believes he should leave his son better off and more successful than he was. My father is brutal, unrelenting, and cruel when he needs to be, but he's also the best fucking father a man can ask for. It's why the people in this town don't cower from him like they do with me.

"That's why you know my name," she whispers. "You're like my...boss." Her head tilts, flashing me with that long scar under her ear.

I fight the urge to ball my fists at my side.

An unexpected feeling of disgust with myself surfaced when I used that imperfection against her. But I had a job to do, so I pushed past it and ignored the buzz in my fingers that itched to tangle in her soft waves instead. She was already trembling, but I didn't miss the way I injected an extra dose of fear into her bloodstream when I dragged the blunt end of my knife across it.

Interest is pulling at all sides. The scar is too clean. Too seamless to be an accident.

Usually, a woman calling me boss would set my dick off behind my zipper, but it's nothing compared to the warmth that fizzles across my skin when she calls me Captain. "Does that mean you'll finally be a good girl and listen to me?"

Her features drop, her lower lip quivering. "Please, don't call me that."

Now I'm really fucking interested in this girl.

Where she came from.

What darkness plagues her past?

I'm a very intuitive man. Every time her eyes flit to my knife clenched in my fist, I have this gut-wrenching inclination that she isn't a stranger to one.

Which further solidifies my distrust of her.

It's not a secret that Luciano and the Calco Cartel are bleeding into our borders. It's clear that he will do whatever it takes to destroy us and establish ownership of the East Coast, expanding his operations.

It's why Tayla and my mom's hearts were carved out of their chests and succumbed to a styrofoam box like they were nothing. But out of all of us, they were pure. They were more than flesh and bone that protected their souls. They were kind. Exuding the type of warmth that burrows so deep it can't help but shatter the frigid darkness that infests anyone enslaved to a world like ours.

It was a horrific and immoral motive that left us distracted and vulnerable. While we were mourning, Luciano took out some of our men positioned on our borders. The bloodshed five years ago hit us like a flash flood amid a drought.

We got our shit together. Recruited more men. Arden and I came back stronger on the outside, since nothing remained on the inside.

It's been a year since the last attack, but that doesn't mean he's given up.

What better way to destroy us than from the inside?

Kate's scar makes me think she crossed someone unmerciful. The uneven healing tells me it wasn't stitched.

What if this is his plan?

Sending a pretty distraction to worm her way to the heart of our operation.

Not on my fucking watch.

My voice is unrecognizable. "Get up."

Her chest stills. "What? Wh-Where are we going?"

"Your sentence starts now, darling." I reach for her forearm, tugging her upward as she struggles to stand like a newborn giraffe on those long legs that would perfectly wrap around my waist while I thrust between them.

"I'm sorry. I'm so sorry, I won't let it happen again. Please, just let me go!"

I tug her through the room, keeping her tucked alongside me. She seems slippery. Like she'll slide through my fingers if I don't keep her exactly where I want her.

Darkness seeps through my words. "There's only one way I like someone begging. So, I suggest you keep your mouth shut before I decide to force you to your knees and shove all these useless apologies down the back of your throat with my cock."

She gasps in shock, the sound making me wonder if that's what she'd sound like the first time my dick slides into her.

*Goddamn. Get it together.*

Surprisingly, she listens for a moment before her mouth parts, hitting me with a question that is just as frustrating. "You're just going to leave him here? Like that?"

Yep. That's precisely what I'm going to do.

Twenty-four hours from now, the stench will be so horrendous that I'm hoping it might entice someone else to come out with the truth. Rowan wasn't alone in collecting that shipment, and I'm hoping that when I sit Cathal down in front of his friend, he won't think twice about keeping secrets from me. Unlike Rowan, Cathal has a clean record with me. He might not end up dead like the bastard who was with him, but he won't escape unscathed either.

Pushing Kate out the door, I close it behind me, forcing her down the opposite end of the hallway she ran down. She nervously nibbles on her bottom lip as I march her to one of the military-grade utility vehicles we use to navigate the tunnels. Moving to the passenger side, I toss open the door and gesture for her to get in. Kate peers at me with hesitancy before I fold my arms in a silent challenge.

She swallows and crawls in, folding her hands into her lap, anxiously fiddling with her fingers as I shut the door. I move around the front and slide in beside her, firing up the vehicle as we take off, covering the half mile of tunnels that lead from the park to Lachlan Estate.

# ELEVEN | PRESTON

"**A**bsolutely fucking not." Carter crosses his arms over his chest in defiance, not bothering to keep his voice at an inaudible level.

Kate peeks up from her knitted fingers in her lap from the accent chair she's sitting on in one of the guest rooms at the estate.

Her new home for the next month.

She hasn't spoken to me since I told her I was going to leave Rowan's body in that room. I may not have delivered the final blow to his life, but technically, he's still dying by my hand as he goes in and out of consciousness from blood loss.

Pretty anticlimactic if you ask me.

I inwardly groan. I fucking hate not finishing things.

On second thought, I could have Imogen fix him up so I can play with him more; keep him in the cells under the park so I can drag out his sentence.

Kate is just another distraction I have to deal with, which is why I'm trying to hand her over to Carter, who is irritatingly trying to hold his ground. He knows I'll win this battle no matter how persistent he is about protesting.

"I have enough shit to deal with as it is. You know that. All I'm asking is that you keep an eye on her."

"Babysit," he growls. "You want me to fucking babysit."

Kate stands from the chair. "I can hear you, and I'm not a child." Her eyes snag on the expansive yard, lit up in the night through the massive windows.

She glares out as if it's the first time she's seeing the impeccably mowed lines across the grass, patio, and the blooming garden beds. It isn't. She was so zoned out and lost in thought when I drove out of the entrance to the tunnels, located in one of our armory buildings, through the trees. I sped across the yard, and then I ushered her inside through the back door quickly, like I was a teenager sneaking in a girl behind my dad's back for a quick fuck.

This three-story estate is elegantly ominous enough to stop most people, but it was evident that her exhaustion and fear from the last few hours had taken a toll on her. She followed me like I had an imaginary leash hooked to that pretty little neck.

An idea triggers.

I ignore her, turning my attention back to Carter, who's fuming enough that I wouldn't be surprised if smoke starts curling out of his nose. "You've got to be fucking with me, Preston. Do you think this is the best use of my time, given that these shipments are going missing? You know I'm more useful than this!"

Placing my hands on my hips, I turn away from Kate so she can't read my lips. My voice lowers. "Will you calm your ass if I tell you that my reason for keeping her under surveillance is because I think she's related to this damn mess?"

His brow quirks at that.

"Remember when I got on the boat the other day when we took inventory, and I said I found someone on our dock?" I refresh his memory.

His tone softens for the first time since I called him into the guest room, but it still contains that dangerous edge. "That's *her*? And you found her in the tunnels?" My sharp nod has him muttering, "Fuck." He drags his fingers through his mussed hair in contemplation. "Yeah, I'll keep an eye on her. If it will help."

"I have an idea to keep track of her. Just give me some time."

His probing gaze is trying to pull the information out of me. I don't let up. Not when I know Kate's listening to our every word.

Carter's mouth pulls up at the corners. "You're losing your edge, *deartháir*." I know he's serious when he calls me brother like that.

My father and I only speak Gaelic when it's necessary—when words need to be exchanged between us in public. Carter may not have Irish blood, but he made it his duty to learn the language to prove his loyalty and dedication, after Arden gave him a roof over his head and a financial status most would kill for.

The artery in my chest jumps. "I don't know what you're talking about."

"*Mhmm.* Then I'm sure you won't mind if I suggest we solve this little issue in the morning when the boats head out. I mean, you do remember what happened the last time a park employee found themselves in the tunnels?"

The reminder screws and twists into my abdomen, leaving behind an excruciating burn that claws at my flesh. Besides my mom and sisters' hearts arriving in that box, the second worst day of my life was when I fed that fresh twenty-something boy to the sea. He was unconscious, but it doesn't make up for my wrongdoings or my guilt. It has fucking eaten me alive for the last ten years.

I watched the waves devour him.

Pull him under, along with the weight attached to his feet.

Whatever remaining humanity I had left disappeared with him.

But that night, when I was at a low that felt unescapable, Tayla was there. There was no hiding the all-consuming shame rotting me from the inside out. My sister sat with me on the rocky shoreline below our estate and didn't need to say a word. She rested her head on my shoulder, her dark waves cascading over my arm, and just existed with me when I wished that I didn't.

It's peculiar that even the purest love in the world still finds beauty in the things that are broken.

The moment I tossed him over the side of the boat, the remorse weaved like invasive vines through my conscience. There was no going back on my decision. His body found its final home one thousand feet under the sea, and I'll be damned if Kate joins the skeletons I keep buried.

But if she is working with the Calco Cartel, the man responsible for the bloodshed on my family, drowning her would be too kind.

That thought still doesn't stop his name from tasting bitter in my mouth at the suggestion. "Carter," I warn.

Out of the corner of my eye, Kate is still gazing out the window. It's the same view of the yard I have with the ocean beyond. There are spotlights at the edges of the grass, illuminating the trees on the forest's edge. The garden maze in the distance glows with those twinkling lights, inviting and warm.

"You do realize a month is plenty of time for her to learn things," he whispers. "And if she isn't involved with Luciano—if he's even the one behind these missing shipments, you plan to just let her go? Let her disappear with the knowledge of what the Megalley Syndicate is capable of? There are enough rumors as it is floating around Lachlan Harbor from those attacks and murders that happened in the park."

Fuck, I need a drink.

It's almost one a.m., and I'm too tired to make any rational decisions.

The only thing I'm certain of is that I need to keep track of her when she doesn't think I'm watching. The security cameras littered throughout the estate aren't enough. If tonight is any indication, there are flaws in our system.

Lifting a hand to my temple, I rub in a circular motion—a pathetic attempt to clear the turmoil. "I need to see Arden. Can you keep a post outside her door until tomorrow morning?"

"What about the balcony?"

Goddammit. Visiting the tech room will have to happen tonight.

Unease tightens my muscles. "Fine. Stay in the room with her." The words taste sour, but at least there is an en suite for her to use. I make a mental note to tell Gretta to go shopping for some clothes to fill her closet.

Stepping away from Carter, my eyes are drawn to those steadfast green pools glaring at me from the other side of the room. Our eyes remain locked the entire time until I'm boring a hole through the door after I shut it.

Walking down the hall to the grand foyer with a spiral staircase, I remove my jacket as I ascend the steps to the third floor. The hallway is dark, except for the glowing strip coming from beneath my father's office door. My knuckles rap on it a few times before his deep voice tells me to enter. When I open the door, he's lounging comfortably in his desk chair, his back turned to me as he gazes out at the blanket of night encasing the estate. His hand lifts, bringing his tumbler of scotch to his lips.

His office, with its dark wood accents and deep greens, is as intimidating as it is inviting. It's somewhere in between.

Silence passes between us, and I'm sure he knows I need a drink before I tell him about my day, just like we do most nights, since we are both shit at sleeping. I approach the wet bar, roll up my sleeves, and notice my red-stained hands that I still haven't cleaned. It's not like cleansing them would wipe my soul.

The damage is done.

The amber liquid flows into the glass. I take a sip before sinking into one of the chairs across from his desk. It's that kind of night.

Dad slowly turns around, his tired eyes hitting me with a war that rarely ever shows on the outside, unless we're dealing with business.

On the streets, Arden Lachlan Megalley is a beloved figure in this town that my great-grandparents founded in the early 1930s. People address him with warm smiles, and he returns them.

However, that hospitality is shown when it's deserved.

Behind closed doors, his violence even terrifies me. Which speaks volumes, considering I'm desensitized to most things. I watch him in awe, respecting the power and authority he commands. Ever since Mom and Tayla were murdered, anyone who crosses him not only has their body destroyed, but it's like he tries to crush their soul in his fists, echoing the fractures in his own.

We only have each other now.

His sleep-ridden tone carries through the space. My Irish accent may be slowly slipping from me, but his is still as thick and deep as it always has been. "You must think I'm blind if you think I didn't see you sneak that girl in here. Who is she?" he speaks through the rim before taking a sip.

Shit. So much for him not finding out. But a new face around the estate wouldn't go unnoticed.

I do the same, letting the smooth, spiced flavor glide across my taste buds. "Kate." I'd say the husk in my voice is from the scotch, but it's not.

"Kate," he repeats, nodding. "She's pretty."

"Oh," I cough, choking on the liquor. "It's not like that."

He arches a brow. "Not like what?"

"I'm not fucking her." Yet.

*Not. Going. To. Happen.*

Doesn't mean I can't fantasize about wrapping those dark blonde waves around my fist. Wonder what that lying tongue would feel like gliding up my shaft. Picture what Kate would look like while I assault that goddamn mouth until she can't distinguish her tears of pleasure from her tears of pain.

I shift slightly in the chair to relieve the growing bulge in my briefs.

If just the thought of her can unravel me, what would claiming her do?

Dragging a hand over his salt and pepper beard, he sighs, giving me a flash of those crow's feet on the corners of his eyes. They used to be a warm brown like mine, but are now dull like the dirt he wishes he were buried six feet under—a testament to how the last several years have aged him quickly.

My father studies my face. "I was wondering when you'd finally start to settle down."

"Fuck no. She's not—" Goddamn. How can I avoid telling him about her real reason for being here? Didn't she briefly mention something about having a medical background earlier? "She's joining our medical team," the words pour out of my mouth before I've carefully considered them.

"Oh? I didn't realize we were looking to add another person."

"I figured with missing product and not knowing if the Calco Cartel is behind it, it's best to be prepared." Just because nobody's made a move in a year doesn't mean we're not still at war.

He nods thoughtfully, but I don't miss the glint of suspicion that lingers. "So, she's staying here? In the estate." His lips twitching grate against my skin.

I prop my foot on my knee, lean back, and get comfortable as I pop a few buttons. Fuck, it's getting hot in here.

"She just moved to town. Thought she could stay here for a month until she finds a place. We have plenty of space."

"Ah, I see." His hand rocks, twirling the amber liquid in the glass. "Well, I'd like to meet her when she has a minute. You know, considering you employed her without my knowledge, and my life might rest in her hands."

He's too perceptive to see through my bull shit. My dad may not know the exact reason she's here, but maybe letting him wonder if something is stirring between Kate and me would be better than the truth. If he thinks she's involved with the Calco Cartel at all, proof or not, it's not just her heart and her kidney she'll have to worry about.

He'll leave nothing left of her.

# TWELVE | KATE

Early-morning light pierces through the skylights above me, energizing the indoor plants that surround the perimeter. Vines cascade across the ceiling, their growth lacing through the rafters and dripping down the spaces of the wall between the massive windows.

Though it's a beautiful breakfast nook with a view of the forest to the right and the yard and ocean beyond to the left, it does little to dispel the exhausted fog that's been hovering in my head. My eyes are fixed on those looming watchtowers and fences, with guards—their solid statures look like gargoyles keeping watch. For what, I'm not sure.

This isn't just a family that owns the town and an amusement park. There's more lurking in the depths that I accidentally dipped my toes into, and it's sucking me in.

From the little I've seen of this three-story estate, I know it's massive. The kind of place you walk into and instantly feel small and meaningless. Weightless compared to the elegance, details, and expanse only money can buy. For example, the room they kept me trapped in last night. Where I come from, that isn't a guest room. Not when it's nearly the size of my entire one-bedroom house and the en suite is as big as my kitchen with its white tiles and realistic-looking rock walk-in shower.

Sleep only found me for a few short hours last night. It's hard to doze off into a peaceful slumber when a brooding man lounges in the same room, arms crossed, observing your every move. Not to mention, my mind kept bombarding me with flashbacks of an unconscious man covered in blood as his life slowly drained from his eyes.

Carter would've rather been doing anything else than babysitting me, I could tell that much from his harsh voice. It wasn't until I fully turned around that I got a good look at him. The recognition hit instantly. Just like Preston, he has a beautiful face and frame that's hard to forget. Jet black hair that's effortlessly styled and cropped short at the sides, complemented by tattoos that stretch over every bulge of muscle. Both he and Preston look like they were carved from stone. Hard, mouthwatering physiques that would feel glorious against your tongue and below your hands.

Carter was the one on the boat talking to the man I watched Preston murder. The only reason I know his name is from when Preston growled it last night, when he thought I was zoning out while they were discussing what to do with me, as if I were a petulant child.

After Preston stormed out, I considered starting a conversation with Carter to see if it would help disperse some of the tension and allow me to settle enough to fall asleep. The words never came.

I used the en suite bathroom, stripped down to the t-shirt and shorts I wear under my uniform, and lay on my side, facing away from where he was sitting. He dragged one of the accent chairs over to the door and settled into it like he had done something like this thousands of times. His unrelenting focus on my back the entire night had my skin buzzing with unease.

He sips his coffee in the seat across the table from mine,

those brown eyes boring into my face as I ignore the beautiful breakfast spread a kind woman set in front of Carter and me.

For being a prisoner, it sure seems like the meal of a queen. A pile of French toast is stacked like a carb-loaded tower. There's a bowl of strawberries, sunny-side-up eggs, grapes, and bacon crisped to perfection, all accompanied by orange juice and a carafe of coffee.

My stomach grumbles as I inhale the delicious aroma deeply, as if the scent alone will quench my hunger.

As if he can hear it, Carter lifts his mug to his lips. "Eat."

What if they laced it with something and are trying to poison me? Carter hasn't touched it yet, so why would I?

I don't even know where the hell Preston is. I haven't seen him since he stormed out of the guest room last night, leaving his friend to deal with me. At first, I thought they might be brothers, with similar strong, gorgeous features that made my heart race, but whereas Preston has a more angular jaw and lighter hair, Carter's skin is a shade darker. His face is more heart-shaped with a shadow that makes your fingers want to dance over his jawline to feel the groomed stubble below your fingertips.

My eyes flit down to my spotless plate and back to him. It's a non-negotiable command, but I ask anyway. "Is that a command or a suggestion?"

"Are you always this stubborn?"

"Asks one of the men who's holding me hostage in a castle."

He raises a brow. "It's not a castle."

Folding my arms and bracing them on the table, I lean over them. "Could've fooled me. All it's missing is a moat and some archers. But I have a feeling that's not your style, since the men in the watchtowers are holding guns. If I were to gamble on my life, I'd say there's more going on here than just a little lobster and amusement park business."

His mouth quirks, taking another sip. "And what is it that you *think* is going on here?"

I try to swallow the nervousness scratching my throat. "The Evisceration Cellar. You're running an organ trafficking business for the black market."

He chokes on his coffee, placing his mug on the table. He swipes his mouth with the back of his hand. Once he composes himself, he draws those handsome eyes, flickering with amusement, to mine. It's not him who answers me.

"If that's your perception of us, then the truth will make us look like saints." Like my body is already in tune to his presence, that deep tenor floats across and lathers into my skin.

My gaze snaps to the doorway of the breakfast nook. Preston is leaning against the door with his hands shoved into his pockets. Unlike yesterday, there isn't a speck of blood on him. A pair of gray sweats hangs low on his hips, a white t-shirt stretching across the hard planes of his body. Ink with patterns and script cascades down his arms and onto his hands. I was hungry a minute ago, but now I'm starving in a different way.

Now I know what it's like to be entranced by the devil.

"Will it?" I counter, doubtfully. I watched him stab a man and leave him to die.

Preston breaks the threshold, stalking into the room. "Depends."

I reach for the bowl of strawberries, plopping one into my mouth to distract myself and appear more unaffected than I feel. For a brief second, I remember why I wasn't eating. Well, shit. If it's poisoned, I'm screwed. Although I feel like using such a simple method to kill me isn't his style.

I get the sense he finds violence entertaining. In using his hands...

My tongue darts out to lick the glaze of sweet juice off my lips, Preston's eyes tracking the movement. "Enlighten me then,

Captain. I've heard the rumors about the tunnels and those massacres that happened in the park."

"Drawn to a little darkness, darling?" Preston and Carter are wearing matching arrogant smiles.

"What," I blow out. "No."

Preston's head slants. "Are you sure? You said it yourself, you've heard the rumors, yet you still found yourself wandering in the tunnels. If I had to gamble your life," he throws back at me. How much of our conversation was he listening to? "I'd say you're dangerously captivated by your curiosity and wanted to see what it would be like to dance with the dark." My mouth parts, words escaping me. "I'd know precise knifework anywhere. By the looks of that long scar on your pretty neck, I'd say maybe you already have been."

I've been trying to run from it. And somehow, I've found myself in this reality I can't escape.

Out of the hands of one monster and into the hands of another.

Bolting up out of my chair, I push it backward with the backs of my knees. "I'm done with this conversation. I want to go home. I'm not responsible for whatever it is you think I've done."

Storming past Preston, his eyes track me, raking over my body in the spanks and t-shirt I still have on. Feels like I'm naked beneath his stony expression.

Behind me, Carter exhales, "She's all yours."

Rushing out of the room, I turn right, trying to locate the nearest door to the outside. I need air. I need space. Funny how such a vast space's walls can creep in on you.

I don't get very far before I'm shoved forcefully into an alcove. My back slams against a hard surface, my body wedged between the wall and a rigid frame that has desire flooding to my core despite his cold demeanor.

Preston slaps a hand against the wall above me, trapping

me beneath him. The heat from his skin drenches every inch of mine. "Where do you think you're going?"

My eyes draw up to Preston's. His smoky scent, twisted with a hint of fresh earth, envelops me, numbing the part of my brain that wants to fight back. To slam my fists against those sculpted pecks that will probably shatter the bones in my hand. My head is a warzone—the blasts and explosions igniting that sweet, sensitive spot between my thighs. A flicker that damn well shouldn't be there.

He effortlessly charges the few particles of air between us.

All my words come out in a rush. "If I'm going to be here a month, it doesn't mean we need to breathe the same air."

My fingers reach out, gripping onto the cotton of his shirt. But I don't push him away, and he must notice because his lips shift into a smug grin that could have any woman submitting to his orders.

Too bad I'm not that girl.

Using all the force I can muster, I shove him backward. My features harden to stand my ground, though it feels like it's crumbling below me.

"Careful, Kate." My toes curl at the way he says my name. "Your fight turns me on as much as your fear."

I shake my head, attempting to move past him, but he seizes my wrist. In one quick, smooth movement, he spins me around, slamming my chest into the wall. He takes a step forward, pressing me against the wall with his pelvis. The weapon growing against my ass has my breath shuddering. I'd say I wiggle a little to prove it's not his gun, but we both know it's a lie. My traitorous sex-deprived body is acting out and defying my command to find this man repulsive.

He gruffly groans in response to my ass moving against his front. His fingers drift across the slope of my neck, pushing my hair to one side while the other wraps around my waist. The strands gliding over my neck make me shudder, jerking me back harder against his erection.

Yep. That thing could break me as easily as his hands could.

Preston's hand cups the front of my throat before tilting and forcing my head back over my shoulder to meet those brutal, striking eyes. I swallow against his palm. "Lucky for you, I have business to deal with tomorrow and will be gone for the next several days."

I try to withhold the relief from my tone. "Oh?"

His warm breath fans across my lips.

Doesn't matter if this devil is in a suit or sweatpants. He holds the power to incinerate all my rational thoughts and command my body like it's his to own.

I am his prisoner after all.

"Don't sound so excited. I said I'd keep you under surveillance for the next month, and I meant it. You aren't going anywhere. Just because I won't be here to track you, doesn't mean I won't be able to while I'm gone."

What?

Without warning, his hands move hastily, wrapping something smooth and cold around my neck. Terror claws up my throat. I squirm beneath him, but it only reminds me of his hard length, fully aware of my body flush with his.

*Nooo.* Why are my panties dampening?

The cold feeling of heavy metal nips at my skin as I hear two clicks that have my heart plummeting into my gut.

Preston steps away, the loss of his warmth adding to the chill that skitters across my body when I reach up and drag my fingers over the collar ensnaring my neck.

# THIRTEEN | PRESTON

I prefer my hand cupped around that beautiful throat instead, but the collar will do.

Kate's eyes are little balls of fire, meant to burn me alive, yet I'm too distracted by the way she's awakened my cock with the curve of her ass and the thin gold chain gleaming against her lightly tanned skin.

The gold lock I fastened there, hiding a tracking device, rests between her collarbones. I made sure it's tight enough that she can't slip it over her head. I lift the key between us so she sees it, then tuck it back into my pocket for safekeeping.

"What is this?" she snarls, hooking her fingers through the chain that looks like it should belong on a feral dog.

The kind of chain that chokes them when they're misbehaving.

"A gift." I fold my arms over my chest. "And a way to keep track of you while I'm gone. Not that you'd be able to escape anyway. Just wanted to take extra safety precautions."

"It has a tracker?" Kate claws at it frantically. "You're insane if you think I'm going to keep this on!"

"You don't have a choice."

The high-pitched rumble in her chest is swallowed by a heavy exhale. "You can't expect me to sit in that room for the next month with nothing to do, Preston."

It's the first time she's said my name, and it rewires my brain. I short-circuit. Instantly, I'm hit with all these ideas for how I could get her to repeat it as I brand her with my cock. My mouth. My fingers as they follow the rhythm of my tongue.

*Brand her as mine.*

Well, fuck. It's only been a few days since I first saw her. This girl is already nestling under my skin. My empire isn't the only thing she's infiltrating, and that's a problem. The reason for her being here pierces through the haze of desire.

She thinks I'm a villain, but little does she know the man she might be working for made me one.

My throat clears. "Which brings me to another reason why I'm here. You'll have free rein of the estate when you're not working."

She sputters a laugh. "I'm sorry, did you say working?"

"I'm going to put you to use. How do you feel about working in the medical unit?"

Her laughter dies instantly.

"Last night you mentioned you have a medical background, did you not?" I press.

Her lips roll in deliberation. "I mean, yeah. Before Lachlan Park, I was a nurse."

"Perfect." I grip onto her arm, dragging her out of the alcove.

Her eye roll is audible in her scolding tone. "You don't have to keep dragging me everywhere, you know. If you were a little more approachable, I might listen. A please can go a long way."

"In my line of work, people don't respond to approachable."

"Well, I'm not in your line of work."

"You're about to be."

Her heels dig into the marble floor, making me halt. I drop

her arm, crossing mine over my chest. She narrows her eyes at me, looking for me to elaborate.

A look of disgust bathes her face right before I calm the oncoming hurricane of questions by saying, "I don't work in organ trafficking."

As I said, I'm not sure whether she's working with Luciano or not. I'm hoping a month of surveillance will provide enough evidence to prove she was in the wrong places at the wrong times. Until then, I'll keep her busy. For her safety and my own, because if my father finds out why she's here and that I lied to him, we'll both be dealing with his wrath.

Those light green pools clash with mine. "And you think I should just believe you after everything you've done?"

"Would you rather sit in your room alone and bored for the next thirty days?"

Her chest rises and falls heavily, making the gold chain with the lock glisten and sparkle in the light above us. "No."

My tone is firm. "Then it's settled. You'll start on Monday."

She huffs out a breath, peering up at me with indecision. She doesn't want to accept it, but she also doesn't want to be bored. There is something else swirling there, too.

When she doesn't speak, I leave her with one last warning. "And I suggest you act like working in the medical unit is why you're here. Other people are living on the estate who are more unforgiving than I am. Your life doesn't rest only in my hands, darling."

The tremble bolting through her body tells me she heard me loud and clear.

I don't know why a part of me is hanging onto hope that she might be harmless. Yet there's a possibility she is a rat, trained and conditioned to slip in and gather information to destroy us. If she is involved with the Calco Cartel and is a reason our product has been going missing, she already knows everything about the Megalley Syndicate.

However, if Kate is as oblivious as she pretends to be, Carter is right. She'll learn a lot about our mob in a month while she's staying on the estate. Letting her go with that kind of knowledge carries the same weight and is just as dangerous.

Honestly, at this point, I don't see an ending where she gets to keep her life.

# FOURTEEN | KATE

"Stop touching it. It's not coming off."

My fingers fall from the *gift* Preston gave me, hanging heavy on my neck like an anchor. Another thing keeping me fastened here. I may not be imprisoned in a cell with chains, but it feels the same.

Even if it's an elegant one wrapped around my throat.

I side-eye him from where we stand in the grand foyer of the estate. His hands are tucked into the pockets of his sweats, those dark eyes void of emotion. They have been for the last hour as he gives me a lazy tour of my home for the next month.

A large chandelier with delicate crystals hangs overhead, its light reflecting off the gold embellishments that drip from every corner of the room. The grand entrance, fitting a spiral staircase, is tall enough to fit one of those massive Christmas trees I always admire during the holidays.

For such a dark man, his space is bright, with cream-colored walls and tan-marbled flooring. Too bad it doesn't inject warmth into anything else besides the facade that screams wealth. This place has a kind of emptiness that stretches. It feels lifeless, though we've passed a few people here and there cleaning rooms. They've all given Preston some acknowledgement, then their heads drop, and they get back to work.

He gestures to the right. "Down this hallway is the gym. The door at the end of the corridor is where you'll find the indoor pool and spa." His glare sears into the side of my head, and my eyes are drawn to his. "Top floor is off limits. That's where my office and room are. As well as other rooms, I highly suggest you stay away from."

My sarcasm is unmistakable. "Great. Glad I can be as far away from you as possible."

He cocks his head. "Is that why your ass was grinding against my dick this morning?"

Preston's raw, unfiltered words have heat fluttering straight to my clit. The red flags flying around this man are as bright as the crimson that drenched his hands yesterday. But my pussy doesn't seem to care. She has a mind of her own.

Guess she's not satisfied with just my fingers anymore.

*Hungry little bitch.*

It doesn't help that my captor is by far the most handsome man I've ever laid my eyes on. The soft, golden light from the chandelier overhead cast shadows across his tanned skin, highlighting his muscles. They occasionally ripple in a way that stirs a bloom of desire in my belly. And the tendons in those hands… dear Lord. My pussy may be tired of my fingers, but his—

His eyes narrow. "You look flushed. Do you need a drink or something?"

I catch myself ogling his frame, again, and shake myself out of it. "If I say yes, are you going to get me a dog bowl to drink out of?"

Shadows spark behind those bourbon irises, his hands shifting in his sweatpants pockets. "You're playing a dangerous game, darling. I like it when pretty things crawl for me."

My attention lingers on the way he called me pretty.

I straighten my spine and lift my chin. If I keep acting like he intimidates me, he'll keep getting a reaction out of me, which I assume he finds amusing. Darkness follows this man. I can't let my guard down or fall for his erotic words.

His steadfast gaze feels like he's using the shadows that follow him to sink into my soul and pick through the fragile pieces. It's as if he's looking for something specific in the rubble.

I tuck my arms against my stomach, shifting to relieve the dull thrumming between my legs. "You're sick."

A corner of his mouth quirks. "Are you saying that to me or your cunt? Because, from where I'm standing, it looks like you're rubbing your thighs together. Maybe we're both sick, darling."

Oh. My. God.

I purse my lips. "Are you done giving me this little tour? I want to take a shower." And get myself off so I can think rationally and not be tempted by my traitorous body. It doesn't seem to register that this man is dangerous.

He doesn't have hands that care.

He has hands that kill.

I wonder what his body count is, and I don't mean sex. Well, maybe I'm a little intrigued by that number too.

No. Nope. *Don't go there, Kate.*

"As I said, I'll be gone tomorrow. If you need anything, you can ring Gretta. There's a button on the wall in your room."

I inject some enthusiasm into my tone, so he registers how happy I am that he's leaving. "Where are you going?"

He regards me skeptically for a moment before responding. "Virginia."

"What's in Virginia?"

His head slants, flashing me with those thick cords in his neck. "Why do you want to know?"

I nod. "You're right, I don't care. I want to get on with this so

I can get it over with." Pointing toward the corridor where my room is, I ask, "Can I head back to my room now?"

He gestures ahead of me, and I start walking up the stairs to the second floor, completely aware of his constant presence. When I get to my door, I throw it open and walk in. So does he. He somehow sucks all the oxygen out of the air.

I turn around on my heels, grabbing the collar in my fingers. "You following me kind of defeats the purpose of this, Captain. Are you going to stalk me while I'm in the shower, too?"

He leans on the doorframe, knitting his arms over his chest. "Is that an offer?"

I disregard that. "You can't expect me to live in these clothes for the next month."

"Gretta will handle it. And as for the medical unit, Imogen will give you scrubs."

"For being your hostage, you're sure allowing me to have nice things. Does that mean you're starting to trust me more?"

He doesn't say anything; instead, he electrifies the space between us with something uncomfortable, making my skin crawl. Why is he glaring at me as if I'm plotting something? Preston has been looking at me with this spiteful expression since I asked why he is going to Virginia.

I'm not scheming anything.

If there's a chance I can escape out of here with my life and not end up with his blade plunged in my stomach like that man, I'll suffer through this next month.

Because if there's one thing I've learned, it's that I can survive. Thriving, on the other hand, has eluded me for the last several years.

This won't be any different.

I can handle this, even if there's a stabbing pain behind my ribs that tells me I'm being reckless, believing in hope.

Hope hurts. But there's a chance I'll hurt either way.

# FIFTEEN | KATE

The evening sea breeze whips through my hair, blowing a lock across my lips. I tuck it behind my ear and close my eyes, inhaling what seems like my first deep breath since I found myself trapped in the walls of the Lachlan Estate.

I didn't realize how fatigued I was until my head hit the pillow and my body sank into the cloud-like mattress in the guest room. I slept for almost fifteen hours, and I'm not sure whether it was the fear that took the most considerable toll on my body or the thought that if I slept long enough, maybe I would wake from this nightmare.

I didn't.

I sat up in the same, quiet seclusion of my room with a collar adorning my neck.

The only relief was knowing I had a few days left of peace, free from Preston's irritatingly handsome face that entices me to put my fist through it.

In any other circumstance, I might find the gift sweet. Maybe a little excessive, but I find a little possessiveness attractive in a man.

*When he's not slicing open my body and hunting me to the ends of the earth.*

Preston hasn't done that yet.

Yet.

But this chain was given to me solely to track my whereabouts. It wasn't a kind gesture, even though the weight makes my stomach churn with the realization that I might be wearing a few grand. Given the estate's stunning appearance, its prime coastal location, impeccable grounds, fountains, circular driveway, gardens, pool, and three-story palace, I wouldn't be surprised if it costs more.

It makes me nauseous thinking about it. Doesn't matter if I think it's beautiful or not. It's been over a day since Preston left, and I've tried everything to remove it. I'm sure the back of my neck is bruised from trying to yank it off. It was stupid to hope that the chain wasn't as durable as it looked.

That little keyhole below the lock still mocks me every time I glance in the mirror.

After I woke up, the thought of leaving my room had me on edge. I know Preston said I have freedom to roam the estate, but it feels menacing. Like, I don't belong here and have no right to explore the grounds I'm temporarily living in.

It wasn't until Gretta, the housekeeper, cracked open my door and startled me. She appeared to be in her early to late sixties, given the way her full head of gray hair was tossed in a low bun. Her warmth and kindness were refreshing compared to what I endured with Preston and Carter. I haven't seen Carter either, so I'm guessing he's accompanying Preston in Virginia.

Doing God knows what.

The moment she found me awake, she left and quickly came back with a tray of food. And the second she did, I couldn't help but scarf most of it down like a caged ravenous beast who had its food withheld.

I've never had Shepherd's Pie, but I have a gut feeling most aren't as delectable as that was. My mouth is watering just thinking about the creamy potato-and-beef dish. If one thing might make me compliant while I'm here, it would be if I were consistently served food like that.

*I'm like an animal they're preparing to slaughter.*

I grimace outwardly at the unwelcome thought.

Apparently, Gretta had checked on me multiple times while I was sleeping because I also found my closet full of clothes in my exact size. Usually, I wake to even the slightest noise, and noticing someone in the walk-in closet surely should've alerted me. I've never passed out that hard. How she or Preston knew my size baffles me, but it felt good to change out of my shorts and t-shirt and into something more comfortable, which is why I settled for black leggings and a tank top that hugs my body.

Which may have been a colossal mistake, because the men walking the perimeter of the property and in the watchtowers are observing me with firm eyes that are somewhere between hungry and interested. They're all dressed head to toe in the same uniform: black t-shirts, cargo pants, and boots, with one gun on their hips and another in their hands.

I couldn't escape if I wanted to.

The deep blue water has transformed into a sea of color, with glittering pastel strokes of peach and red. The canvas of rich ombrés looms above the sun dipping below the horizon, a speck of bright light in the distance, where the ocean stretches out as far as I can see. A clear pathway cuts through the vegetation, down to a long, rocky stretch of coastline where a ten-foot fence secures the property, extending past where the waves lap at the beach until it sinks into the water and out of sight.

I turn from the elevated yard that sits above the beach, ambling toward the gardens, sprawling with tall, maze-like hedges and beds on the outer edge filled with brightly colored flowers that fill the summer air with the scent of spring.

As I enter the maze, I walk for a little while. I inhale the sweet, floral scent into my lungs, trying to calm myself and locate some silver lining. I appreciate having some freedom. After all, it's my snooping around that got me here.

Things could always be worse.

Like the fact that I could be trapped in that concrete room below the park for the next twenty-eight days.

Like the fact that Xander could've killed me, but he was fascinated watching me suffer instead—repeatedly.

It's the thought that I haven't sunk to the bottom yet that gets me through. I may be floating barely above the bottom, but I haven't hit it yet.

It's not long before I find the center of the maze, decorated with dainty string lights that weave across the expanse above, against the ombré that drenches the sky. Concrete walls encasing the space are adorned with magenta flowers, and benches surround a fountain that soothes the area with the rush of water.

The beauty and details nearly take my breath away. It's the kind of place that signifies a lot of love. Time and care are reflected in the plants that thrive here, as if they were meant to be rooted exactly where they are. I feel it in the way the tension in my body eases like the water that ripples outward into the small pond below the fountain.

My body gravitates to the closest bench, plopping down onto it with the same weight that has rested on my shoulders since I foolishly found myself in the tunnels.

I scan the center of the garden, not missing the video cameras. The same ones I've noticed placed throughout the house.

This entire place is secured.

Feels secluded, though I know we can't be far from Lachlan Park, considering we took the tunnels all the way here that first night.

If I can't get out, that means nobody can get in without an invitation.

My blood pumps into my ears, stirring that thought.

Up until now, I've thought this is the most dangerous place I could've found myself in my life.

But what if the security of this hell helps me stay hidden from another?

If I can't escape, maybe that means Xander will never be able to get in if he somehow tracks down my location. I let that idea seep like a tea bag in hot water right before I take that first sip that's supposed to soothe my soul.

I'm delusional.

Am I really considering that staying might be the answer to my—

"Beautiful. Isn't it?" The gravelly, unfamiliar voice filling the spaces makes me jump.

My head whips to the side, taking in the middle-aged man with his hands shoved into the pockets of a flawless gray suit with a burgundy tie. He looks like a model that stepped off the cover of a Calvin Klein magazine. His lightly styled hair and short, groomed beard may not be completely gray, but he is the definition of a silver fox.

When he catches me staring, he closes the distance, keeping those whiskey-colored eyes on mine. "It's Kate, isn't it?"

It takes a heartbeat longer than it should to register his question. His Irish accent is stronger than Preston's. It's magnetic and graces my ears.

Between Preston, Carter, and this mystery silver fox, it's enough to make a girl feel like she's in a candy store with endless options.

I try to find my voice. My answer feels weak, even though it is my name. "Yes, sir."

Judging by the silver watch adorning his wrist and the suit that doesn't have a wrinkle in sight, he appears to be the kind of man who appreciates being addressed with the type of power he exudes.

"I was hoping I'd get to meet you soon."

My mouth opens, the words fumbling out of my mouth. "You were?"

He keeps strolling toward me until he's standing beside me in front of the bench. "May I?" he gestures to the spot next to me.

I struggle to nod.

He sits down, wiping his hands across his thighs, and sighs. "I like to know who might hold my life in their hands." A look of genuine confusion washes over my face before he explains. "Since Preston went behind my back and added another person to the medical team, I told him I wanted to meet you. That boy," he exhales, shaking his head, but there's a hint of something there. Adoration maybe?

Oh right. I'm supposed to be acting like the reason I'm here is to play nurse. Which may work in my favor now that I'm not working that goddamn ride anymore, and it might just save me from something as terrifying as I find this place. It's a coin toss at this point. Maybe it's a false sense of safety, but I'm starting to think that being contained in Lachlan Estate might be exactly what I need to survive this life that has haunted me for far too long.

I reach out my hand, giving a strained smile.

God, this man makes me nervous.

He briefly glances down before placing his in mine. It's heavy and calloused. "I'm Arden. It's nice to meet you, Kate."

"Likewise," is all I can manage.

It may seem unusual, but we don't shake. More like we hold hands that slightly bounce while we analyze each other's expressions as if it will open a door to all the questions we both have about each other.

I swallow, stepping into my imaginary armor.

Preston told me other people on the estate hold my life in their hands, and I'm one hundred percent certain I'm shaking one of them.

We release each other.

I feel like the pulse point in my neck is going to burst out and onto his lap. "I wasn't aware he went behind your back. But I will do everything to make sure that if it's your life in my hands, or anyone's for that matter, I'll do absolutely everything I can. But in a field like this, it's foolish to make promises that I'm not sure I can keep. Depending on the situation, of course."

Actually, I'm not exactly sure what I will be doing or how I will be aiding Imogen, the doctor Preston told me I'm under. I'm just anxiously pulling things out of my ass, hoping I sound professional and pushing the narrative.

"I respect that. You'll find that Preston and I value honesty. Speaking of, how did the process with Preston go? He didn't scare you away, so I'm taking that as a good sign."

"Scare me away, no." I breathe, wiping my clammy hands on my leggings. "But he is calloused. And detached."

He said he appreciates honesty.

My focus falls on his sad smile. "Have you ever lost someone, Kate?"

My heartbeat drains into my ears. "No."

I'm lucky to still have both sets of grandparents.

He stares straight ahead, keeping his voice steady. "My son lost his mother and his sister. Everyone heals differently. It's not a straight path, even when you think you're just starting to get the hang of grief. And when someone you love dies by a violent death they didn't deserve, it sticks with you. Changes you." Sounds like he's speaking from experience.

My blood solidifies to ice in my veins.

If I thought this man was oozing power before, he's radiating it even stronger now. "You're his...father?"

*Arden Lachlan.*

Which means he lost his wife violently…

His daughter.

The emotion whirling in my chest cracks my heart, bringing with it a little more understanding.

"He didn't mention me when he was hiring you?" He blows out a dark, melancholy laugh.

"I mean, he did. You just," I land on, "look different than I expected."

Besides the faint crow's feet near his eyes and mouth, nothing would give him away that he's Preston's father. I mean, I see the similarities now. Arden is handsome. Has aged in a way that makes me wonder if I could be into much older men. His short facial hair has gray woven throughout. His body is still hard and muscular, as if he makes a daily effort to stay fit. Strong. Powerful.

He must have had Preston in his *very* early twenties.

"So," he changes the subject. "How did a beautiful thing like you find yourself working for the Irish mafia? It's not every day you come across a job like this one. And we're very selective."

My eyes widen before I think better of it.

Did he say the Irish mafia?

"I—" How the hell do I answer this question? If he's giving me a second interview, I'm failing miserably.

So, it's not organs. However, I'm unsure if this is any better.

Narcotics.

Money laundering.

Extortion.

Gambling.

Corruption.

How is this my life?

It's probably a stupid answer, but I settle on it. "Must have been luck, I guess."

A throaty laugh escapes him, and I can't help the way it makes my body warm.

Is that what Preston's would sound like?

Why do I suddenly have the urge to try to make him laugh?

I'm guessing he doesn't do it often. If ever.

He scans the space leisurely, his features softening. "If you're hungry, Gretta has food ready." The way he says it makes me think he wants to be alone.

So instead of crowding his space, his home more than I already am, I rise to my feet. "It's nice to meet you. I look forward to working with you." Since I'm unsure how to address him—Mr. Lachlan, Arden, Boss—I make my exit short and sweet.

Arden's head tilts up, giving me a suppressed smile that hides the pain of a man who's seen more than most in a lifetime. And I can't help but think about his son, the man who brought me here, and who is half his age.

Preston's hard and jagged edges aren't carved from nothing; they're from enduring more loss than anyone ever should.

As I walk away, all my little ugly truths don't seem so different from his. Because who am I to judge someone by the scars they never asked for?

# SIXTEEN | KATE

"This is what you do all day?" My vocalized amusement has Imogen and the rest of the table smiling.

She studies her cards, placing two fours down face up on the six I laid on the center pile. Her bright white grin clears some of my reservations. "Sucks, huh?"

From the short time I've known her, I've already gathered that she has recently turned forty-two, is married with two kids, and has been working for the Lachlans for the last twelve years.

In the past five hours, she has given me a rundown of the medical building I'll be working in, along with several other employees, located on the left side of the estate, where a small private airport is also hidden among the trees. With everything else I've seen here the last few days, I'm not surprised they have a personal runway.

After I went into depth about my previous experience, she gave me a tour and a list of my day-to-day tasks. Then she decided to toss me into a card game called Clear, without any understanding of how to play, with her and two of my new coworkers. Synthia, who is a little older than I am, and Declan, one of the sons of a helicopter pilot who works for Arden and Preston.

My nerves are still crackling like live wires, but I couldn't be more grateful for the distraction. From what I've heard, this position appears to be quite similar to the life of an EMT. Well, in some aspects. It's almost as if we're on call, waiting, and can fill our time with other tasks when there's nobody in dire need of attention and our work is done—ensuring rooms are stocked, and inventory is accounted for.

"Don't lie to the girl," Synthia smirks.

"Better to let her know what she's getting into now," Declan adds.

Imogen pushes her dark, medium-length hair behind her shoulder, re-contemplating her response while her fingers drum through her cards. She looks as if she were born to wear that white coat over her black scrubs. The entire look is pulled together by those reading glasses resting on her head.

"Sometimes, it's easy," she sighs. "They're right. I'm not going to pretend it's a fucking walk in the park because this job is demanding when it wants to be. Every member of the Megalley Syndicate is blood, as you know now."

*Megalley Syndicate.*

Their real business has a name.

The one that's under feet of concrete, ride tracks, and a Ferris wheel, fried food stands, and gleeful laughter that conceals the true malicious nature. The one that appears as lobster boats instead of vessels that smuggle narcotics and other things from God knows where.

"We'll do anything to save and protect our own, which is why you'll learn that sometimes, we do things untraditionally when the time calls for it. Like the fact that the mob has its own medical unit instead of sending our men to a regular hospital or urgent care for treatment. We do everything on the estate when we can. I'll ask you to do things that may be outside your comfort zone. We'll administer drugs that you may not recognize or understand. It's okay to be curious, but don't ever question me or my methods."

Now I see why they hired her. She just straightened my spine to be pin-straight with that last comment.

I almost say, "Yes, ma'am," out of pure nervousness.

Synthia suppresses a chuckle, placing a ten on the pile in the center and says, "Clear." Wiping away the pile to the side, she places down three queens. "So, in retrospect, don't ask questions and do what you're told."

My fingers flip through the cards in my hand to release some of the tension in my body. This is so different than what I'm used to. But that doesn't seem like the accurate way to describe how I'm feeling.

It's like they play by their own rules.

Play their own cards.

This is the mafia, after all.

A world that I knew existed but never thought I'd be thrown into. Now I have no choice but to shed my layers and adapt, even if it goes against my morals. I don't want to find out what happens if I don't.

I'd rather be safe in these walls—a different kind of safe—than work the haunted mine ride and constantly scan faces at the park, as if Xander would appear and shatter my world even further.

Here, Xander can't get me. Can't hurt me.

Sometimes we have to do unconventional things to survive.

I paste on a grin, but it is quickly wiped off my face as a blaring alarm drowns the living room and break room combined into one. The unexpected screech grinds against my skin, raising the hairs on my arms. It's so loud, I nearly press my palms to my ears to block out some of the noise.

Synthia and Declan's faces pale, their eyes meeting each other's as they share a knowing glance.

"Shit," Imogen hisses. She tosses her cards haphazardly on the table, reaches into the pocket of her lab coat, and stands, rushing out of the room.

"What's happening?" I yell over the earsplitting alarm, pulsing the space with red-and-white flashes from the light on the wall in the corner above the doorway Imogen slipped through.

Declan shakes his head. "Whatever it is, it isn't good."

A minute later, Imogen marches back into the room, tugging at the bottom of her jacket. She had a look of alarm when she left; now, a professional poise has replaced it. I don't know why that unsettles me so much.

She exhales the breath she's holding. "In an hour, we're going to need all the hands we can get." Her pointed and worried look finds me. Then she says something that has every ounce of blood draining from my body and pooling at my feet. "Synthia and Declan, you're in the surgery room with me. I hope you're ready to get your hands dirty and know how to administer stitches, Kate. This is going to be one hell of a first day."

# SEVENTEEN | PRESTON

Red clouds my vision as I shove open the passenger door and step out into the air that does nothing to extinguish the inferno blazing behind my sternum.

We were set up.

Ambushed at one of our borders.

The scent of smoke, explosives, and carnage that permeated the air still clings to my clothes. My skin. The rancid smell is seared into my pores, a reminder that this war is only beginning, and we've already lost one of our territories.

I'm not sure how I managed to get onto the helicopter and back to the estate. All I remember is Carter hurling his body at mine after the first few gunshots pierced through the night as we were unloading cargo. Not even the illegal weapons we were moving could've saved us from the attack.

Thirty-seven men.

Thirty-seven brothers whose bodies were left in the rubble and dirt in and outside of that warehouse, as if they were nothing but a pile of bones. I didn't want to leave them, but getting out of there was a priority.

Now, only sixteen of us are returning home—less than half of the men I took to Virginia.

That's not including the ones who were stationed there and already dead when we arrived. I knew something was wrong the moment we landed—the kind of silence that is suffocating because *he* had already taken out everyone before we got there.

Their blood is on my hands.

It's always On. My. Hands.

The back of the military-grade vehicle lowers, and several of my men wheel out their friends on gurneys into the medical center that shares the same grounds as our estate.

*Those who survived the flight, if they weren't left behind.*

Luckily, Arden was safe at the estate, letting me handle this one on my own.

There may have been burning skin, hair, and the stench of blood that stained the air, but I could still pick out the unmatched scent of a cigar that threaded through the aftermath. At first, I thought it was my brain playing tricks on me, wanting me to seek him out like a bloodhound. There was no time to find him, not when we were taken by surprise.

I thought we were prepared for anything. Ready for everything. But it's not until someone strikes that you realize you underestimated their power.

When the plane carrying our survivors took off, I hopped into the helicopter with Carter, and that's when we saw him below. He strutted out of the warehouse in his gray suit, puffing on one of those cigars that makes me want to release the acid in my stomach. His fucking son, Nico, was beside him.

Our cargo.

Our men.

Our fucking territory.

My. Territory.

I'll be damned if I let him take everything we've drained our blood, sweat, and tears into, which means finding the imposter he's implanted in our walls.

Anyone will betray you when the price is high enough—when the gains outweigh the losses, the gamble is worth the risk.

In their case, I hope it was worth the fucking risk, considering Luciano took out one of our top locations and has his vile hands on our biggest shipment of the year. Which is why ever since our wheels left the ground, dark blonde waves have weaved through the red blanketing my vision.

My little rat might be a mole.

And if this bloodshed is on Kate's hands, the last words she'll speak are her begging for her life through the air I'm robbing her of as I grip her gold chain in my hand and tighten it around her pretty little throat.

The gurneys with men who are clutching limbs and struggling to keep their hearts beating are rushed inside, while some of my other guys limp through the doors. The medical center was alerted a few hours ago through the alarm system. When I enter, the medical staff are flying from one side of the room to the other, taking my men to rooms and attending to the most critical injuries. The entire place is abuzz with chaos, but my radar is zeroing in on one person.

I swear to fucking God, if she's not here...

My footsteps are heavy as I march through the waiting area, as if I can somehow feel her presence bubbling under my skin. As I enter the hallway with doors to the patient rooms, I toss open the first door, but it's someone else wrapping the arm of one of my men. I throw open the next one, but she's not in there either.

Her name is a growl in my chest.

A curse on my tongue.

Intoxicating rage consumes me as I barge through the

second-to-last door at the back of the building near the surgery room.

As if she's as affected by my presence as I am by hers, Kate's shoulders stiffen. She's monitoring one of my men's vital signs when he registers the look on my face. Luckily, his injuries are minor. There are bruises on his arms and a gash cutting through his chin that will need stitches and leave a scar—just another story to mark his skin like the rest of us. Without a word, he stands and scurries out of the room, leaving us alone.

I shut the door, ensnaring the rodent with my presence as my rage charges the room. The fear radiating off her is palpable. So sweet and potent that I'm eager for her to face me.

When she does, I'm nearly knocked off balance by how beautiful she is. Her round face is brighter, a sign she's gotten rest since I've been gone. Her long, slightly curled hair is pulled up in a high ponytail, looking so much lighter than it usually is against her black scrubs.

The swells of her cheeks are vibrantly painted a beautiful rose that pops against the ghostly color of the rest of her face. Her green eyes fix frantically on mine.

I don't want to come clean about how often I've thought about her while I've been gone. How the vision of her absent-mindedly wiggling the perfect swells of her round ass against my erection when I gifted her that collar was on a rotating track. Then I spiraled, wondering what it would've felt like to shove those tight shorts around her ankles and use my dick to test if she was as wet as I thought she was. Those manifestations fell behind my eyes as I languidly stroked my cock, drawing out my release. A release that wasn't fucking satisfying in the slightest because it wasn't her cunt gripping my cock like I imagined.

Seeing her now reminds me of how distracted and unhinged she makes me. How dangerous she is to everything I've worked so hard for.

She's obliterating my control.

Robbing me of my fucking sanity.

*Exactly like he wants.*

I barely recognize my voice. "You're not going to run?"

Her lips part, and I track the movement. Her gulp is audible over the thrashing in my chest. "Why would I run?" She studies my face, then her focus instantly falls to my shoulder. "Preston, you're bleeding."

My pace is deliberate as I stalk toward her slowly. She instinctively tries to retreat, but her back hits the paper covering the treatment table. "I suggest you carefully consider how you answer my next question, or I'll add another name to the list of the dead."

She audibly sucks in a breath.

I tilt my head. "What did he promise you?"

"Wh-What?" Her voice trembles. "Who?"

"Don't," I snap, making her jump. "I fucking know you're working for that bastard. The one who has destroyed everything in my life," I point my finger at my chest. Her ass perches on the table, and I use the opportunity to step between her legs. "He's taken everything from me!"

"Preston, I—"

The rage increases tenfold, injecting into my bloodstream that rushes to pound against my skull. I snatch her throat in my fist, leaning over her as Kate's back bends under me.

God, she is so fucking fragile.

If I bend her under my weight anymore, her spine would snap like a twig.

My fingers pulse into her flesh, trapping her gold collar beneath my hand. She gasps for breath, tears slipping over her bottom lashes and onto her cheeks. Her pulse—so beautifully alive—flutters against my palm.

It would be so easy to break this pretty neck.

I lower my face to hers, my breath fanning across those

tempting lips. "It's unfortunate that the prettiest things are always the most lethal."

Kate nods in my grasp. She struggles to speak through the airway I'm crushing in my fist. Her mouth is an inch from mine. "The feeling is mutual, Captain."

Then Kate does something I don't expect. She lifts her hands to cup both sides of my face, drawing my focus from her puffy, tear-soaked lips back to her bloodshot eyes. I blink, the cool green of her irises fresh against the fire licking every inch of my skin. My grasp on her neck loosens just a little.

She sinks her teeth into her lower lip, shaking her head. "It's not me, Pres. I'm not the one who did this. I don't know who *he* is."

My resolve hardens. "You're lying!"

"Kiss me." It's a whisper.

Now I'm the speechless one. What kind of witchcraft am I yielding to, where I'm considering shoving my tongue in more places than just her mouth with that plea?

My heart screeches to a stop. "What?"

Her soft hands against my face are a different kind of heat that penetrates the unbearable inferno covering my skin in a sheen of sweat, dirt, and other grime from the grenades that detonated the ground I stood on. It's trying to burn me alive, but her warmth blooms out from where she's touching me, pushing back, and extinguishing the flames that are a living, breathing thing against my flesh.

Her tender fingers dance across my cheeks, those eyes firm like she's somehow going through the archives of my life.

Kate is somehow looking at me with fresh eyes. This isn't what they looked like when I left her.

"I want you to kiss me," she whispers again, another tear gliding down her face.

My heartbeat slows more than it was, pulsing wildly for an entirely different reason.

I slam my eyes shut.

Maybe I'm an idiot, or perhaps I'm saving myself when I speak the rejection across the small space between our lips. "I'm not going to do that." Moving my hand from her throat, I lightly grip the back of her neck instead, blowing out a shaky breath.

When my eyes snap open, hers are bouncing between mine. The column of her throat moves as she nods. "Okay."

Okay?

What the fuck is happening right now?

Then it dawns on me.

The rage is muted. A subdued buzz in my veins that allows clarity to seep through the hurt.

The anger.

The wrath that would've had me demolishing anything in my path.

Demolishing her.

It's the kind of lucidity that brings back a little bit of my humanity, even if it's just a sliver that got lost somewhere in the rubble I piled up when my life fell apart five years ago.

How did she do that?

I drop my hand from her and step back, letting her suck in the breaths I deprived her of. I know she wants to reach up and touch the reddened skin decorating her neck that will surely bruise, but she doesn't. She pushes to stand, wiping at her wet cheeks with the back of her hand.

She gestures to the table, shuffling to leave the space between me and the table empty. "Sit. I need to take a look at your shoulder."

I glance down, noticing the deep red color that's staining through my white dress shirt. At least the bleeding has slowed. The downside to her clearing my head is that the pain is a bitch. I was shot when the bullets first started flying. Luckily, I was only hit once before Carter shielded my body with his, sending us both crashing to the ground.

Carter was in the helicopter with me, but I don't know where he is now. Worrying about his condition has me moving toward the door. He said he was fine, and he is physically. However, I know deep down there's a goddamn war raging in his head for letting me get shot at all. Carter barely spoke on the flight home, his knee bouncing up and down violently with his arms folded over his chest. His body language conveyed how furious he was with himself.

I'm glad it was me, and he needs to know that. If he had shielded me sooner when the bullets first started ripping through the air, the one in my shoulder would've been lodged in his back, and I don't even want to consider what that reality could've looked like.

"Where are you going?" Her genuine concern makes me pause.

"I need to find Carter."

"An empire can't rebuild without its king." I turn to look at her hesitantly. When I don't answer, she answers the questions bombarding me, "So... The Irish mob, huh?"

A corner of my mouth curves, feeling foreign against the fury dissipating. "Have you made some friends while I've been gone?"

If she's free to roam the estate now, I'm not the only one who will recognize how gorgeous she is. That is why tomorrow, my men will know she's off-limits, or else actions will be taken.

But only because I'm still suspicious of her.

Not because my dick is already wanting to stake a claim.

I might just kill anyone who touches her.

"I met your father." Her response distresses me. "I'm assuming you were talking about him when you said that my life isn't only in your hands." She waves a hand over me. "Take off your shirt."

I do as she says, too tired to fight her, though I'm worried about my best friend and about what words she and my father exchanged while I was gone. Fire shoots up my arm, and I grit my teeth, struggling to undo the first few buttons. I've been through worse. It's not the first time I've been shot—I have five scars to prove it. But, mixed with the exhaustion and being blindsided, my muscles ache.

After Kate pulls out some gauze, bandages, and other medical supplies from the cabinet over the sink, she turns, watching me struggle.

She blows out a breath and gestures her head to motion to the table again. I drop my hands, leaving my shirt partway open to reveal the tattoos gliding over my skin, and sit down, the paper crinkling below my weight.

Moving to stand between my legs, I'm hooked to the way her delicate fingers pop open each button. When she finishes the last one, her hands gently move under the fabric, her hands grazing my shoulders as she gently pushes it off to let me wiggle out of the shirt. Her eyes flit over the mapping of ink over my abdomen and chest before magnetizing back to mine. She's already seen my arms, but somehow it feels like she's memorizing every stroke and line that's decorating my skin.

And not just ink.

All of me.

She's undressing me to fix a damn bullet wound in my shoulder. Yet the way she's touching me, it's like she's undressing more than just my body and trying to dissect my head and read the scars that penetrate my skin.

It's been days since I've seen her, but with one heated inter-action, she's cracked my barriers, and I can't help but want to do what she stupidly asked. Claim her mouth with mine and taste every inch of her, even if she's the sweetest poison that was meant to annihilate me.

She's a distraction I can't indulge in.

Her fingers dancing over my skin makes my cock twitch.

Before I'm possessed to shove Kate to her knees and force her to make my dick feel better with her hot mouth instead, I snatch her wrist, drawing a quick breath from her lungs. "I've got shit to do, darling. Hurry this up before I rip the bullet out myself and settle for a band-aid."

She presses her lips in a line at my command, leaning to pick up some supplies off the counter while I can't help but lean toward that twinge of belief in my gut that tells me maybe Kate isn't involved with Luciano after all.

But if she isn't, then who is?

# EIGHTEEN | KATE

I've never experienced lingering glances. The kind of tension that's thick and uncuttable, somehow connecting two people even when they don't understand why.

I've barely seen Preston the last few days. I tell myself he's not avoiding me because of whatever cracked between us, and that it's the fact he's been calling emergency meetings and plotting with his father since the attack in Virginia. But it doesn't feel like the truth.

Something snapped and left a mark on us both the moment I asked him to kiss me.

His father's words to me on that bench about Preston losing his mother and sister to something sinister dissolved so many of the things I've judged him for.

When his fist snatched my throat and squeezed, I saw the pain stirring in his dark eyes. The hurt. The life of a man who was born into this world but was robbed of the only things that made it beautiful.

Maybe it was my survival mode, wanting to distract him from the demons infecting his head so he wouldn't choke me to death. However, I can't ignore the fact that a part of me wanted his mouth on mine. To steal away some of that pain and give him relief, even if it was just for a fleeting moment.

Stupid? Probably.

But he didn't do it. The mixture of relief and sting of rejection has been battling in my head ever since.

It's been a few days since they returned from the attack. Two men died in surgery, and another was lost to an infection that was too brutal to fix. Imogen did all she could, but I recognize the way she sees it as failure in the way she's carried herself since those alarms went off. Exhaustion lines and dark circles are her companions, but it doesn't stop her from keeping up with check-ins and administering more treatments and drugs to survivors as they need, giving them more attention and care than I've ever witnessed.

To her, it's personal.

Which is why it's been so easy to spend my days alongside her and the team I was tossed into. It's nice to know my time and talents are finally making a significant difference. It didn't feel like that when I was working at Lachlan Park. Strangely, it's almost like a gift in itself. I may be trapped, but I've been able to rediscover something I'm passionate about and handle lives with the delicate care they deserve.

Imogen said the Megalley Syndicate is a mob bound by blood.

A family.

I see and feel this in every interaction, having worked tirelessly beside her to fill my time and distract myself from the flicker of worry in my chest that is concerned about Preston.

It's silly to think that something switched so fast that I'm seeing him through a different lens.

I can't help but sense that maybe he's feeling the same about me.

Remember when I mentioned those lingering glances?

When I'm leaving dinner, he's going to get dinner.

When I'm taking a walk outside, he stands in that same window watching me from the third floor.

When I'm outside on the balcony before I go to bed, he's sitting in that chair a few stories up, where I can see him, and he can see me at an angle.

It's unnerving and thrilling at the same time.

The estate is big, but it's as if we orbit each other.

Or he's using the tracking device to his advantage and avoiding me.

I lift the glass of red wine to my lips, taking a sip while my feet sway back and forth in the water from the edge of the pool I'm perched on.

The afternoon sun glides through the pool room windows, spilling across the floor and into the water. Ripples I'm creating with my feet span out across the surface, sparking where the sun touches. Marble pillars extend to the ceiling, accompanied by skylights and high beams that stretch from one side of the room to the other. There's a waterfall at the end that dribbles into the pool, on either side of which two giant palms stretch out their greenery and disappear into the rafters.

The sound of a door clicking shut over the whirr of water snags my attention. My pulse jumps in response, my eyes darting to the door.

Carter stops when he notices me, a towel draped over his shoulder and bare chest. His black swim shorts hang low on his hips, where his defined V-line disappears below the hem. "Oh. I didn't think anyone would be in here."

I frown. I haven't talked to him since he guarded me on my first night here. It's hard to push past the awkwardness that hangs in the air. But I also can't ignore my relief that he was one of the few who got out of Virginia unscathed a few days ago. Preston was worried sick about him and nearly avoided medical attention altogether. He pretty much burst out of the room the second the stitches were done to check on Carter.

Tossing a leg onto the ledge, I push myself up, pausing when he says, "I didn't mean you needed to leave."

I settle back down, gliding my foot back into the water as he walks to the nearest lounge chair and tosses his towel down before padding to the deep end and diving in. He disappears for a moment, his splash reverberating off the walls before he reappears in the shallower end. Standing, he glides his hands over his wet, jet-black hair to smooth it back.

Water droplets cascade down the hard planes and divots in his abdomen, drawing my eyes to his tattoos. The one that holds my attention is a giant octopus on his upper chest. Its tentacles drape down his arm, across his defined torso, and over his shoulder. It's a work of art, and I can't help but stare at it.

Maybe a little too long when he cuts through my distracted state. "You're not swimming?"

Probably a good thing I'm not, considering there are only skimpy bikinis in my closet.

*I wonder if Preston selected those.*

I'd prefer not to give Carter an eyeful of the strokes and blemishes decorating my stomach. He would ask questions. I try not to show them if I can help it.

Someday I'll wear them with pride. The marks of a survivor. Not a runner.

That day is not today.

"I was looking around and found myself in here. It's peaceful." I take another sip of my wine.

His tongue darts out, swiping the water off his lips. "Yeah, I like coming in here when I need to think." He peers around, something unspoken in his eyes. "It's one of my favorite places on the estate."

"Have you been here long?"

"What's your definition of long?"

I shrug.

He wades through the water toward me, his hard body

gliding through like a predator. "The Megalley Syndicate has been my family, this has been my home, for the last twelve years."

My eyes lock onto his. "You say family like this was the one you were born into."

I know he wasn't, but I say it because I'm being nosy. Digging for more information about this mob as if it can reveal a complexity that extends beyond their criminal activities. They are still human. They have blood running through their veins, even if they drain others.

The world may be as beautiful as it is dark, but there are various hues of gray blended through, too.

I'm just not sure what shade *they* are.

Luckily for me, Carter entertains my question. "I wasn't. But blood means nothing. Family isn't a physical tie, it's a feeling."

Setting my wine glass down next to me, I ponder that. "Preston said you threw yourself on top of him when he was shot."

The natural light casting shadows across his face moves as his jaw flexes. "Yeah. Well, he shouldn't have been fucking shot to begin with. I should've reacted sooner. That bullet should've been mine."

My brows furrow. "You would've taken a bullet for him?"

His stern gaze makes me think I'm pressing too hard, but my eye contact doesn't falter. It takes a few heartbeats, but he responds. "Yes—and it's not just because it's my job. He's my family, and I'd do anything for him and Arden, even if it means putting my life at risk."

I brace my elbows on my knees, leaning over them, hoping he'll elaborate more about his past. Unlike Preston and Arden, Carter has no Irish dialect in his tone, which I find interesting. "So, you don't have any blood relatives?"

He leans back, floating on the water. "It's complicated."

I stare at him until he sighs, fed up with my steadfast attention ruining his peace, and sits back up. "Questions can put you in danger around here."

"I'm in danger anyway. It doesn't make a difference," I mumble honestly.

Slits appear in his eyes, but then they soften after a moment. "I was a drug addict. Lived on the streets in Boston for a year before Arden found me."

That catches me off guard.

My chest stills. "Arden found you?"

When I think he won't say anything else, he swims closer, bracing his wet, massive hands beside me on the ledge to hold himself there.

I listen intently.

"I was staying in an alley near one of their clubs when I walked past in the middle of the night and saw a few men trying to take advantage of one of the bartenders outside the service entrance." He rolls his lips, a look of disgust pulling up his lip. "One of the men was holding her body against his chest with a gun to her head, while the other had his hand down her shorts. I thought I was hallucinating. I might have been tweaking at the time, but somehow, I managed to pull myself together enough to register what I was seeing. I was able to wrestle the gun out of the hands of the one, and a few seconds later, their bodies were lifeless on the concrete. Arden and his men heard the shots from inside and found me with the girl. The next thing I knew, I was on their plane, and they had brought me here." He glances around the space before finding my face again. "Arden gave me a home. Helped me get clean because he saw more than just my addiction. He gave me a purpose."

I blow out a raspberry. "And your real family?"

"They cut ties when I started using. I don't blame them. It wasn't until I got clean and something happened," the column of his throat moves, "that I realized how important family is. I reached out and started mending what was broken."

I hook onto something he said. I tread carefully. "You said you've been here twelve years. Was it Preston's mom and sister's deaths that brought on that realization?"

His eyes slice to mine, something ominous rousing there. A hurricane that's threatening to destroy anything in its path. For a moment, I think it might be me, but then he blinks, and sadness replaces it, combined with something else I can't quite place.

Determination maybe?

But that doesn't seem right.

He pushes off the side, swimming away from me. "You've been busy. Knowing Preston, I doubt he's the one who told you that."

I pick up my wine glass, staring at the contents as I swirl it, the red liquid gliding up the edges of the glass like spilled blood. "What happened to them? His mom and his sister?" I mutter.

His raspy chuckle has my head tilting upward to find him scrutinizing me. "It's not my past, so it's not my story to tell."

If anyone should understand that, it should be me. But I can't help the little fireball of interest that scorches my chest, wanting to dive deeper into the man whose callouses run deeper than his hands.

I ask a different question. "Did you know them?"

Carter drags his wet hands over his face from where he stands in the center of the pool. When his attention finds me again, he groans. "If she were here, you two would get along. Both of you are stubborn in your own ways."

The moment my mouth opens to ask who he's talking about, the door to the pool opens. Both Carter and I gaze at Preston, standing shirtless in the doorway.

His hardened, suspicious look bounces between us. "Did I miss something?"

Avoiding his eyes, I chug the rest of my wine in one gulp as Carter swims to the other side of the pool.

Preston's eyes feel like they're attached to every inch of my body. They are solid. Deadly. Untrusting, though something snapped between us in the medical center that day. He still doesn't trust me, but something he said that day ferments in my gut, turning sour.

*"I fucking know you're working for that bastard. The one who has destroyed everything in my life."*

It registers now.

Someone took his mom and his sister from him.

Sure, this is the world he was born into and destined to rule, but after my conversation with Arden in the garden, I caught onto the hint that Preston wasn't always this cruel and unforgiving. Maybe he was never entirely soft, but there's a chance he's far different now than he was then. Back when the good parts, the best parts, of his life were intact.

I always thought evil was ingrained in someone's DNA—woven into their very being.

But now, as I stare into those dark bourbon eyes, I'm reminded that monsters can be made, too.

# NINETEEN | KATE

I toss my towel onto the boulder and slip off my flip-flops, turning around to take in the murky waters lapping at the rocky shoreline. Stars twinkle above, the ocean alive with moonlight that glitters across the surface like an earthly galaxy that's pulling me in.

It's nearly two in the morning, but the nightmares flooding my sleep had me breaking out in a sweat. When I finally woke, hot tears drenched my pillow. The dream felt realistic, as if Xander had somehow slipped through the walls and stood in the shadows of my room, wearing that smile I used to find handsome but is now sinister and haunting in a way that has rotted my insides with fear.

I pulled my trembling body out of bed and tugged on one of the swimsuits Gretta put in my closet—a pink bikini that ties on both sides of my hips and around my neck. It's so late, nobody will see me. Or my scars. I can swim in peace, knowing I'm alone with whatever lurks in the water. Those creatures no longer scare me.

Heading to the pool crossed my mind, but something about the bright moonlight drifting through the windows pulled me to the beach. Even in the summer, the waters greeting Maine are cold. I'm hoping freezing my ass off will chase off the demons and give me some reprieve before I try to sleep again.

Ambling down to the water, the first touch of the ocean has me sucking in a sharp breath. The further I walk, the more my skin pebbles with goosebumps. If I wasn't awake before, I sure am now. And I don't see prolonging my torture anymore. Inhaling a deep breath, I sink below the surface. The cold water rushes around me, attacking my skin like millions of tiny needles. The icy blanket extinguishes the blistering terror that's had a hold on me. When my lungs start to burn, I pop out, sliding my hands over my hair to smooth it away from my face.

Just like that, the heat returns, but it's different.

An awareness.

I knew the men in the watchtowers would be watching me, but it's not their eyes that have my body stiffening.

Swallowing, I turn around to see Preston on the shore, his hands shoved in his sweatpants pockets. His brown hair is mussed, but not from sleep; his mouth is set into a scowl. How did he know I was out here? It's two in the morning.

Instantly, my body becomes aware of the weighted metal around my neck.

He tracked me out here.

"You think drowning yourself will help you escape me?" he calls out over the soft lapping of water along the beach.

Clutching my arms to my chest, my voice quivers from the cold. Luckily, it's too dark for him to see my stomach. "Don't flatter yourself. You're not the one I'm trying to escape, Captain."

The moonlight washing over his frame makes him look ethereal. Otherworldly, with his rippling, tattooed muscles painted silver.

Preston's head slants curiously.

I swallow, nearly choking on my sandpaper tongue. "I couldn't sleep."

"So, you decided to take a late-night swim?"

I don't know why I tell him. "I'd rather swim with the monsters that lurk in these waters than submit to the one that haunts my head."

He peers at me momentarily across the tens of feet separating us before turning and walking back up the beach. Just as I think he's leaving me, he surprises me by plopping onto the boulder my towel is on. I need that, but his firm, perfect ass is trapping it below him.

Preston folds his arms over his chest, watching me. That's fine, I'm not ready to get out yet. I'm hoping he'll leave before I do. He already saw the scar under my ear and used it against me. I don't need him noticing the ones that lacerate my lower belly.

For a while, I wade through the water and float on my back, letting my worries wash away with the waves. But Preston's not leaving; his presence is as constant as the cold that chills me to the bone. When my teeth start chattering, I know I can't stay in any longer.

I wade back toward the beach, keeping my arms folded across my stomach, hoping it's too dark for him to see the imperfections that mark my skin.

My body is so numb I can't feel the pebbles digging into my feet. I stop before Preston, trying to disregard the way his eyes trace over every part of me, coiling that familiar desire I'm trying so hard to ignore.

I may be covered in a small bikini, but it doesn't feel like I'm wearing one at all. Those bourbon eyes strip me bare.

My body trembles from the icy chill penetrating my muscles. I clutch my arms tighter around my stomach. "Can I have my towel?"

The shadow falling over his throat moves. His chest rises

and falls, like he's trying to keep control. Calculate his next move. Or his next words. I'm not sure.

"Can I please have my towel? I'm cold." I reach out a hand, palm up, keeping the other tucked into my belly. Is it too much to wish that he'll stop being so broody and tenacious and give it to me? I release a frustrated breath. "Preston—"

The air whooshes from my lungs.

With one swift movement, he snatches my outstretched arm, pulling me on top of him. All it took was one heartbeat, one fluid and smooth motion to have me on his lap. My legs are parted, straddling his. Absentmindedly, my hands fly out to brace on his shoulders like I'm bracing for an impact I may never recover from.

I'm dripping, but he doesn't seem to care as water slides down my thighs, seeping into his gray sweatpants.

My nervousness floods the silence. "I'm getting you wet."

Preston rolls his hips, grinding my covered, soaked center against his erection. "Not in the way I want." His hand glides up my spine, threading my wet hair sticking to my back around his fingers.

My lungs fill with a rabid breath. "I thought you didn't trust me?"

"Hate fucking is more fun anyway."

I glare at him, and he growls his answer. "I don't. Especially now that I know you're more terrified of someone else. What are you running from, darling? Because it certainly isn't me." His hand, tangled in my hair, moves to the side of my neck, his fingers ghosting over my scar. "Or shall I say, *who*?"

And just like that, I'm scrambling off him, slipping my flip-flops on, and forgetting the towel. Preston's question slices through the lust and arousal, filling my head with the one person I can never seem to rid myself of.

# TWENTY | PRESTON

Now she's running.

But still, I get the sense I'm not the one she's fleeing from.

There's something else.

Someone else.

The jealousy I feel, knowing another person is taking up that fucking space I want to be mine, is unexpected. It has me chasing after her.

*"Don't flatter yourself. You're not the one I'm trying to escape, Captain."*

Everything in my body is demanding to find out who.

Is it too much to fuck it out of her? Hope that filling her with my cock, my cum, will push out the answers she's denying me.

She's quick, pacing across the yard, though I'm closing the distance one stride at a time, like there's this tether that's straining, and I don't want to let it snap whatever is transpiring between us. I feel the eyes of my men on us as we race across the sidewalk to the house. They're just doing their job.

While I, on the other hand, am entirely distracted from mine.

Kate enters the house, taking the steps two at a time, but I'm hot on her heels, trying to ignore the fact that she's practically naked in that tiny pink bikini that gives her skin a glow. Her hair is slicked back, the long strands dripping and gliding over her back. My focus lands on a drop slipping down her spine and below those bikini bottoms that enhance her curves and pull at my sanity.

If my dick wasn't already hard, it is now.

God, she's a beautiful specimen.

When she reaches the second floor, she heads to her room, not looking back. But she knows I'm following based on her stiff shoulders and strained movements, like she knows if she breaks out into a run, I'll chase.

"Stop following me, Preston. I want to be alone," she huffs as she opens the door and steps inside, slamming it behind her.

I lunge for it, stopping it with my hand, and barge through. She stops partway in the room, lit only by the glow of the lamp beside her bed, facing away from me. She stares at me through her reflection in the windows of the French doors.

Lightning crackles in my chest, my heart creating a thunderous roar that pulses in my ears. "Turn around and say that to me again because I don't believe you."

A subtle mocking laugh shakes her back. "Do you always get everything you want?"

"Usually. But not right now, apparently." I swear I hear her swallow through the space. I can't deny that the one fucking thing I want is her.

Under me.

On top of me.

Seeping further into my soul, she somehow cracked to break through to the parts I thought died long ago.

I. Fucking. Want. Her.

And I know I shouldn't, considering why I brought her here.

"You had your chance. I asked you to kiss me, and you said no. Not very uplifting to a girl's self-esteem."

"I was about to choke you to death. I fucking thought about snapping your neck, Kate, and you asked me to kiss you. So, yeah, I was a little taken aback by those words." Her eyes hold mine in the reflection of the doors. "Can you tell me with all certainty that you still want that, even after that day?"

*Please say yes.*

She sinks her teeth into that plush bottom lip.

There goes another fracture in my control.

When she nods, the air is knocked from my lungs. It's barely a whisper. "But we can't take it any further than that."

"I'm a patient man, but *fuck*, darling. That's a lot to ask of me when I can smell your arousal from here. When all I've thought about since you first opened those lips to lie to me is what they would look like wrapped around my cock."

The blood rushing to my dick is making it strain painfully in my boxers. At this point, I'd happily settle for her beautiful fingers choking it. Maybe a little flick of her tongue to collect the bead of precum that is waiting eagerly for her mouth.

I'm about ready to get on my damn knees and grovel when she closes her eyes briefly and turns around. Her eyes remain locked on mine, but I don't miss the way she's trembling. I slowly take her in, like the most beautiful artwork that was created just for me, when my focus lands on the discolored, raised skin on her lower stomach. Her bikini bottoms conceal others I can't see.

I stop counting the haphazardly placed scars when I get to fifteen because it doesn't matter to me.

But it also fucking matters a lot. Whoever the fuck did this to her is going to wish they could use the knife they carved her with to end their pain that I will drag out. I'll use my blade and then let Imogen heal them.

So, I can inflict pain again.

And again.

I'll be the devil in their living hell. No escape. Just torment and torture for hurting this beautiful creature who is still the most gorgeous woman I've ever laid eyes on.

My hands ball into fists at my sides. The familiar coil of rage is starting to stake a claim again. But seeing Kate, the tears falling down her face, all I want to do is soothe whatever pain she's been living with.

Lucky for her, I know endless ways to torture a man till he's begging for death. And I have a team ready to haul their ass to me on a silver platter.

"A name," I growl.

Her eyes bounce between mine. "Preston—"

"Darling, I'm going to track that sick fuck down whether you tell me or not. But this," I wave a hand over her, "doesn't change a thing. I want you."

She exhales a disbelieving breath. "These scars are from someone who took everything from me and never gave an inch back. Sex has never been about me, Preston. I'm not even sure I know what that feels like. My body is broken—I can't get off without some pain mixed with the pleasure because that's all I've known. Running is all I know. And I don't want to taint anyone, you," she clarifies, "with something I've never healed from."

In one heartbeat, I'm consuming the distance, wrapping my arm around her waist, pulling her into me. "Look at me, Kate." Her eyes are diverted to the floor, but when I whisper, "Please," the request feels foreign but right coming out of my mouth.

Her heavy, glazed eyes lift to mine.

Seeing her like this breaks my heart. Which is baffling, considering I thought there was nothing left.

I press my finger below her chin, so she feels the truth of every word. "You are not broken. You were just dealt a fucking shitty hand and had the strength to run and get yourself out of something you never deserved. Trust me when I say, I know how hard it is when you don't have closure, that the person who did this is still out there wreaking havoc on your life, and won't let you rest. Healing takes time and the right people to help you through it, because it's too heavy to do alone. Healing isn't a straight path. Let me help you heal, even if it just removes a little bit of the weight you carry."

A tear glides down her cheek, and I absentmindedly swipe it away with my thumb.

A ghost of a smile plays on her lips. Her voice is as soft as she feels in my arms. "Your dad said the same thing when he was talking about you."

I swallow. "You aren't alone."

She sinks further into me, gripping my t-shirt in her fists.

Tonight is about her and what she needs from me. Because whatever she wants will satisfy us both.

My thumb brushes across her flushed cheek. "Tell me what you want. I want you to trust me, and in return, I'll trust you."

She considers that for a moment, rolling her lips.

"And if you need time, I'll give you time." No matter how fucking hard it will be. "Whenever you're ready, I want to give you everything you deserve." And more. "I want to make *you* feel good. I want you to come on *your* terms. Darling, doing that for you, and only you, will be more than enough for me."

Her eyes flutter shut, her gasp floating in the small space separating us.

When she mutters, "Kiss me," like a plea, I don't hesitate.

I'd be a very, very stupid man to walk away this time.

# TWENTY-ONE | PRESTON

My arm snakes around her waist, pulling her flush against me as the hand on her face slides to her neck, guiding her full lips to mine. The moment our mouths fuse, blood surges to my groin, straining painfully against fabric meant for comfort.

My body may be aching for her, but I let hers tell me what it needs. At first, her movements are so gentle it's torturous. When her mouth parts, granting me entrance, I eagerly memorize her taste and the way her tongue twists with mine.

Her fingers weave around my neck, threading into my hair.

Kate tastes like minty sugar and wildfire. Her flavor seeps through my defenses, making me want to drop them altogether —to never put them back up, at least not with her.

I slowly back her up to the bed, turning us so that when the backs of my knees hit the mattress, my ass collapses onto it. Her mouth is still welded to mine. Electricity sparks across my nerves, turning me savage for her and the way she feels against me. It's starting to unravel the sexual tension that's buzzing and alive behind my sternum.

It's deliberate, but hungry.

The kind that wrenches your soul from your body.

That's the way I'm kissing Kate. I'm fucking her mouth with my tongue, and she lets me. Like I can capture and seize her soul, tangle it with mine.

Too many clothes separate us. Well, mine, since she's wrapped in this skimpy pink bathing suit that my fingers itch to remove.

My body is an inferno, but every move is hers tonight. If she wants me to burn, I'll gladly be the ashes she walks on.

She pulls back, a cold from the loss of her touch washing over me. Her eye contact is steady as she stands, hovering above me. I'm witnessing a goddess who fell from heaven. Her eyes don't leave mine. She reaches behind her, pulling at the strings that keep her breasts confined in that bikini that I wanted to rip off the moment I saw her walking down to the beach from the window in my office.

She tugs at the strings, letting the pathetic excuse for material pool on the ground at my feet. She stands before me, her perfect tits and perky rosebud nipples making my mouth water for a taste. I bet they would fit perfectly in my hands, as if they were sculpted for me. Nipples that were crafted to be grazed by my teeth and twisted by my fingertips.

God, I crave to touch her, but I don't. She's in control, and I'm surprised I'm letting her be, considering I have a dominance kink and get off on power.

Surprise, surprise.

Now I'm thinking I have a Kate kink.

How could I not?

Her fingers dip below her bikini bottoms, and she slips them down her long legs, giving me a full view of that pretty pussy that I'm hoping she'll let me play with. Suck. Fuck with my fingers.

I swipe a hand over my jaw. "God, you're killing me, darling."

Her lips curve nervously, but I reach out for her, and she puts her hand in mine, letting me tug her back onto my lap to straddle me. I hope it's not just water soaking through my sweats now.

She slams her lips on mine, leading our kiss again. Rising, she pushes my head lower, my cock jumping in excitement. When Kate straightens her spine to lift her breasts to my mouth, I nearly come in my pants. Seeing her like this is the fucking sexiest thing I've ever seen.

I draw one of her perky buds into my mouth, invigorated by how her hands move in my hair—a silent request for more.

Kate whimpers as my tongue moves in slow circles around her nipple, then she moves my head to the next one. I know she said she can't get off without pain mixing with the pleasure, but it's her call. The beast inside of me is roaring to stake a claim, but I suppress those urges.

Her skin is so soft against my tongue. I give the other nipple the same expert attention, giving her what she deserves as I suck it into my mouth.

What she wants.

*What she needs.*

"Fuck, Preston," she breathes, rolling her hips over me.

When my cock creates friction against her wet center, it takes all my willpower not to toss her onto this bed and destroy that perfect pussy till she's screaming my name instead. I release her perky bud with a pop and peer down. The mess she's making on my pants, chasing the friction to satisfy her clit, has me entranced.

"Look at how wet you are, darling—taking what you want from me, knowing damn well it's driving me crazy that I can't fuck you yet."

The soft, pleasure-induced smile that appears on her face engrains into my skull like the ink covering my skin.

She grinds down on me again, using her arms around my neck to help her momentum. "What would you do if I let you?"

I grumble in frustration at the question, and she grins. Removing one of her arms from my neck, she grabs my hand, dragging it to her sensitive center.

When my fingers glide over her seam, she's so soaked that my jaw clenches. "Goddamn. Do you know how wet this pussy is for me right now?"

She bites her lip, nodding. "And it's not the first time."

"Fuck," I drawl huskily. Since she's straddling me, I position my feet further apart, watching the way it spreads her thighs more for me, which gives me more access. "You can't tell me things like that. Now whenever I see you, I'll be distracted, wondering if this cunt might be ready for me to take it, whenever I want, however I want." I rub circles on her clit before slowly sinking a finger in her tight cunt. She feels like warm velvet and sin.

I greedily soak in her whimpers and moans, answering her question. "First, I would flip you on your back and use my tongue while my fingers stretch you, prepare you to take my cock. But you'd be so wet that the moment I bend you over the side of this bed and hike your leg up, you'd perfectly take every inch of my dick like this pretty pussy was made for me. You'd be so full of me, darling. Then, when I finally come inside you, it will demolish the traces of anyone else who had you until the only name you remember is mine."

"Oh my God."

"Do you need my cock now? That's not my name."

When I slowly add another finger, cursing as I meet some restriction, she trembles in my arms. "Preston—" Her forehead falls against mine.

"That's right, darling."

Her eyes flutter closed. "I need— More."

"What do you want?" I ask across her lips.

"I want your tongue on me. In me."

My arrogant smile emerges. "You're in control here, darling. You had my tongue in your mouth. Is that what you want again? You'll have to be a little more specific—"

"I need your tongue against my clit. In my pussy. I want it with your fingers like you said."

Her neediness scratches at my ego. "So desperate for me to make you come."

She whimpers as I strengthen my arms around her. I stand and flip us, laying her gently on the duvet. She sinks into it, not wasting any time as she parts those gorgeous legs for me, granting me the first view of her glistening center.

Keeping her big green eyes locked on mine, I drop to my knees for her. Like her giving herself to me like this is a knife straight to my heart. If the last few breaths I take are while I'm ravaging her pretty cunt, then it will be one hell of a way to go out.

*Better than I deserve.*

Wrapping an arm around each of her thighs, I tug her ass to the end of the mattress, releasing a hot breath across her pussy. She shudders, gripping the sheets in her hands. The wet strands of her hair fan out around her, her back bending at the first touch of my tongue pressing against her seam.

I gaze up at her, writhing while my tongue swirls over her sensitive bundle of nerves, my dick painfully begging for attention as her taste blooms in my mouth. Her eyes are glued to a spot on the ceiling, little murmurs I can't understand falling from her lips.

"My eyes are down here between your legs, Kate," I speak her name against her so she knows how fucking serious I am that I want her eyes soaking in what I'm doing to her.

She breathes heavily, as if tearing her gaze back to mine is hard. I insert my middle finger, watching her struggle to meet my eyes. When she does, I find that sensitive spot inside her and curl my finger, mesmerized by her velvet walls tightening around me.

Realization dawns. I press my tongue to where my middle finger is thrusting into her entrance, and I glide up to her clit before I place a soft kiss there. "You've never had a man taste this sweet pussy, have you?"

She shakes her head. That one answer hurls a grenade at another one of my barriers. "I-I don't know, it was a part of foreplay that was skipped."

"I'll take any firsts I can get." My ring finger joins my middle, and she releases a moan that vibrates through her. "Now that I've had you this way, I'm afraid my tongue will need a taste every time before my cock gets one."

A mischievous smile lightens her features.

"What?"

"I want you to reach into your sweats and stroke your cock while you play with me."

*Oh, sweet fuck.*

Her filthy words make me wonder what else that mouth is capable of.

She doesn't have to tell me twice. Reaching into my boxers, I wrap one hand around the base of my aching cock while the other is inside her. My strokes are languid, from base to tip, in time with the thrusting of my fingers. It's never been this erect before, and somehow her sweet breathy sounds, the feeling of her soaking my fingers and my tongue, have my balls tightening quickly.

When I add my tongue again, it's game over. Her fingers turn white, clenching the sheets in an attempt to prolong our time before her orgasm hits. With the way her barriers are tightening around me and throbbing, it won't be long.

"Preston, I'm going to—"

"This is your night, darling. You don't need to ask, just come for me. Take what you want from me."

Then she does.

Her walls collapse, a moan blended with a shriek filling the room from those beautiful lips as mine suck on her clit to drag it out. She pulses around me, filling my mouth with her, and it's the most beautiful thing that could satisfy a man for life.

Her body trembles with the aftershocks, her skin glowing from the orgasm. When her fingers weave through my hair, tugging me upward, I pull my fingers out of her. I release my cock with my other hand and crawl over her body, sprawled out below me like she wants.

"That was—" Kate shakes her head. She's naked below me. Stunning. Breathtaking as her brows draw together and she asks, "What about you?"

"I don't break my promises. Tonight was about you and only you. And if you need more nights like this one, days, mornings, that's exactly what I'll give you. I need you to tell me you understand that."

Kate nods sheepishly, exhaling an exhausted breath. "Yes, sir."

Jesus Christ.

I almost say good girl, but I catch myself. I know that fucker from her past ruined those words for her, and I'll never let them come out of my mouth.

The future is for new memories. Healing. And Kate deserves a new beginning.

So do I, and I can't help but feel like maybe I'm holding mine.

# TWENTY-TWO | PRESTON

"Are there any ex-boyfriends buried in that research somewhere?"

Brody turns in his computer chair, lifting a dark brow over the rim of his black-framed glasses. One of his five monitors has tens of tabs open. A timeline of Kate's life is sprawled out before us, my fingers clenched into balls at my side to keep from reaching over him and digging through it all like the bloodthirsty killer I am.

One name. That's all I fucking need.

"Not that I know of," he drawls.

I cross my arms. "Then you didn't do enough digging."

He shoves his tongue into his cheek, a habit he resorts to when he's annoyed. "Kate pretty much fell off the map entirely a year ago. No bank records. No digital trails from a credit card. No housing records. No social media. Nothing, Boss. She was thorough." He rocks back and forth in the chair, the hinges whining beneath his weight. I dig my nails into my biceps, so I don't cave into my urge to punch him off it. I'm in a bad mood. His constant rocking, combined with the slight squeak, is irritating my nerves.

"You want to tell me what this is fucking about?" A cynical expression pulls at his features. "Because at first you thought she was involved with Luciano, and now you're asking me about her love life." I don't like the way he glares at me knowingly, like he's in on one of my secrets.

"What's that?" I point at a picture on the screen.

"Oh. When I did a facial recognition search, that's the only thing that's popped up with her face in the last year."

I study the dark image, the focal point a blonde teenage girl popping a piece of pink gum with her hair twirled around her finger, wearing a pair of the haunted mine ride overalls. Kate is in the background, near the loading platform, looking completely oblivious as the image is being taken, her gaze fixed off toward the line of guests waiting to get on the ride. The background of the social media image is blurry, but there's no denying it's Kate.

"It was posted on Instagram a few months ago," he clarifies.

The door opening has the hairs on my neck raising at attention, and with the way Brody's spine shoots upward, I don't need to look to know who walked into the room.

I lower my voice to a low growl only he can hear. "Dig more. I suggest starting the year before she fell completely off the map. Get your hands on any deleted data that hasn't been overwritten. There's a reason we hired you."

"Yes, Boss," he acknowledges, pulling himself back to his desk, typing away like I asked.

A rough hand clasps my shoulder, but I refrain from letting it jolt me out of my skin like it usually does. Arden may be my father, but he elicits the same reaction from everyone when he's in boss mode.

His deep, interrogative voice accelerates my pulse. "What's going on here?"

From this angle, only I can see the way Brody's eyes are blown wide. My father has a view of the back of his head.

Brody doesn't say anything.

Good.

He knows the real reason I brought Kate here and is aware that under no circumstances can Arden discover the truth.

Rubbing the back of my neck, I muster up a lie. "I'm having Brody pull up all communication records transferred between us and the Virginia location, trying to see if there's any digital footprints from someone who might have hacked the system."

Brody's shoulders stiffen further. To an outsider, his typing might seem like the kind of speed that suits a hacker and security expert. But I hear the inconsistencies. Namely, that backspace button he keeps jamming with his finger. I just hope my father doesn't.

When my father drops his hand from my shoulder, I turn to see him nodding. My gut twists at the cynical look pulling at his features. "Conference room, now. There's been a new development."

My heart hammers in my chest. "About the ambush in Virginia?"

His golden-brown eyes study mine, the dim sconces on the wall in the nearly black room casting shadows across his face. His stoic expression causes me to shift uncomfortably on my feet. I've never lied to him. At least not when it comes to the Megalley Syndicate. It would be foolish to underestimate him and believe I wouldn't find myself subjected to his wrath.

"Brody, won't you join us?" My father isn't requesting his presence; he's ordering it.

Arden struts back out of the tech and security room. I follow him down the dark concrete hallway under Lachlan Park, with Brody hot on my heels. My father slips a hand into his gray suit pocket and pushes the door to the conference room open. A massive television is mounted on the wall, positioned in front of a long mahogany table, with chairs and a scarlet carpet beneath. Even the amount of red dye coloring the threads wouldn't amount to the blood we have on our hands. It would drown this room.

Carter is already here, lounging back in one of the chairs with his arms knitted across his chest. I take a seat across the table from him as Brody sits in the chair next to mine. My father takes the head of the table. He doesn't sit; he stands, like he always does, since I started coming to these meetings long before I was thrust into my role. But at that time, I was a young boy watching my father command attention and lead with respect.

The tendons in Arden's jaw flex under the fluorescent lights, his eyes shifting to Brody, then cutting to Carter.

"What?" I demand harsher than I intend to. Why am I the only fucking one out of the loop?

Arden braces his hands on the table. "If you weren't so distracted lately, you'd remember that, yesterday, I told you that I had Brody go through records on all our communication channels. *All* messages back and forth between every location from the time we discovered our first shipment of missing product three months ago up until the attack in Virginia."

Brody's frame hardening shifts the air in the room.

*Fuck. Fuck. FUCK!*

Somehow, I manage to keep my face straight as my father's untrusting eyes bore into mine.

There's no pushing past the transparent lie that fell from my mouth, but for now, I avoid it. "And? Did you find a digital footprint someone left behind?"

"Yes." Arden blinks, something darker injecting into his glare. "Someone hacked into the communication channels between the New York and Virginia locations." My brows furrow. "From Lachlan Estate."

Shit.

My dad gestures across the table. "Want to elaborate, Brody?"

I turn to glare at him. He doesn't look at me. Can't say I blame him, not when he knows that my father is the one he fully reports to.

Does that mean he knows about Kate?

She flashes across my mind, flooding me with images of her from around the estate over the last few days. We have fallen into a state of comfortable coexistence when we cross paths. The electric snap in my fingers always wants to reach for her when I'm not working, and she's not at the medical center. It's taking all my sanity not to give my cock and soul what is craving since I didn't indulge the other night. I left her and went straight to my room, settling for my hand that was still covered in cum from her climax, imagining my fist was her tight pussy.

I've been so busy dealing with this fucking Luciano mess and this war on our hands that I've barely spent five minutes with her. So, I have no excuse for ignoring my father yesterday when he told me Brody was checking all of our communication data.

I've been working a lot; I've just been...distracted.

I briefly replay the moment now—sitting in his office with a glass of scotch, the way we always end the night. But instead of focusing on him, I was too busy plotting my first move for when I finally get my revengeful hands on whoever gave Kate those scars.

It's knifework. It's only fair that's how they suffer. Let them watch me with one eye while I gouge out the other with the blunt end of my blade.

Guilt rushes through me, remembering when I ghosted my knife over the scar on Kate's neck. No wonder she was in hysterics seeing me with that blade.

Which gives me an idea.

I make a mental note to go shopping later today.

"For fucks sake, Preston," my dad grits out. He taps a stern pointer finger on the table enough that I think he'll put a dent in the furnished wood. "I need your head here."

Carter gives me a sympathetic look before instructing, "Keep going, Brody."

"Yeah," Brody clears his throat. "It looks like whoever it was hit at just the right moment. Our estate's IP address was recorded in a series of secure messages that happened three months ago between Arden and the Virginia location. That was when you two were in New York for a week," he gestures to my father and me. "The same week that shipment came in with missing product for the first time." All three of us peer at Brody, listening intently. "Whoever hacked into those messages from the estate knew the exact date that we would be transferring the biggest shipment of the year to Virginia. They knew how many men we were taking, and then the ambush happened, which we all know was expertly planned and not impulsive. You get the idea."

The vein in my forehead throbs and pulses in time with my chaotic heartbeat as I focus on the details.

Our biggest shipment of the year, lost to the Calco Cartel in Virginia, arrived at the harbor the same morning I found Kate. But the messages between Arden and the Virginia location had been hacked months earlier from inside the estate—the same week the first shipment went missing, back when we were in New York.

It couldn't have been Kate, unless she is working with someone on the inside.

I squash that thought. Maybe it's reckless and will come back to bite me in the ass or kill me, but I'm starting to believe she isn't involved.

My father pinches the bridge of his nose. "You were here the week Preston and I were in New York, Carter. Do you have a recollection of any suspicious activity or anyone who was in the estate at that time that may be worth interrogating?"

Carter pulls his fingers through his dark hair. "I'd have to think about it. I was only at the estate for a few days. I was supposed to go to New York with you, but you had me stay back to collect the shipment that arrived early. And then my mom was in that car accident, and I had to rush back to Chicago."

Arden nods, sighing defeatedly. "That's right."

"But if I remember correctly," Carter adds, "We had a fresh wave of recruits training the week you were in New York. The estate was crawling with them."

I fold and brace my arms on the table. "Brody, we are going to need a list of all recruits who were initiated that week." This time, he meets my eye. "If that was when that first shipment went missing, this is a good place to start. Specifically, ones that were granted access to any computers with the estate's IP address."

Brody sharply nods. "Done."

When I glance back at Arden, his eyes are narrowed on me. He blinks, whatever was swirling there dissipating just as quickly before I can catch it.

He slams his fist against the table, the vibration solidifying our spines. "I want to take this fucker out and have his organs in a chum bucket by the end of the month. He's taken enough from us. I don't care if it's a fucking bloodbath, this Italian pussy is going to get everything he deserves." He scrubs a hand over his jaw. "Now get to work. It's not a war if we're sitting here on our asses willingly taking the punishment for something that wasn't our fault to begin with."

Five years ago, it was the 90th-anniversary party at Lachlan Park. The party we threw at the park had the biggest attendance we've ever had. After closing, my family ended the night, as we usually do on anniversaries, by taking the Ferris wheel around a few times. I'm not sure when that tradition began for the boss and his family, but Arden remembered doing it every year on the anniversary as a child and kept it going.

My father and I never made it on the Ferris wheel that night, but Mom and Tayla did.

They got in their car first. By the time my father and I were ready to board, gunshots pierced the night air from inside the park. Pops that still ring in my ears today as a reminder of how easily it can be to create a distraction.

A diversion that we fell for.

My father left his right-hand man and three other guys with my mom and sister, ordering them to keep them on the Ferris wheel through whatever atrocity was about to take place.

We thought they were safe up there.

We rushed to the edge of the park with a few of our men and Carter, where the old rollercoaster used to be. We encountered Luciano, his son Nico, and six of his soldiers. I'll never rid his smoke-stained, malicious grin from my mind.

Once upon a time, the Megalley Syndicate was looking to form a business deal with the Calco Cartel when it was in the hands of the late Don, Marco Giovanni, Luciano's older brother. We found him respectable. Smart. Well, as decent as a man in our world can be. A deal that would've left us, together, dominating most of the East Coast and southern states.

A business deal that ended with Marco foaming at the mouth and face down in a pile of his own vomit on the conference room table at their sex club in Miami.

Luciano placed the blame on us for plotting and murdering his brother. They believed we had schemed to create chaos, allowing us to expand our borders into their territory while the mob operated without a Don.

Without order.

We ran. Left a trail of Calco bodies through the hallways of the club and in the alley.

The murder of Marco Giovanni wasn't our doing, but that night started a war, and his brother came to collect.

And what's the point of seeking revenge if you don't hit back harder?

# TWENTY-THREE | KATE

My eyes fall shut as my body hits the mattress. The soft duvet envelopes me, wrapping me in the scent of fresh lavender and lemon. The late sunlight pierces through the French doors, spilling warm yellow light across the floor and the end of my bed, where I'm sprawled.

It's hard to miss my one-bedroom house and small paycheck when I'm living like a queen for free. Well, the price is my freedom, but even that doesn't feel like the truth anymore. I enjoy working at the medical center every day, but sadly, it means that Preston and I's paths cross less often than I wish. Which may not be a bad thing, considering every time I see him, all I think about is my mouth on him.

His tongue in me.

The talented strum of his fingers as he gave me the most brutal, overwhelming orgasm that shot me straight up into the cosmos, where I could float among the stars.

Being dominant over Preston was a part of healing that I didn't know I needed. He did everything I asked, letting me take what I wanted from him. That night was about me and drawing out my pleasure. Yet, in a way, I think he was enjoying it as much as I was. Owning him in that way was a power I didn't know I could feel.

Everything about being with Preston felt different.

He listened to me. Heard me.

It gave me a glimpse of what a future with someone could be like, since my body and mind aren't as broken as I've believed. He doesn't understand the weight it holds. He saw my scars but held me in his lap like I wasn't breakable or tarnished. Then he cleaned me up with a washcloth and tucked me in.

His thumb caressed my forehead with the kind of gentle heat that made me wonder if he was going to kiss the spot he was touching.

But he didn't.

He lifted my chin with his fingers, peering into my eyes before leaving me with, "You're so beautiful when you come. I could watch you do that for the rest of my life, even if it meant I'd never get to."

I felt the truth laced in his tone.

He meant it, and each word was like a stitch, pulling back together the confidence I gave up on years ago that sex could be for me. If one time with Preston accomplished something I thought was hopeless, what could more moments like that do?

I'm so attracted to him that one glance lately has me needing to change my panties. When I'm alone at night, my fingers find my clit and sink inside me while I replay his words. His touch on my body. His beautiful bourbon eyes that hungrily lit my body on fire.

My core throbs with need.

I need more. I want more of *him*.

I sit up on the bed, considering taking a shower to clean the day off my body, and solve this wave of desire crackling through my veins. My eyes drift to the dresser, my pulse jumping at the long black velvet box sitting on my bedside table. The moment

I burst through my bedroom doors, I immediately crashed. I didn't see it.

Just looking at it reminds me of the weight of gold adorning my neck. Did Preston get me a matching bracelet or something?

Pushing myself to my feet, I close the distance and pick it up. Rotating it in my hands, my fingers skim over the soft velvet. When I open the lid, my breath escapes my lungs in one sharp exhale.

Staring back at me is a knife, its blade reflecting the dainty chandelier above my bed. The handle reminds me of smooth, black wood after it's been charred. A deep black that draws the eye to the band of pink opal before the hilt meets the blade.

It's so beautiful.

Delicately intimidating.

My heart beats wildly in my ears. Even just the sight of the blade stirs the nausea in my stomach. Why would Preston gift me a knife when he's seen my scars?

Hurt and anger bubble inside me, carrying me to the door and out into the hallway. I know he's been spending a lot of time in his office lately, since I always catch him staring out the window at me when I walk on my breaks.

I've never been to the third level, since he told me it was off limits, but I head up anyway. The box feels heavy in my hand, increasing the panic crawling up my throat. There are five doors on the side of the house facing the garden, but I remember he was standing by the window at the far end, just off center. I choose the second-to-last door at the end of the hallway; the way it's cracked open makes my pulse race.

I knock a few times, barely having to wait before his voice orders me to come in.

Blowing out a shaky breath, I push it open, instantly enveloped in his earthy scent. His eyes are steady on mine with amusement. He doesn't even need to look at the box to know why I'm here.

"I see you got my gift." I haven't spoken to him since yesterday, and the warmth of his voice is a shock to my system.

Preston stands, moving around the dark wooden desk that contrasts nicely with the deep forest tones of the room, lit only by the natural light flooding through the windows.

He stands in front of me, making me swallow.

I turn the box over in my hands. Itching to get it out of my proximity, I hold it out to him. "Most men give a woman jewelry."

Ignoring it, he lifts his arm to let his fingers drift over the chain adorning my neck. Goosebumps skate across my skin when his skin brushes against mine. "I did give you jewelry."

"No," I correct. "You gave me a collar."

"You're right. Maybe I should've gotten you a matching leash to go with it instead."

I slap his hand away with more playfulness than I intend to. I'm kind of hurt that he thought this would make a good gift. My lip trembles. "Why would you give me this?"

His hand bounces back to cup the back of my neck tenderly. "What better way to take back your power than to learn to wield the thing that stole it?"

My brows pull together, my voice small. "You want me to use this?"

He nods. "I want you to learn to fight with it. Protect yourself."

My eyes drop from his to the box as if the knife is going to grow legs and jump out at me—still hurt me somehow despite it being perfectly contained.

I push it toward him through the small space separating us. "I can't. It's too soon."

"Maybe I should've gotten you a gun."

I press my lips in a line, shaking my head.

"I'm going to teach you to use one anyway, because you

should learn. But we'll start with this. You need to be able to protect yourself."

"Protect myself. From who? You?"

"From me. From whoever you're running from." I swallow at the reminder. Preston's gaze locks on the scar below my ear. "To protect your mind from thinking that you can't fight back when you and I both know you're more than capable. Carrying this around will give you a new sense of safety, which is why," he releases me and walks over to his desk drawer, pulling out a black strappy sheath, "I got this for you. I thought it would be safe for you to have it against your thigh. Easily reachable if you ever need it. It's not just for whoever you're running from, Kate —or me. It's for any situation you may find yourself in where having a weapon could determine whether you live or die."

The anger and hurt sizzling in my stomach twist into interest. The way he peers longingly at me stirs a sense of confidence. It's small, but it's there.

"I want to teach you to use it. Please let me."

I always thought I needed to run. I've never felt as hopeless as I did when Xander caught me at that motel and painted the sheets scarlet with my blood as his body took what he wanted from me before he left me with the scar under my ear as punishment. I absentmindedly reach up to touch the raised and rough skin.

But what would it feel like to know I could fight back?

Hold my own.

Take some of Xander's power away if he ever finds me again.

My lips tilt upward, my pulse still racing with uncertainty, but I've made up my mind.

# TWENTY-FOUR | PRESTON

Usually, patience and control are a constant surge that flows through my veins. They impact my actions, my deliberate thoughts, and the decisions I make throughout the day.

I can't function without them.

Today, I'm operational, but I'm spiraling—wanting to get back to the girl who's the sweetest distraction from the chaos swelling around me.

I've been plunging into this deep abyss, where the only thing I see and feel is Kate's body filling my hands. Her frame flush against mine. The brief warmth that wraps around me tightly right before she puts up a fight and tests everything I've taught her.

And I say abyss, because I've buried her in the unfathomable depths of my soul that I didn't know existed. I'm sure as hell not letting anything penetrate and tarnish the only space in my chest that doesn't feel desolate and empty. I have more barriers than I know what to do with. Over the last few weeks, Kate has somehow broken through—slipping between the cracks in my armor to settle behind them, as if she belongs there, as if she's protected by them.

My home somehow feels like hers, too, with the way she goes back and forth to work at the medical center. I'd say we're in this circuit orbiting each other, but that's far from the truth. She's the sunshine, and her pull imprisons me. Drowns me in a heat I never want to escape, so I'm constantly seeking her out with that little tracking device that hangs perfectly between those beautiful collar bones.

Her safety has become my priority.

Teaching her self-defense has been for her own safety. Yet I can't push aside the fact that it's to give me peace of mind knowing she can hold her own in a ruthless world that targets pretty things.

Tayla and my mom couldn't protect themselves. Maybe it wouldn't have mattered if they had the strength to raise hell, but fuck if I let Kate walk around defenseless with that defeated look in her eye that I came to recognize the moment I saw her scars.

The physical reminders of her past.

She hasn't tried to escape the estate once.

Not that she'd be able to, but it's unsettling knowing she feels safer inside walls that could put her in just as much danger as whoever hurt her.

Whoever's hunting her.

Another reason I've been training with Kate in the gym every morning before we head our separate ways is that we don't know Luciano's plans. We may believe we have an impenetrable empire, but there are always hidden faults in the shadows, waiting to be discovered and used as leverage, which is why rebuilding our army to be stronger is a priority.

Nolan, one of our lieutenants in training, peers at the sheet before him. "They started training a few weeks ago and will start their positions next week. All night shifts."

Taking my time, I peer out the window, studying the new faces of men we're training for security at the park. A few of them are built, strong enough to hold their own and give us a wireframe to work with, while others need to be put through the wringer, so they don't look so breakable.

I don't tolerate breakable.

Unless it's Kate breaking apart on my fingers.

Shattering on my tongue.

*Goddamn, Pres. Get a hold of yourself.*

We'll give these newcomers a shot. Hiring for the security staff at Lachlan Park has fewer requirements than the recruits we pull and train for the Megalley Syndicate. Mainly because our men are integrated with the regular employees, so they don't draw as much attention.

I scan the room again, a few of their demeanors piquing my interest. Not even the glass can hide the darkness in their eyes that thrives deeper than the surface. We often promote Lachlan Park security to soldiers once they've proven their skills. They will have eyes watching their every move.

Especially now, as our war with the Calco Cartel escalates.

We need more men than ever.

"Let's make sure we get them to the range and test their hand-to-hand combat. By the end of next week, if any of them have potential, I would like a comprehensive report detailing their strengths and weaknesses. As well as a thorough background check and details about their family lives." My head slants, and an odd sensation curls in my gut as I peer out the window at two who look promising.

The trainees are lounging in the chairs in the briefing room at our main security headquarters for the park. The one-sided glass conceals our scrutinizing glares from view as we analyze our recruits.

Several of them are chatting harmlessly, while others, the two I have my eye on, lean back in the chairs with uninterested looks, pulling at their features. We never hire someone without a headshot with their resume. Vincent and Nolan went through those thoroughly and know what to look for. There are too many snakes that try to slip through our fingers.

I nod my head toward them. "Who are those two?"

Nolan watches where I'm pointing. "Lex is on the right. Brett is on the left."

Lex, with dark, cropped hair and a sleeve of tattoos, braces his elbows on his knees, leaning forward to crack his knuckles while Brett's knees bounce impatiently—his hair a dirty blond that's pulled back into a bun on his nape.

Good.

I can feel the eagerness emanating from them. The flow of their anticipation is threaded with something else, like a whip cracking against my skin, leaving a sting that has me questioning their true nature.

They want to get their hands dirty, and I'm going to let them.

Tone dark, I point between the two men. "I specifically want your eye on these two when they are on duty in the park. Ramp up their training and don't hold back on them. I want to see what they are capable of."

My focus drifts to the brooding man in the corner who's barely said a word. Vincent, one of our oldest lieutenants who oversees all our men in the harbor, lifts a finger to his lips.

Those gray eyes narrow in contemplation, swirling with chaos as they usually do. "I'll push them to their limits. There's something about them I can't put my finger on."

He sees the same darkness flourishing in their eyes as I do. If I trust anyone to get an accurate read of this group, it's him. Not only is he a perfect shot in training and in combat, but he is a terrifying motherfucker that would straighten my spine if I weren't his boss.

Vincent has been with us since before I was born. My

grandfather, who is now retired with Gran at our estate in Ireland, recruited him from the military. He has more blood on his hands than I do. I swear the bodily fluids of his victims are calcified in his callous hands. I'd say it happened back in his prime, but Vincent is always in his prime. Those muscles, hidden beneath his long sleeves, showcase it.

There is a reason we have him patrolling the tunnels and the park, as well as training our men to manipulate them into machines.

A piece of our empire rests in his hands.

If we are going to pull any of these men into the mob, I damn well know he'll find the best. Or fix them until their faults are cowering in the darkness, afraid to emerge.

We don't tolerate weakness.

That means drawing them out early.

A corner of my mouth lifts maliciously. "After the park closes Friday night, why don't we let loose Rowan and Cathal and see what Lex and Brett are truly capable of. No guns. No weapons." Just their hands and their pure carnal need, because our men who broke our blood oath will do whatever it takes to survive, even if it means killing these newcomers.

That first night, after I found Kate in the tunnels and brought her back to the estate, I called Imogen and asked her to do her best to fix up Rowan. I hate not finishing things my way, even if there is a beautiful little distraction that kept me from ending his life at that moment, as I should have.

Now, I'm glad he's been rotting in a cell, battling an on-and-off again infection in the side of his stomach. Cathal is in the cell across from him, so he can watch the motherfucker suffer in pain while I contemplate what to do with them. Turns out, Cathal sealed his fate when he decided to get his dick wet with Rowan and join in on the fun with the girl he paid for.

They've been rotting in a cell under the park, awaiting their sentence. We were going to kill them anyway.

As for Lex and Brett, I want to see if we can get their dark sides to emerge early, if they're as animalistic as they look.

A few days from now, we'll know.

If these two look promising, they may become our new prospects for the mob. This comes with a long conversation, a significant pay raise, and benefits that are more substantial than any other career they might find elsewhere. The only difference is that they sign their life over to us and carve their name on that line at the bottom of the contract in their own blood.

Death is the only way out.

Vincent lowers his hand from his gray beard, his eyes hard on me. "Rushing the process. That's not like you. Usually, we watch these guys for months before we propose a promotion to them."

It's not like me.

However, ever since some of our shipments have gone missing—the attack in Virginia, *Kate*—my control over my priorities has been slipping and shifting. It started with one hole in the bucket when I saw Kate on that dock. Then I saw her in the tunnels, and it was another blow to the metal holding me together.

Then I started thinking about Kate.

Kissed Kate.

Touched Kate.

I haven't fucked her yet, and she's already filling my thoughts so thoroughly that it's draining my other priorities, making room for her like she's becoming one.

And maybe she is.

But the Megalley Syndicate comes first, and if Arden keeps sensing how distracted I am, he won't hesitate to get rid of her. So, though my body is strained from this metaphorical tether stretching through the fucking space between Kate and me that's pulling at my stability, I shove my hands into my suit pockets, glancing out the one-sided glass.

We're waiting with bated breath for Luciano's next move while we sit in the shadows waiting for our perfect moment. The plan has been in place since we received that mysterious envelope from an anonymous person in the mail months ago. Time isn't on our side right now, and we need to be prepared for anything, strengthening our army and our men in numbers and skill.

I'd say it's to protect our operations, this world that is all I've ever known, but I can't shake the feeling that I want to increase protection for an entirely different reason.

Because the last time this fuzzy sense of contentment existed behind my ribs, my world shattered, plunging me into a darkness I never thought I'd escape.

Until Kate.

# TWENTY-FIVE | KATE

My feet pound against the gravel, the thick walls of green closing in on me. Anxiety sears my burning lungs, my mind racing in every direction, not knowing where he is.

I bolt left, trying to train my ears to his footsteps smashing against the earth in tune with mine. But it doesn't matter, I can't hear anything over my rapid heartbeat echoing in my ears and my ragged, uneven breaths.

This was his plan.

Intuition and vigilance can escape you the second your mind is racing as fast as your blood.

In a moment when it matters.

It's more realistic this way if I'm terrified.

With each step, I'm aware of the straps plastered to my thigh. With its constant company, I don't feel completely powerless and terrified of a weapon that only brought me pain. I'm learning to wield it.

Claim back my power.

If working out with Preston these last few weeks, as the sun comes up, has taught me anything, it's that I can be scrappy.

His words, not mine.

He gave me the extra dose of determination I needed right before I found myself straddling his sweaty torso on the mat in the gym with my knife positioned above his heart.

It was empowering. Freeing.

As if I wasn't enslaved to my circumstance anymore and could fight if I needed to. I'd rather die raising hell than be the docile girl I was when I left Oregon.

The way he peered at me with pride, with a loopy smile like he was mesmerized by me trying to kick his ass, increased my confidence. I can't really beat him. Not in the literal sense anyway. His frame not only towers over mine, but he also has the muscle and mass that could squash me in an instant.

Preston is a unique breed.

A man created to crush and annihilate anything in his path, but he's been downplaying his skill just enough that I have to work extra hard to get him where I want him—a slave to my blade. On the other hand, he's not so soft that, if I found myself in a real fight for my life, I'd be entirely vulnerable.

I feel stronger than I have in a long time. Not just physically, but mentally. As if increasing my agility and awareness of what my body can do has chased away the powerless fog that poisoned me for far too long. Sure, there's still a muted sense of paranoia hovering over me, but I'm not as terrified knowing Xander is out there somewhere looking for me.

I have a long way to go, but I've learned a lot in this short amount of time.

Also, I've had to work my ass off against the added distraction of Preston's hard, nearly naked body gliding against mine —being pressed into mine. Every. Single. Morning.

He'd be in the gym before me, taking out his frustration on that punching bag with such controlled movements. Beads of sweat would slide down the ridges of his tattooed back and his temple. The pure force and raw masculinity radiating from him were enough to stun me speechless the second I stepped through the door.

Then, like every morning, as if he's taunting me, he would turn, letting me get an eyeful of the way his gym shorts hang low on his V-line that leads to his cock that I told him to touch while he made me come. Not to mention the beautiful ink that stretches across his bulging planes, where that six-pack of abs leads to the dark, happy trail that dips below the hem of his shorts that my fingers buzz to follow. To touch. I haven't seen all of him yet, and it's pure torture. His body alone holds enough power to soak me on the spot, which is entirely unfortunate since the entire session not only tests my physical ability but also my mental stamina to keep myself from grabbing the hard erection he carries around when our bodies touch.

Like the other day when I found myself straddling him on the mat, our heaving breaths in unison in the otherwise quiet gym. His abdomen flexed below my core, resting on top of him. Preston's hands started gliding along my knees, bracing him, moving them upward until he cupped my thighs, pressing his fingers into my heated flesh, abuzz with need.

I'm not stupid, I know he's been going easy on me. He's a mafia boss; he could snap me like a twig with those hands that I used to think could only inflict pain and torture. But not when I've felt how tenderly they hold me before we somehow pull ourselves apart to go our separate ways for the day. And I say tenderly hold me because even when he has his arms snaked around me while I'm fighting him with my knife, the air between us is charged and filled with sexual tension that is bound to snap and mark us both at any moment.

Unfortunately, I know he's letting me take my time after seeing my scars and knowing my trauma. The thought that he cares so deeply about making me feel safe and valued spurs on the feeling that he is different. Like being wrapped in his arms is the closest to home I'll ever get.

Moral of the story about the last few weeks: he's about as distracting as a dark god emerging from the depths of Hell. I know I should fight for my life, but I can't help but want him to pull me under and devour me with that mouth that beautifully haunts my dreams.

*"I'd say you're dangerously captivated by your curiosity and wanted to see what it would be like to dance with the dark."*

If it were with him, I would.

My mind whirrs back to the present. My heart lurches into my throat, knowing he is hot on my heels even if I can't see him chasing after me. He's smart. Calculating every one of his moves while panic claws at my skin.

If I can pull myself together when he sets my skin ablaze and makes my heart pound, just as it does now, I can do this.

*I can do this.*

Sprinting through the maze, a section ahead emerges where I can take a left and head back towards the yard, or a right that leads to the center, where the fountain is located. Darting right, I see the expanse up ahead opening to the center of the maze. My lungs seize, but I push through, pumping my arms as I break the threshold. A massive body slams into mine, maneuvering me so my back is plastered forcefully against his chest. Preston's forest and smoky scent stir comfort, but I shove it away.

I can't think about that right now.

I have to play this game as he told me: appear vulnerable at first, let their guard down, and strike when they're least expecting it.

Gives me a more significant advantage if my size doesn't.

So instead, the ink on his arms shifts and warps into different ones. I picture cold gray eyes and short dark hair. Xander's hold on me is tightening, trying to squeeze and suck the life out of me before he tosses me down and violates my body with more than just his knife. I inhale a deep breath, keeping the image of that vile man where I need it to be.

It's working until Preston's lips glide against the shell of my ear, making me shiver, and the spell shatters. All I can see and feel is him. Only him. I'm trying and failing miserably to picture the monster searching the ends of the earth for me, but now, all I can think about is the one I'm going soft for.

The deep timber of his voice has heat licking up my limbs. "I hear your heart racing. I feel it against my own. I like that you're scared of me."

Preston's arms tighten around mine, trapping them against my body. I need to distract him enough to free one so I can slyly grab my blade.

I play into the narrative. "Please— Please let me go."

His dark chuckle elicits a flurry of goose bumps that prick my skin. "Why would I do that? You're so pretty. Let me have a little fun with you first."

In any other situation, that would sound creepy as hell and have me trembling, but coming from his mouth, I almost want to drop to my knees and give him what he wants.

These are the cards he's playing. Chase me to illicit terror flowing through my veins and use my attraction toward him at the same time.

Two can play at this game, Captain.

My breaths are ragged. "What do you want?"

His arms around me loosen a little.

Even for the game, his answer seems honest. "You."

"Why me? You could have anyone."

He releases one of his arms around me, lifting his hand to glide his fingers over my bare collarbone. When they dip under my tank top strap and leisurely pull it down my shoulder, I bite back the moan that wants to escape.

*Only one arm wrapped around me now.*

God, I shouldn't be this wet. I can feel how damp my

panties are against the inside of my thighs. I've been on the run for the last year, but this is the first time being chased has an erotic need zipping between my legs.

But knowing it's Preston and not someone who wants to hurt me has me melting in his grasp, no matter how hard I'm trying to role-play this scenario he's created.

"Because I haven't been able to stop thinking about you since I saw you at the edge of my dock. It's like you were a drop of sun that somehow fell into my lap and made me feel warmth I haven't felt in years." His words freeze the breath in my lungs.

I listen intently while I slowly move my right hand along my leg, trying not to make any sudden movements he would feel.

My fingers glide under the slit in my skirt to the sheath on my thigh while he continues messing with my head. "Because you've tested my sanity every. Fucking. Day. You've contaminated my control. My work. My empire." Preston's gravelly tone is a drug, slipping further into my veins. He's giving me a high I never want to come down from. "You've distracted me from this war on my hands, imagining what it would be like to sink inside your glorious pussy I've tasted. Wondering what it would feel like to fill you up with my cum so I can watch it weep with proof of my obsession for you before I thrust inside again and fuck it so deep, you'll never be rid of me."

"Oh, shit," I breathe at the same time I release my knife from its confinement to mask my true motive.

My body quivers against his, feeling every line and stretch of muscle. He is a master of distraction. My clit throbs for attention, my nipples aching for his rough fingers.

His lips fall against the slope of my neck, and my eyes flutter closed at their warmth and the scratch of his facial hair against my skin.

My voice hardens. "Let me go or else."

"Or else what?" he roughly chuckles. "You'll run? Careful,

baby. If you do that again, I won't be able to keep myself from fucking you." I'm supposed to be playing this out as a scenario, but I can't focus. That promise lathers over my skin, soaking into my flesh as he grinds his hard cock against my ass to further his point. "I like it when you run from me."

I'm on the verge of snapping and handing myself over to him.

*Get it together, Kate.* "I said, no."

"Your mouth may say one thing, but your body doesn't lie." With one arm wrapped around my shoulders, and his other hand gripping the slit in my skirt, I ready my knife. "Should I ask your pussy instead?"

Leaning the back of my head against his chest to bring my mouth inches from his, I mold against him and lift my arm. To him, it may seem like I'm folding for his charm, but the second his eyes fall to my lips, I press the tip of my knife into the side of his neck, but not enough to hurt him. One sudden jerk of my hand and I'd impale his carotid artery.

I speak the words across his mouth, but they are feeble. "Let. Me. Go."

His lips lift into a satisfied smile. "Very good. I thought I had you distracted there for a minute."

*If only he knew.* I swear I'm so soaked, I'm dripping down the inside of my thighs.

His arms release me, the removal of his body warmth making me shiver at the loss of him. "I expected you to put up more of a fight like you did in the gym, but this performance was applause-worthy."

I turn around with a smile, my happiness instantly vanishing as my eyes lock on the red drop, dripping down his neck.

Retreating a step, my horror is written across my face. I slap a hand over my mouth, shaking my head. "I'm so sorry!"

Crimson slides down his neck, seeping into the collar of the gray t-shirt he's wearing.

His head slants. "You think a little cut like this hurts me? Don't fucking apologize, Kate. If it comes down to it, and someone isn't listening to your threat, don't be afraid to draw a little blood, darling."

I sheath my knife back against my thigh. "But it was pretend." I don't know why I say it, maybe because I'm fishing for the truth.

Are my senses off, or did he mean those things he said about the day he found me on the dock? That I'm infesting his thoughts as much as he's consumed mine.

When he swallows and says, "Not all of it," we stand there holding each other's eyes, both of our chests rising and falling, trying to catch our breath.

The air crackles.

Electricity sizzles and sparks in the space between us.

My body burns to feel every inch of his against mine.

And then, because I have a death wish, I run.

## TWENTY-SIX | KATE

**I**f I'm being accurate, I have a death-by-dick wish.

It would be one hell of a way to go out.

Warm air whips across my face, my ponytail thrashing behind me as I sprint out the way I came, back into the maze. A tendril of hair sticks to my wet lips as I bolt left, my body prickling in awareness, knowing he's not far behind me.

I can hear his footsteps harmonizing with my own. Beautifully chaotic, like whatever is transpiring between us.

Anticipation skitters to every nerve ending when I turn again and nearly run face-first into the hedge at a dead-end, the same time a hand whips out to grip my neck. Preston whirls me around with ease, effortlessly tossing me over his shoulder with the swagger of an animal that knows it's captured its prey.

And damn do I hope he's about to feast on me.

A smack resonates through the air, my ass stinging where his hand landed. He does it again to the other cheek, eliciting a yelp from my lips. The pain makes the anticipation curl in my belly, eager to see what happens next.

He doesn't say anything, and neither do I. Our thundering hearts and pulses are communicating enough for us.

It's not long before he returns to the center of the garden, lowering me to my feet near the fountain as I wait for his next move.

When he reaches into the pocket of his gym shorts, my brows furrow. He pulls out his phone, clicking through a few things on the screen before he lifts it to his ear. My heart jumps, my breath tattered and uneven as I hold his eyes and step back absentmindedly to give him space.

His jaw flexes, his fingers tightening around his phone. Whoever it is on the other end must not get much of a word in before Preston orders, "Turn off the cameras in the garden."

Oh, shit.

I spin around, my eyes locking with the black device above one of the hedges. It takes a few seconds, but when the small red light shuts off, the reality of what's about to happen has roots growing through my feet and planting me in place with my back toward him.

One rapid heartbeat, then two, and Preston's voice comes from behind me again. "Don't ask questions, just do it." With that, he must end the call when no other words are exchanged.

My shoulders tense as I feel the way he stalks toward me. The hairs on the back of my neck stand on end, vibrating with excitement. When his hands snake around my waist, pulling my body flush against his, beautiful toxins release through my bloodstream.

I release a sharp breath, feeling his lips and words drag against my shoulder. "Fight back. Don't let me ruin you."

My hips roll, grinding my ass against his bulging erection like the day he had me pinned in the hallway when he gave me my collar.

I reach an arm behind me, gripping the scruff at the back of his neck to steady myself. "You already have. Ruin me more."

His fingers pulse into my stomach. Preston's lips fall to the slope of my neck, biting at the skin there and soothing the sting with his tongue. "Don't tempt me, Kate. I don't know how to take it easy with this. I like rough fucking."

That admission ignites a spark, coursing to my clit.

My grip tightens on his skull, and I turn my head to drag his lips to mine, but not enough to touch.

"I trust you," I say, my words brushing against his mouth.

Preston's forehead drops against mine, those dark eyes concealing a raging war. He was so gentle with me last time. His promises about being willing to listen to what I wanted and letting me take control were validated in the way he touched me and pleased my body in a way that has me craving more of him.

All of him.

My pulse is erratic. "I already imagine my fingers are your cock every night. Please, put me out of my misery. Plea—"

I'm cut off by his mouth slamming against mine as my back is plastered to his chest. His arms tighten around me, one of his hands moving to cup my breast. His tongue pushes against my seam, demanding entrance. I willingly open, letting his fresh taste invade my mouth like a toxin that will change how I function, how I breathe.

It's like he's trying to devour my soul with the way his tongue explores my mouth. I release a whimper, and he greedily consumes the sound, releasing a groan. He kisses me harder to the point my toes and ears tingle. I already know the magic of his tongue, and this is only the beginning of what he's capable of.

Lust and fascination have never felt this inebriating.

"You're so beautiful when you beg." He reaches for my hand, gliding both of our fingers below the slit in my skirt to my soaked panties. His knuckles brush the material over my clit, making me tremble at the slight touch.

"Shit," his hiss soaks into my skin as his fingers guide mine to my slick center. "Show me how you do it."

He bunches my skirt at my waist. Using his other hand, he picks up one of my legs, opening me up wide as the fresh air brushes against my needy core. I'd feel unsteady on one leg if he weren't holding my back against his chest. The feeling of him peeling my panties to the side to grant me entrance has me shuddering.

Listening to him, I insert a finger into my wet heat, gripping his forearm braced around me harder from the pleasure that racks through me.

"You want my cock to ruin this desperate cunt? Let me hear how wet you are for me."

My finger moves faster, filling the air with the needy sound of my pussy slick and ready for him with the whoosh of the fountain.

"Holy fuck. Keep your hand there." As if Preston can sense I need more, he slips one of his fingers inside with mine. They move in unison, making a whimper fall from my lips.

"That's two. Do you think you can take three?"

I nod, deliriously.

"Confident little thing, aren't you?" Preston slowly slips in another, opening me wider as both of us work together to draw out my pleasure. This is the hottest thing that's ever happened to my body, and he isn't even inside me yet. "I think you can handle a fourth, don't you?"

I shake my head.

"How do you expect to fit me then, darling? Or do you want to feel yourself stretch around my dick? Didn't you say you can't get off without pain mixed with the pleasure?"

My confessions from that night in my bedroom flood back. The panic is there, sizzling in my gut, but with his mouth colliding with mine again, it melts away. Preston may live a more dangerous lifestyle than Xander, but I feel safer with him.

I trust him.

My oncoming orgasm builds and swirls behind my hips as

our fingers start to submerge me in the euphoria. A bead of sweat glides down my back in this position, with him holding up one of my legs. My limbs ache, but I don't care. He removes our hands and releases my leg, his wet fingers darting out to grip my throat and lather my skin with my arousal. My core is left empty and unsatisfied, begging for more.

Preston forcefully walks me toward the closest bench surrounding the fountain, pressing his hand down on my spine to bend me over it. Knowing where this is going, I lift my leg to rest my knee on the bench while I stand on the other, opening myself up to him.

He takes his time gripping the material of my skirt to bunch it at my hips again. Digging his fingers below the fabric of my lace panties, he drags them down, maneuvering one side over the sheath strapped to my thigh to let them pool at my knees. The warm air is a welcome sensation on my wet center, on display for him.

"You have no idea how much I've thought about this. Every. Fucking. Night. Kate. I've jacked off to the thought of my cock being buried in this perfect pussy." A guttural sound rumbles in his chest as he grips my ass roughly in both hands, spreading me wider as he draws his mouth to my most sensitive part that is already dripping for him.

I cry out.

His tongue laps at my seam, stopping to swirl around my clit. I glance over my shoulder, my elbows digging into the concrete bench, watching him violate my pussy with a mouth that is as dirty as his promises. His facial hair rubbing against me only adds to the sensation building in my belly.

Watching and feeling the soft warmth of his tongue gliding over my clit has muffled curses falling from my lips.

When his mouth disappears, I slouch at the loss, but his eyes don't leave mine as he drops his shorts, letting his massive cock spring free. The cut I made in his neck has stopped bleeding, but combined with his animalistic gaze and his dick in his hand, he looks unhinged.

My eyes widen, my heart jumping into my throat like it's trying to make space to fit him down there. How is it possible that it looks bigger out of confinement? And the way the tendons in his hands strain as he leisurely strokes himself... holy shit.

You know what they say about men with huge hands?

Yeah, somehow his cock is still bigger.

My breath remains locked in my lungs when I watch him drag the head through my core to coat himself with my arousal. He watches his dick swipe through my wetness in fascination while I intently watch him move his cock through my folds. His other hand holds his t-shirt, giving me a view of his chiseled abdomen—a marbled work of art, crafted to perfection by his dedication in the gym. Those bulging muscles are accompanied by dark ink that swirls and cuts across his skin.

"Fuck. You're soaked, darling. Do you feel the way the tip of my cock is slipping right through you?" It's like he's the artist and his cock is the brush collecting the paint from my core.

I should be worried someone will walk through the maze and see us, considering this is where I met his dad, but I can't bring myself to care. Luckily, the cameras are off, or whoever is on his security team would be getting an eyeful.

His cock nudges harder at my entrance, making me suck in a rapid breath. Preston curses. He reaches out, collecting my hair in his fist while the other is gripping my hip. He forces my head back so the blue sky blanketing us in this garden is all I see. Slowly pushing his hips forward, he fills me completely. The pleasure and pain are one as I struggle to adjust to his size. The tremble in my legs is faint, but enough that I'm sure he feels it vibrating through where we're connected.

"Just a little more," he chuckles darkly, enjoying my struggle.

"More?" I gasp, flattening my hands on the surface.

Without warning, Preston's hips smack against my ass, and I moan. Fully satiated inside me, the slight curve to his dick, combined with his girth, has him pressed against that self-destruct button inside me. He pulls all the way out before snapping forward, making me shriek as he thrusts into that sensitive spot again, while his hand gripping my hair makes my scalp sting.

I can't see him, but his words feel just as intimate. "Yes, just like that, baby. Your pussy feels like home, with the way it's gripping me so tightly. This position gives me a perfect view of your hot and needy cunt swallowing my cock."

Preston starts to move steadily, his deep, beautifully punishing thrusts using me like the punching bag he pounds his fists into every day. He's just as controlled with this.

"Preston, your cock," I whine hazily.

"Keep praising me like that, and it won't go to my head." He's not wrong, I feel him thickening inside me.

He nearly pulls out to the head, smacking my ass first before sinking back in and pulling out again. I release a cry, the ache intertwining with the overwhelming pleasure to carry me back to that place where my oncoming climax coils, making me shake.

Thrust. "Keep writhing, darling." *Smack.* "There's nothing that satisfies me more." Thrust. "Than knowing my cock is too much for you." *Smack.*

His foul mouth and his relentless fucking have my arousal dripping down the inside of my thighs. My moan has him rewarding me with another smack on the ass that has my back aching from being arched in this way while he pounds into me.

I'm on the verge of coming, the darkness reaching its claws up through the ground like vines to pierce my flesh and hold me still as he draws my orgasm out of me, sucking me into his depths.

My insides are spiraling, my chest tightening around my heart. I'm so close.

His gravelly chuckle adds to the pleasure. "Oh, goddamn. I think your pussy likes it when I talk like this. Are you about to come? You're already soaking my cock, but there's nothing I want more than to feel you shatter around me."

He releases my hair, bracketing his hands on my waist to pull me against him and thrust against that spot that has a smattering of stars dotting the blue sky.

Preston is ravenously sucking every ounce of strength out of my body. My chest falls to the bench, my shaky arms unable to hold me up any longer, but my ass is still in the air, letting him claim me.

It sounds more like a plea from my lips. "Yes."

"Come for me, mo ghrá." His Gaelic words somehow hold the power to launch me upward, letting me float with clouds as my orgasm crashes down on me.

My pussy pulses around him. I cry through the aftershocks, about ready to pass out from the intensity, when he wraps his hand around my throat and tugs my body back up to the position I was in before. I'm still coming as he snatches the hair at the base of my skull, tilting my head back to meet his stern gaze, mixed with amazement.

"My eyes are back here, darling. I want your full and undivided attention while I pump all my cum into your pussy. You'll keep it nice and warm for me, won't you?"

It's like he pulled a trigger inside me. How can his words alone make a second orgasm build? While my eyes are on his, he slaps my ass again, my mouth opening on an O.

Preston's cock starts to pulse inside me. "I feel that you're there again, baby. Does knowing I'm filling you right now get you off, you dirty little slut?"

The shock that I love him degrading me hits as hard as my

second orgasm. My walls tighten again, feeling him throb as his warmth coats my walls.

Tears swell in my eyes, but they don't part from his when he slows. I'm panting, my limbs shaking as he pulls out, letting me adjust to the loss of him. He tucks himself back into his shorts, then takes my panties from around my knees and pulls them back up over my satiated core.

He gives my clit a small smack, and I jump. "What was that for?" I whine.

"My room, now. I'm not done with you yet."

"Again?" My sigh is a blend of nerves and interest. "Don't you need a break or something?" I push myself up onto my trembling legs, nearly tumbling from the wild ache that shoots through them.

Preston steps forward, letting me grab onto him for support before he hauls me into his arms to cradle me.

He presses his lips to my temple before his mouth curves into an arrogant smile, with that darkness swirling in his eyes. "It will take a few minutes to get up to my room. That's all I need before I lay you on my bed, spread your legs, and admire the mess I've made of your pussy with my cock."

The obscurity in his gaze has a sensation of soft wings batting around in my stomach, instead of frightening me like it used to. His promise courses through my body like molten sugar, sticking in all places I know I'll never get rid of it.

Preston Lachlan is going to break me, and for some reason, I want to let him. Because if he cares enough to carry me all the way there when I'm too weak before he breaks me again, I know he won't hesitate to put me back together after.

# TWENTY-SEVEN | PRESTON

As the future boss, I used to take pride in being an overachiever. Drowning myself in work was the only thing that muted my demons. I say muted because they're relentless little fuckers that have thrived and rotted corners of my soul that are unreachable. An infestation that I began to ignore because I didn't deserve to feel better.

Not when Luciano should've drained the life from my eyes instead.

I've kept myself busy ever since the weight of Tayla and Mom's deaths crashed onto my shoulders like an anchor that can't keep a ship at bay in stormy waters. Wave after wave of grief slammed into me with the force of a hurricane, determined to splinter and crush my stability and the world I had worked to keep up with.

The one that I'm prepared to take over.

Dedicating myself to the Megalley Syndicate was easy when sleep evaded me. When I'd get swallowed into that place that had those voices echoing in the darkness, telling me it was my fault they died. That their final breaths taken in violence should've been mine.

After all these years, I'm still not sure I've come to terms with the fact that it isn't my fault. And it isn't my father's.

Marco Giovanni's—the late don of the Calco Cartel—death isn't written on our souls like the countless others we've stolen over our lifetime.

No. That one we are clean of.

Yet it's somehow worse knowing that my mother and sister died for a war that isn't ours.

Tayla always told me I was too protective. It wasn't until my father and I ran back to the Ferris wheel to find their guards' lifeless eyes staring blankly into the night that I realized I wasn't protective enough. At the time, I agreed with her, but I didn't care, knowing the kind of monsters we coexist with. Men whose hands were once clean and were conditioned to inflict the type of agony and malice that's demanded if you want to survive and earn respect.

The kind of monsters that flood our property and whose eyes wander to pretty things.

Tayla was our wildflower growing through a brutally hard world.

She was soft-spoken. Kind-hearted. Gentle.

Had a smile that was as bright as her eyes. Blue, like moms. Eyes that looked ethereal against her dark brown hair, with the way they make you feel like you're drowning in sunlit glacial waters.

I used to be able to remember her voice, her unique warmth when she clung to me, just like a younger sister would who looks up to her brother. There may have been three years separating us, but it didn't feel like that. We were close. So close that I went against my father's rules and would sneak her out of her room to come to parties with me. Because I knew if I didn't, she would disappear anyway, and at least if I helped her, I could keep a watchful eye on her when she was with her friends.

Without trying, I'm dragged back to a moment that replays

on a constant loop. I'm pulled into the night that I took Tayla to one of my family's clubs an hour away in Portland. A secret twenty-first birthday trip that should've landed us both front row seats to my father's fury. But I was careful. Crafted a story made up of beautiful lies to see her smile return after she'd been locked away in her room, suffering through her first heartbreak.

I'm still not sure who she was seeing. Probably good considering I would've killed the bastard who hurt her.

*Still would.*

That night, I lurked in the shadows and watched her dance and drink until she felt better. Luckily, I ran into Carter, and he kept me company before a call from my father came in, and I had to step away to spew more lies to keep him in the dark about where we were.

I live in those moments more than is healthy.

Recounting that memory and all that transpired in that month before she was taken—before Luciano crushed her petals in his fist, destroying the only bright and innocent life that didn't make mine feel so dark and bleak. Before he cut her heart out of her chest like a vile, bloodthirsty motherfucker he is, acting like he wasn't already happy to be on top, ruling without his brother.

Like I said, I hurled myself into my work to mute my demons, but with Kate lying naked in my bed, somehow her sugary scent and sweetness have slowly started seeping into all those places I could never reach. The kind of depths that until now have left a constant ache behind flesh and bone, stirring a pain that hardens you on the outside because there's not enough space to harbor any other feelings on the inside.

From that moment I saw her on the dock, a part of me thawed and melted straight through the wooden boards, disappearing with the tide.

The first time I watched her fall apart on my fingers, on my tongue, her taste invaded my bloodstream, leaving behind a comfort that I don't feel deserving of.

And yesterday, when I fucked her for the first time, I wrapped that beautiful hair around my fist and clung onto her like she was my lifeline. The one supplying oxygen to my lungs. A drop of sunshine through a crack in the cavernous void I've adapted to.

The faint glow of moonlight drifts through my open French doors, cascading long, fingered shadows across the room. The black curtains billow in waves from the breath of the breeze, circulating the room.

I thread my fingers through Kate's hair, lightly stroking the strands near her temple, caressing her ear as I tuck them behind. Don't get me wrong, ears aren't a turn on, but hers are cute as fuck. They're delicately adorned with small diamond studs, with a slight point to them. The only reason I noticed is because I've been staring at her for the last few hours before reality comes crashing back. She's filling my head and my room with her soft, even calming breaths that make this place feel more alive than it has in five years.

*"Come for me, mo ghrá."*

That declaration echoes in my ears. Calling her that came naturally despite how much it terrified me after.

If I could stay here in the confines of my room with her tucked into my side forever or coming on my cock, I would.

But I have shit to do.

For example, I'll meet my father in a few hours for another shipment that's coming into the harbor.

And tomorrow night, when we release Rowan and Cathal in the park after it closes, we'll see if Lex and Brett are worthy of being proposed for the opportunity to live and die for a kingdom, rather than wasting their purpose and skills on an amusement park. Exhilaration thrums in my veins thinking about the show we'll get from them. Releasing Rowan and Cathal will be like freeing two rabid dogs with gnashing teeth. They are men who will stop at nothing to survive.

My fingers push aside Kate's hair, floating down the delicate slope of her neck, where the risen and angry skin slices through perfection. She tenses where she's cradled into my side, the slight movement causing her ass to stir my half-erect cock.

I shift my arm, resting behind my head on the pillow, to get comfortable again and make sure there's still blood flow to my limbs. I move the collar adorning her neck out of the way, lightly brushing the pad of my thumb over the scar.

Her voice is as delicate as my touch. "I was with him for three years."

My body stills.

She has enough scars on her stomach to tell the story of a lifetime. I know, because I have them. I remain silent, my gentle movements in her hair turning mechanical with the ire burning behind my sternum.

"He was a phlebotomist at a blood drive I went to while I was attending OHSU School of Nursing in Oregon. He was the one who drew my blood that day, and he asked me out after."

I remember Brody pulling up information about her college years when she was attending nursing school, before she started her internship, which eventually turned into a full-time position at OHSU Hospital. She was renting a cute little house on the outskirts of Portland and attended a yoga studio in Beaverton. Her mother and father still live in Oregon, and she has an older sister named Natalie. The amount of information he pulled up could tell me anything about her and her younger life, besides the one fucking thing I wanted to know, which she is telling me now.

My fingers continue to pull through her hair. I'm not sure

whether it's to comfort her or me. Probably both, given the way our heartbeats thrum and string together, where she's braced against me.

"There weren't any signs at first. Or maybe there were, and I was too naive to see them. It wasn't until a year later that he told me about his kink." My lungs collapse. "He told me blood play was normal. That I'd learn to enjoy it as much as he did."

She still faces away from me, which is probably good considering all my blood just rushed to my face. Anger simmers below my skin. Her sad chuckle has me removing my other arm from behind my head and snaking my hand around her stomach to tug her closer to me as if I can protect her from the memories rushing back to her.

From where my head is propped on the pillow, I can see her picking at a loose thread on my sheets. "I should've known then, but between how rough he was and the knife cutting me, I froze, fearful of what else he was capable of when hurting me like that came so easily." She sighs. "God, that seems like a lifetime ago. I was twenty-one then."

I don't realize I'm clenching my jaw hard enough to shatter my teeth until she shifts beside me to her other side, giving me a glimpse of those beautiful green eyes still vibrant in the darkness engulfing us. She places a hand on my chest. My heart is about to explode out of my chest. I know she can feel it.

The soft column of her throat works as she swallows. "Even when I found my voice, it was too late. There wasn't enough evidence to charge him. The only thing I could do was run until he caught up to me in Wyoming and nearly killed me. That's how I got the scar." My blood turns to sand, scratching against my veins, the weight making me drop my hand from her neck. "I've been running for a year."

For the first time since she turned to look at me, my eyes dart away from hers.

Kate's delicate fingers grip my chin, lowering my face back to meet hers as she rests against my chest. She wets her lips. "Lachlan Harbor, working at the park, it was the first time I felt far enough away. I feel safe here."

She still doesn't give me a fucking name.

*The only darkness I want consuming her is me.*

A disdainful laugh leaves my lips. The word is bitter. "Safe? You think you're safe here?"

Pushing herself up, she hovers above me, clutching the sheet to her naked breasts, which is good. I can't be distracted by how beautiful her tits are and how they contain their own gravity that calls to my hands. My mouth.

*I bet they would look pretty pressed together with my cock thrusting between them.*

Apparently, not getting distracted isn't an option when it comes to her.

Creases form between her brows, but she doesn't say anything. The confusion painting her face is enough.

"For one, he's still out there doing fuck knows what to look for you. And two, you traded one monster for another."

She purses those lips that were sealed to mine a few hours ago, shaking her head. "That's what I used to think, but I don't anymore. You couldn't be more different."

"Monsters come in different forms. I've killed people. *Inno-cent* fucking people who will never be found. You could've easily ended up as one of them!"

Her soft voice is calm. Steady. "I don't believe you would've hurt me."

I hold my hands up between us. "These hands are stained with blood." They are cruel. Unforgiving. "I'm not a good man either, darling. I might not have had a knife, but I've been just as rough with you tonight."

Surprisingly, she slips her palms into mine, opening up my

arms. Kate crawls on top of me to straddle my hips, letting the sheet fall away to expose her fully. She gazes down at me with resolve so pure that it takes my breath away. I don't realize I'm wrapping my arms around her naked form inattentively until her lips lift in a soft smile.

Maybe I'm afraid she'll run if she has a moment to contemplate my words. Recognize the darkness that thrives and threads through my body like its own nervous system.

Those fears vanish as Kate leans over, cupping my neck. "Good is a subjective term." I swallow the acid in my throat. "To me, a *good* man doesn't hurt a woman and then continue to shatter what's left of her after. Yes, you're rough with me, but you collect the pieces once you're done and put them back together while also mending parts that aren't your responsibility to fix." Her eyes hold mine. "That's the difference, Preston."

She sits up, her core grinding down against my aching cock. My palms flatten against the curves of her ass, lightly gripping into her supple flesh. The feeling of her wet seam pressed against my dick has my muscles tightening, forcing the breath out of my lungs in a growl.

Kate rolls her hips again. My eyes drop to where her slick heat rubs against me, entranced by her movements.

Goddamn, she is a sight to behold like this, all warm and ready for me.

"Break with me." The power of that request hangs between us with bated breath. It's heavy. Pure. Contains so much meaning that Kate burrows into my fractured soul a little deeper. "Shatter with me. Let your pieces tangle with mine for a little while so I can care for the parts you've been too afraid to let anyone see. I want all of you, and in return, I'll give you all of me." She grips my face in one hand, drawing her lips to hover above mine.

I'll give her anything she wants if she keeps looking at me

like this. Like a beautiful angel from heaven that isn't afraid of colliding with my dark.

Kate lifts, gripping my cock in her fingers to sink onto me slowly, letting me get lost in her.

Truthfully, I already have been.

# TWENTY-EIGHT | PRESTON

Dark gray and black swirl overhead, the relentless clouds unleashing a heavy rain and wind that slightly obstructs the view of the marina lights in the distance. Boats rock back and forth, bound to the dock ties but still imprisoned by the angry waters that stir the surface, the sea dark while dawn draws nearer.

The pads of my fingers dig into my biceps, my eyes steady on the large box van that's backing up to our main tunnel entrance with our new shipment of narcotics and illegal weapons that arrived earlier this morning. And when I say early, I mean four a.m. because it's one of the easier times to smuggle our shipments in and out of the harbor.

It's nearly five now, the slight chill from the wind and mist blowing through the open overhead door torments my body with the reminder of the peaceful warmth of Kate's limbs tangled with mine before I slipped out of bed. The peace I felt is now replaced with dread as I watch a few of our men pull up the hatch, revealing the tens of blue and white crates piled into the back of the truck.

The scent of salt and sea quickly overtakes the dank tunnel

air as its breath collides with the freshness outside. Workers wheel down the crates filled with the day's lobster catch, soon to be processed in the warehouse and distributed to local markets and suppliers. Meanwhile, the most valuable part that fuels our empire, concealed in the middle of the stacked crates, will be wheeled into the tunnels that lead underneath the park.

Arden's orders echo through the space, the chill in his tone penetrating deep into my bones. His demands leave no room for negotiation: he tells them to wheel the crates down the ramp into the large processing room, then to wait silently for further instructions. Anyone in proximity to this shipment is to be held in rooms until they're all interrogated by my father and me until we're sure none of them is our mole. We're still searching for the scum under our nails that Luciano planted to destroy our operations while he works toward encroaching on our territory.

Stealing what's *ours*, thinking it will divert our attention and buy him some time before we hit back harder and obliterate a kingdom that was never supposed to be his.

His brother, Marco, had many enemies back then.

But we weren't one of them.

However, because we were the only outsiders in that meeting when the life slipped from Marco's eyes, it was easy for his brother, Luciano, to place blame. Blame that ended with my mom and Tayla being murdered for a sin that isn't ours to bear.

After years of planning and calculating our revenge, a new plan was set in motion six months ago when an anonymous person sent an invitation in the mail to one of Luciano's exclusive parties.

*Time to celebrate. A new era is beginning. You must show this invite at the gate to join us for Luciano's 50th birthday party on April 12th @ 7 p.m.*

A birthday party he's throwing himself, which is a pathetic excuse to indulge in more sex, drugs, and alcohol.

Lucky for him, I've always been a good gift-giver.

And when our plan comes through, and we get him alone, he'll have front row seats to watch his birthday bash blow up. Literally. Then I'll give him the rare experience of eating his entrails instead of cake while watching his empire burn. His last few breaths will be tainted with his metallic flavor filling his mouth and the tangible stench of smoke, while his life and anyone he loves goes up in flames, including that spawn of his.

Eight more months.

Instead of over the hill, he'll finally be buried six feet under it.

A death that's five years overdue.

My father shoves his hands into his suit pockets, his untrusting eyes following our men as they wheel the crates down the ramp into the dark that swallows them whole, along with the evidence of our illegal operations.

He scrubs a hand over his salt-and-pepper beard, walking back toward me. "We've got enough fucking messes to deal with as is and can't afford to miss anything. You and Carter are sure it's none of the recruits that were on the estate when we were in New York?"

"We interrogated them all, and I have no reason to suspect any of them were behind it." Even if they somehow sent word to Luciano about us taking that shipment with a team to Virginia, it doesn't explain how the other shipments went missing before they reached the harbor. "Those shipments were full when they left our partner facilities. Someone is intercepting them before they arrive, stealing enough that it is noticeable but not detrimental to our operations."

Enough to throw us off our game and distract us while Luciano plays a bigger one.

The tendons in Arden's neck flex, the words sounding like

venom off his tongue. "That bastard is smarter than I give him credit for." He folds his arms over his chest. "If Carter were here, we'd be out of here faster. I saw this week marked off on the calendar. Where is he?"

I try not to let the words affect me, but fail. "His sister is getting married."

A look of sadness passes behind my father's eyes. "Good for him. It's an exciting time for a family."

I choke down the unwanted emotion slithering up my throat and tearing at my insides. "Too bad we'll never know what that's like."

Creases form between his brows, his eyes holding mine captive. "That's not entirely true—"

"No?" I spit with too much hatred. The admission is out before I can stop myself. "Because last I checked, you don't have a daughter anymore to give away someday, and I don't have a sister to pester about how her future husband will never be good enough for her."

Nobody would've ever been good enough for her.

Usually, my father carries himself like a god above men. I'm almost as tall as him, and with the way he holds himself up, it's always like he is looking down at me. But right now, it's like my comment slaps him across his face, and his shoulders drop.

Unlike other mafia fathers who rule with an iron fist, Arden has never laid a hand on me. But now I wish he would. He didn't deserve that.

His Adam's apple bobs, his voice hoarse. "I was going to say that I still have you." It's like the chill of the air freezes the oxygen in my lungs. Then it ruptures into shards of ice and punctures through my chest when he says, "Just because I lost the love of my life doesn't mean that you don't deserve to find yours. At least one of us deserves to find peace at the end of all this."

I haven't dated or fucked anyone since we lost Mom and

Tayla. Just the thought of love has my stomach coiling into knots.

It's so temporary.

Fleeting.

After watching my father for these last five years, I recognize that losing it makes you feel hollower than if it didn't exist in the first place.

But it doesn't matter because I'm not falling in love with Kate.

Kate just fell onto my lap when I found her in the tunnels.

And then my cock.

And now is somehow tied to every strain of thought, even when she shouldn't be.

Arden sighs. "It was clear to me that there was something you were hiding when you brought Kate here. I'd rather you fuck Kate out in the open—date—whatever, than continue lying to me. You've been different since sneaking around, and it's not hard to understand why. This life can be long, and you shouldn't hide the good parts of yours just because I lost part of mine. What kind of man and father would I be if I didn't want a better life for you than the one we've both been stuck living these past five years? It might be too late for me, but it's not for you."

He doesn't need to lay a hand on me because his comment punches me in the gut just as hard.

Maybe coincidences do exist. An anomaly that brought me a girl who has just scratched the surface, healing the parts of myself I thought were dead and too broken to fix. I never made the effort to try.

I used to think that there's nothing to lose if you have nothing to begin with. But it's an empty life all the same, avoiding love or losing it.

Kate's sentence is nearing an end, and each day there's more dread that circulates in my stomach and tightens my chest.

Weeks ago, I thought there was no way out for her but death. I wouldn't have been able to let her go knowing our secrets. The blood we're drowning in. But I don't want to let her go anyway.

I want to keep her.

Claim her.

Make her mine in more ways than that pretty collar around her neck.

*And you say you're not in love with Kate.*

I tell my conscience to shut the fuck up. Because I'm not.

Would she stay if I asked?

Stay because I'm infiltrating her soul as much as she is mine, and not because she's in survival mode running from someone?

If she wanted to stay protected behind my walls—even if she didn't harbor the same feelings—I would let her. Protect her until I can slay her demons. Or watch her drain the life from his eyes while I peer up at her with admiration from my knees.

I know the feeling in my chest isn't just fascination anymore, but putting a name to it terrifies the fuck out of me.

I shove my hands into my slacks, bringing my eyes back to my father's knowing ones. "Peace. You make it sound so simple."

Arden nods thoughtfully, his eyes far off. He's thinking about my mother, I'm sure.

I always used to watch them. Their lingering glances. Their wandering hands around the estate. The muttered words between them in secret that I couldn't hear, but my father's smirk and my mother's sheepish smile were proof enough of the kind of conversation that flowed between them. For those moments, I'm glad they were whispering. I probably would've been scared knowing my father's tongue can be as foul as mine.

After twenty-three years of marriage, they never extinguished their flame. It burned until it was snuffed out, and still,

I see the love that loiters in his gaze. In the way he speaks about her. Thinks about her as if a part of her will never die, even if she did.

I flatten my lips. "Do you think you'll find it? Peace."

Arden is fifty-one. Still has half a lifetime, if he's lucky, to find someone who makes him feel alive like she did.

It takes him a second, but his focus finds me again. The rain outside the door is relentless, the water cascading down the slope of the tunnel around our feet and into the void, only dimly lit by sconces on the wall.

"Finding one soulmate is rare enough. Two—" He shakes his head, the expanse of his throat moving in the dim light. He changes the subject. "I haven't talked to Kate much, but I like her. Which reminds me." His eyes ignite with something that has my gut rolling. The darkness that washes over his brown irises is alarming. "I can't find her contract. Or any paperwork for that matter."

My sternum tightens. I fight to reach up and rub away the tension as it flows to every muscle, pulling them tight.

"I must have forgotten. I'll have her fill out one." Can he hear my heartbeat laced with my tone?

"Yeah. Strange," he repeats, glowering. It's that look of his, where it's like he's using his rough fingers to pick apart my brain and search for the information I'm denying him.

Fuck. How could I have missed that?

I need Kate to sign a contract, or he's going to know something is off, and my lies will catch up with me.

But the moment her blood touches that paper, she's not just mine, she's *ours* in every way, shape, and form. Her life belongs to the mob.

She'll never be able to escape.

But at this point, I don't think I'll let her either way.

# TWENTY-NINE | KATE

My spoon nudges around the beef in my bowl, my eyes locked on the tender meat bobbing in the broth of my stew like it's the most interesting thing in this massive dining room.

Right now, it is, considering I'm the only one occupying it. It's nearly 9 p.m., and exhaustion consumes me from our fuck-fest last night. I've showered since then, yet Preston's scent still clings to every stretch of exposed skin. It's become a comfort I lean on—one I don't have to seek out when it's seeped into my pores and follows me around.

All day I've meant to ask Preston if he wanted to eat with me tonight, since we usually dine separately in our rooms, but I haven't seen him. Not to mention it's a little too late now. Unfortunately, I waited this long hoping I'd run into him, despite my stomach grumbling when I got off work. I should be hungry, but unease has settled in my stomach instead.

Something monumental changed when he ravenously claimed me in the maze, and I'm starting to crave that deeper connection that only time together can offer. I want those ordinary moments since I said I'd give him all of me if he gave me all of him.

Then, when I woke, the cold sheets from his side soaked into my back, and I knew he was gone. He had cradled me all night, tucking me safely into his side like a lover would. That's where he was when I fell asleep, after he let me ride him until I had us both coming undone again. At some point, he slipped from the bed, and I haven't seen him since. So, I got up and went on with my day at the clinic, replaying everything that happened.

Is he regretting what transpired in the garden?

It wasn't just that one time. He made good on his vow and carried me back to his room. He removed my clothes, placing me on his gray duvet that felt like heaven until he took me there with his cock. He did what he promised and admired the mess he made of my pussy by sliding back into me. I was leaking with his arousal and my own, and he fucked it back into me.

Then he added more, repeatedly, until I was so drained that I passed out. I think I was holding my breath when that last orgasm shredded through me.

I've never been fucked and come that hard in my life. He dragged my soul to the depths with his, then brought me back to consciousness before diving in again until my pussy had memorized every vein in his shaft.

Nervousness blooms in my belly at the thought of him being stressed about whether we took things too far.

Or was it my ugly truth that came out in the middle of the night when we were both awake that sent him spiraling?

Those things are weighing on me; however, I can't ignore that flicker in my chest that tells me I'm being ridiculous. Just because he was gone this morning when I awoke doesn't mean anything.

He's so caught up in whatever mess I found myself in that

I'm surprised he's had time for me at all. Not just to pleasure my body, but to teach me self-defense every morning. But it doesn't dissipate the eager feeling in my bones, which is impatient to see his handsome face.

There is a large fireplace on one side of the room, the hearth looming and empty since we're nearing the end of summer. Various abstract art pieces line the far wall, with spotlights highlighting the masterpieces featuring chaotic brushstrokes and swoops across the canvas. I used to think I could easily do that. Then I took an art class as a filler in college and nearly put my fist through the canvas.

It's more complicated than it looks.

Now I have an appreciation for that kind of artistic eye and creativity, which I admire whenever I'm in their presence. From where I'm sitting, my attention is drawn to the signatures scribbled in the bottom corner. I wouldn't be surprised if each painting costs six figures.

Or more.

I'm guessing the latter.

Wiggling my nose, I scoop a potato onto my spoon. I've barely touched my stew, my mind wandering to where Preston might be.

The sound of footsteps echoing in the hall has me adjusting my posture and features to appear less bored than I actually am. I peer expectantly at the door, attempting not to slouch when I see Gretta walk into the dining room holding a tray of food.

Is that for Preston?

When Arden enters, my spine aligns unnaturally, despite the disappointment that curls through me. His presence holds the power to command anything in his vicinity. Tonight, I'm that thing.

"Oh, hi Kate," he says with a hint of surprise.

"Hi—" I'm still not sure how to address him. "Mr. Lachlan," I try with the confidence of a flea.

I feel like one when he's in the room.

Gretta places his food at the head of the sixteen-person dining room table, pulling out his chair for him. By the way she veered directly to that spot, I'm assuming he always sits there.

"Thank you, Gretta." His appreciation for her is sweet.

Sometimes it's flustering to know he's the head of an organized crime group because you wouldn't think that otherwise. On the streets, in that suit, I would've pegged him for a real estate agent. Or a sexy professor who teaches an entrepreneurship class. Just like the front he puts on for the people of Lachlan Harbor to conceal his illegal activities, he personally has one, too.

If Preston is that unhinged behind closed doors, what is Arden like?

Gretta strolls out of the room, leaving us, while Arden peers at the bowl of stew on his plate, accompanied by a slice of freshly baked bread. The head of the table is a few chairs down from mine, but I watch in fascination as he picks it up and approaches me, pulling out the seat next to mine. As he settles down, I try not to notice the way the tendons in his strong hands move as he places and folds his napkin across his lap.

When I'm pulled back to the moment, I look up, seeing him peering at me inquisitively. "And you can call me, Arden, Kate."

A faint, uneasy smile pulls at my mouth. Did he catch me looking at his hands? What can I say, they are nice.

I fumble the words. "Yes, sir." A few heartbeats pass before I interrupt the silence stretching between us. "Is Preston going to join us?" I ask a little too eagerly.

He picks up his spoon, digging around in his stew. "I'm afraid not. He has some business to deal with in the park tonight."

*Business.*

Lachlan Park or Megalley Syndicate business?

I try and fail miserably to hide my disappointment. "Well, thanks for keeping me company."

He places a piece of beef in his mouth, chewing slowly. I do the same with a potato.

"I take it that you've been settling down nicely and everything is going well at the medical center? Imogen is a very talented woman. She has saved my life more times than I can count."

"I love it, and she is," I agree, in a rush. "And yes, to the settling in. Thank you so much for letting me invade your space."

Arden waves a hand before hitting me with those whiskey eyes. "How's searching for a place coming along? Preston told me that you had just moved here when you got hired, which is why you are staying on the estate."

My stomach sinks. We never talked about that.

It takes a second, but I remind myself that this was our ruse before everything started feeling all too real. I don't know what facts Arden knows about me, but it's clear he doesn't understand much about my past or what brought me here. From what Preston has said about Arden's power, it's better that way.

Preston may not completely trust me yet, but he knows I'm not involved with whatever is going on out there that I'm still oblivious to.

I still don't fully understand why he brought me to the estate—I've almost asked more times than I can count. What I do know is that he gave me a death threat unless I came with him for a month so he could validate my honesty about being in the wrong places at the wrong times. In that same first week, he thought I was working with whoever was responsible for the attack that happened in Virginia, and I assume for what happened to his mother and sister. Not even Imogen or the other staff will tell me why that is or what's going on. Believe me, I've asked. They say there are too many ears listening, and it's not their place to clue me in.

"I've been looking." Shit. Why are my hands so clammy?

My breath is strained as it comes from my lungs. Somehow, He's sucking the oxygen out of the room to make space for his intimidating energy.

He nods slowly.

Picking up the knife from the butter dish Gretta had given me, he glides some over his bread. My focus is drawn to his movements. "I've been meaning to mention, did Preston have you sign the contract and complete your paperwork in your first week?"

My heart swoops violently. "Yes, he did."

Why does this conversation feel like it's tightening around me? Something is off, but I can't sense why. I didn't have much of an appetite before, but I was still eating a little. Now the emptiness in my stomach is replaced with concern.

"*Hmm.* Maybe I just misplaced it." The way he says that makes me think he never misplaces anything.

The air shifts in the room.

The floor below my feet turns soft and muddy as if I'm going to start sinking into it. Alarm is a painful spark skittering in my veins, raising the hairs on my arms. When I meet Arden's gaze, I swear his irises somehow shift to black. His jaw is set. Those eyes, framed by dark salt and pepper brows, pulsate into mine with a fervor that has me trying not to tremble.

Static fizzles in my head.

I blow out a shaky breath. "It was a long day at the clinic. I think I should head to bed." Placing both palms flat on the table, I push to stand.

Abruptly, the man in the chair beside mine thrashes a hand out in front of me. A bang reverberates through the dining room, stopping my heart entirely to a point I don't think it will ever restart.

Dropping my gaze in horror, my eyes zone in on the butter knife, speared into the wooden table between my outstretched fingers. A hair over and he would've severed my pointer finger.

But Arden's too controlled for that. And he knows it.

I bite my lip, my eyes welling with tears.

Slowly, I drag them back to his, void of emotion, as an entirely new definition of fear materializes. "If you lie to me again, the last sound you'll ever make will be gurgling through this knife lodged in your vocal cords before I remove them from your neck."

# THIRTY | PRESTON

Unhinged, anticipation curves through my organs. There's a twisted, gruesome need inside me that desires watching these two new security guards get their hands dirty. Let their inner beasts out to play. Tear apart these two traitors, whose internal clocks are ticking down, as if I can see them hovering above their heads on the screen, where they stand in the center of the park near the fountain.

If they don't kill them, I will.

And I'd much rather have a show tonight because I'm not feeling very murderous. I want to relish in observing this chase, the carnage, and then return to the girl waiting for me.

A part of me feels bad, knowing I slipped out of bed before the sun peeked over the horizon, the only goodbye being a kiss to her forehead, which she didn't even wake for. I've been gone all day—had that meeting with my father to gather the new arrival of narcotics that came in, and then was working out the details of tonight's *festivities* with Vincent and Nolan.

The shipment this morning was perfectly intact and untouched. Everything was there. My father and I stood in shock after reconvening and triple-checking because we didn't want to believe it. My mind has been reeling in bewilderment ever since, with the added distraction of Kate and the state I left her in.

I exhausted her. Fucked her thoroughly all evening till our last round, when my fingers strummed her clit while she bounced up and down on my dick until she came so hard she passed out and slouched to my chest. Fuck, she was a sight to behold. But I was already being hauled into the unfathomable depths of my own darkness and couldn't stop. I wrapped my arms around her fragile frame, thrusting up a few more times. It was lights out for her, so she didn't get to feel me come inside her again around two in the morning after telling me to break with her.

I did.

We broke together in that moment.

And it was the best fucking feeling in the world that I've been high on all day. But tonight, I'm on edge, waiting like an addict losing their mind for another hit. Those images of her naked and bending beneath and on top of me have been replaying in my mind all day.

Today has been one big clusterfuck of things I'm spreading my attention between, and all I want to do is get home.

Bracing my elbows on my knees, I temple my hands and rest my chin on them as the two idiots on the screen dart their eyes every which way. The park, lit only by a few rides, is shrouded in a soft, rainbow glow.

Rowan and Cathal's directions were clear. At midnight, they can start running and try to reach the edge of the park. If they make it, they live. If they start running before the horn blows, or they get caught by Lex or Brett, they die unless they kill the two newcomers first.

Those morons probably believe it, even though they know the only way out of the mob is in pieces. But it makes for an entertaining show, especially with no weapons involved.

The only way Rowan and Cathal will be exiting this park is with their body parts and organs in buckets that will be dumped the next day off the lobster boat, tens of miles out at sea.

It's one minute till midnight, which means their adrenaline and fight-or-flight instincts are kicking in. God, if I focus hard enough, I can sense their blood pulsing in their veins.

Lex and Brett are being held in one of the restaurants across from the fountain. Vincent and Nolan informed them that this was a high-stakes, realistic training exercise, and they could use *any* means necessary to seize the targets.

How they process that information will vary.

If they are as deranged as those looks flickering in their eyes, my body hums to observe how they handle this situation. You'd be surprised at what people resort to when their life is on the line. Or maybe they have been waiting for the perfect moment for their vile nature to come out and play like the rest of us, if it hasn't already.

We're in tune with people as disturbed as us. Plus, Vincent and Nolan have been watching them closely for the last few weeks. Vincent is never wrong with these things. He knows which security guards we present this *opportunity* to. If he had any ounce of doubt, we wouldn't be here.

Brody is sitting to my left, with a bag of popcorn, like it's a usual Saturday movie night. A few other men surround us, all eager to watch the show start.

He puts some in his mouth and crunches. "We haven't had one of these in a while. It's about damn time."

Rowan and Cathal's heads chaotically whip back and forth, and Brody leans over, typing and clicking places on the screen to ensure the monitors update in sync with catching movements throughout the park.

When I see their fists clenched by their sides, their legs apart in a ready stance, I grin. "Here we go."

A horn blows. The sound may be muted through the speakers, but I feel it vibrate through my bones like I'm standing there in person, watching this shit-show go down. Rowan and Cathal take off in the same direction, toward the roller coaster at the far end, where the edge of the park meets the forest line that crawls up the hill to the Lachlan Estate. Cathal blows past his friend, Rowan, who's struggling to sprint against the agonizing pain of everywhere I stabbed him. But it's the wound in his stomach that he is gripping as he runs.

I let Imogen heal him enough to keep him alive, and I'm glad I did.

Reaching for some popcorn, I pop it into my mouth.

This is entertaining as hell.

We all lean closer to the monitors as the restaurant doors fly open, the two new security guards racing across the park's center in the direction of the two bastards who should already be dead.

I inwardly sigh. I should've killed them weeks ago.

I guess I do have a minuscule shred of humanity left somewhere. For some reason, I recognize it more now with Kate around. Perhaps that's why I don't feel like having more blood on my hands tonight and finishing this job myself, as I should have the moment I found out they defied our orders.

Reaching for the popcorn again, I think better of it. Is that why I have an odd sensation, cutting through my gut, as I think about Kate and watch this game unfold simultaneously? Watching the four bodies dart across the screens, I recognize the feeling as distress. Alarm.

Over what, I'm not sure.

I train my eyes on the monitors, ignoring the voices of my men behind me as they make commentary about the chase.

Cathal is far ahead now, while Rowan is falling behind, spitting curses into the air that barely drift through the speakers. There is some delight in knowing this is taking place above us. We may not be able to hear their blood pumping, their frenzied heartbeats, and hectic breaths through the five feet of concrete, but somehow it vibrates the earth, injecting it into my bones.

I'm sure Rowan hears the oncoming rapid footsteps pounding the earth, but he knows his time is up. He'll put up a fight, though. That bastard is as obstinate as a goldfish you wish would die but won't. Proving me right, he turns, getting into a stance that has a wicked smirk pulling at my mouth.

Brett blows past him, headed for Cathal as the next security guard, Lex, screeches to a stop ten feet in front of him, tilting his head in challenge as they stand off.

Their mouths move; words are exchanged that the security system can't catch enough to be intelligible. Lex stalks toward him, and everyone surrounding the monitor leans closer in anticipation.

Rowan growls, sprinting at Lex with his fists flying. His stomach wound must have popped open when he was running, because his hands are caked in blood as he swings a fist. The security guard barely dodges it, his cheek getting swiped with Rowan's knuckles.

For only a moment, shock registers, Lex's eyes widening at Rowan's bloodied state and hysterics. Lex stumbles, trying to regain his ground. When he takes a second to steady himself, his metaphorical armor, I know his true nature has overtaken every other instinct. His hands snap out to grip Rowan's t-shirt in his fists.

Their bodies do the deranged dance, which usually gives me a pang of satisfaction, but it's not there. Instead, I watch, my eyes narrowing at them while I try to ignore the discomfort scraping at my skin.

On one of the other screens, Brett has Cathal in a headlock, the man's face looking like those red balloons children carry all over the park.

But it's this other confrontation that my focus won't stray from.

Rowan flails around in a chaotic whirr of limbs, howling as Lex swings him around by the collar, tossing his body across the pavement like a leaf caught in the wind. He crawls, his bloody, calloused hands clawing at the pavement for leverage. Lex grabs his legs to flip him over. Rowan is a big man with a beer belly that accounts for most of his weight, but Lex rolls him over like he's nothing more than a feather. Swinging a leg over, he straddles his waist.

In a split second, Rowan manages to land a fist to the center of Lex's face, his vile mouth dispensing rage-filled words I crave to hear. It's as if the bone cracking splits through the air, the hairs on my neck standing on end.

Both their bodies are still.

Every breath in proximity to the monitors is being held.

The security guard swipes the back of his hand under his nose, peering at the red streak across his skin. Not wasting another valuable second, he rears back, his fists pummeling into Rowan's face. Rowan's body flails under him, but Lex doesn't stop, giving us the relentless and unforgiving hand-to-hand combat we've been anticipating.

Skin meets skin—bone cracks bone.

He persistently pounds the motherfucker's skull in with his naked knuckles while Rowan's bloodied and swollen face whips back and forth. There's no doubt that Lex is bleeding too through cracked skin, but I know this kind of grit. It numbs the pain until the only thing you see and feel is a wall of scarlet clouding your vision. Lex pulls back his arms, landing one blow after another until Rowan's features are coated in crimson and engorged. Bloated beyond recognition on the screen. Rowan stills, his body limp under Lex's strong build.

I'm sure his heart is still beating, but it won't be for much longer.

When Lex bends forward, I think he's about to push off Rowan. But what he does next is like a crack of lightning zipping through the air, stilling me entirely. He wipes his fingers across Rowan's cheek, drenching them in blood. Then, I'm nearly fucking blown out of my chair when he raises his fingers to his lips.

"Jesus fuck," Brody exhales.

I have seen many deranged things in my lifetime, more than most, but this is...

He dips them again and touches his face, but I can't quite see why from this angle until he looks up.

I stare at him while he glares into the void of night. The rainbow lights from the rides glide off his face, making the scene appear like a horror scene from a carnival. Lex is not looking directly at the security camera, but somehow it feels like he is, his eyes revealing the crimson smudged under them like war paint.

# THIRTY-ONE | PRESTON

Something ugly snakes through my ribs, seeping through my pores to lie heavy on my skin.

I shouldn't be judging another man for having dead eyes, but there's something about tonight that has me on edge. Brett had to knock out Cathal, but Lex beat Rowan enough that his decayed heart stopped beating thirty minutes after Vincent and Nolan intercepted them.

By that time, I had had enough.

I pushed away from the monitors and stormed out of the room, my hands itching to wash off the unknown feeling from my body and send it down a drain that I'm sure is as black and disgusting as my soul.

Everything has felt off tonight. I'm not sure why.

It's been nearly twenty-four hours since I've seen Kate.

Is this what it feels like to have an obsession?

To be so utterly consumed by someone that the withdrawals attack your insides like an illness destined to destroy you. It could be in the best way or the worst way, but it doesn't fucking matter because without it, you could be just as miserable.

I blow through the front doors of the estate, letting that thought simmer. The cool rush of the air conditioning washes over me, useless against the heat that envelops my body with every move I make.

In this life, Kate will constantly be a target.

Be in danger.

But she is out there anyway.

Losing her or letting her go would be just as excruciating.

Is fighting to hold onto something beautiful, even if it's fleeting in this lifetime, better than regretting never having tried to begin with?

After one night of having Kate in my bed, I want her to keep infesting it with her warmth. I want her sugared scent to permanently intertwine with the particles in the air. I want it to fill my lungs constantly.

Driving me fucking crazy.

Her sentence is almost over, and I wonder if a part of her is dreading the approaching deadline. The only way to know what's going on in that beautiful head is to ask her to stay.

Turning the corner, I march down the hallway to her bedroom. I need a shower, but not after quelling these rampant thoughts causing a ruckus in my head. She's probably asleep, since it's almost one-thirty in the morning, but I don't care as I knock on her door softly, so I don't startle her.

My sternum is so tight that it's pushing my heart violently into my throat.

I knock again, with more of an edge this time out of pure nervousness. When I stop, the silence taking over is deathly still. All too quiet. Reaching for the door handle, I slowly push the door open.

"Kate," I murmur.

Forcing myself through, my eyes slowly adjust to the swallowing darkness. The dim room, lit by the moonlight pouring through the French doors, highlights the emptiness that I somehow felt in my bones the moment I entered the house.

The cream duvet on her bed is untouched, the pillows perfectly in place. Dread pools in my gut. Not at the immaculate space, or the emptiness that devours the warmth that once thrived here, but it's the object glistening on the nightstand.

Soft, white light reflects off the gold chain, replacing the heat that consumes my bones with ice. Rage simmers under my skin, sizzling enough to melt it off my flesh to seep into the carpet. My footsteps are weighted as my anger drags me to the nightstand.

I grip the collar in my fist as if I can crush the pure gold into shards that will fall to my feet.

Kate ran.

Lowered my guard with that gorgeous mouth and that sweet pussy and a soul that I naively thought might be made for mine.

The collar dangles in my fist, my eyes fastened on the jagged edge where one of the chains was cut. The lock, still perfectly in place, taunts me. Gripping the collar with one hand, fueled by every ounce of fury coursing through my veins, I reach into my pocket and yank out my phone, dialing Brody.

The line connects, but he says nothing.

"Where the fuck is she?" I growl. "I swear to God, if you don't find her in the next five seconds, I'm going to lodge my knife up your—"

"Preston." His words are a trigger, nailing my chest straight on like they were meant to. "Arden has her."

## THIRTY-TWO | KATE

Trails of my tears sear my fevered cheeks, enough that I think—if I make it out of this alive—I'll have permanent burn scars on my face.

Another reminder that danger is inescapable.

Tied to me in a way I'll never understand.

I'm a magnet, somehow always sucking it in with my pull.

I fight to lick my lips again. The bitter taste of the duct tape adhesive is already filling my mouth. Zip ties bind my wrists to the arms of the metal chair and my ankles to the legs. I'm powerless, but that's the point. This is the second time I have found myself in this chair and in this room. The first was when Preston found me in the tunnels.

Now it's the man who created him holding my life in his hands.

I know why they use metal chairs now. They are easy to clean. Sturdy. Cold in a way that makes me think they keep them in a freezer before use, so that insufferable chill soaks into your flesh and penetrates your bones. I doubt it makes the torture any less painful.

I'm trembling profusely, trying to refrain from letting the

muted sobs from leaving my taped lips. I wouldn't doubt Arden to make good on his promise and impale my vocal cords if I make too much noise. But in this case, it would be with a bullet instead of the butter knife he threatened me with at dinner before stabbing my arm with an unknown injection.

I've been in here for hours. Falling in and out of consciousness until the nightmare decided to be a solid thing I couldn't rid myself of. I almost miss the oblivion tugging me under to pass the time. At first, everything was hazy and blurry when I came into consciousness before I was dragged under again. Then I fully woke, realizing I was bound, with my mouth taped to keep me from talking. The weight missing from my neck had dread filling my stomach almost as much as the livid and brooding man sitting in the chair across from mine. At some point, Arden removed the chain from my neck that held the tracker.

Then my eyes would meet his, still black and lifeless compared to the warm whisky I had grown accustomed to in our brief interactions.

The plastic zip ties dig into my skin enough that I can see the marks forming. My ass is numb, along with my limbs, from being immobile for this long. My chest is still heaving, my eyes puffy, but I'm exhausted from fighting the restraints.

At first, he found it amusing. Arden's been lounging in a chair across from mine, with his Glock rested on his thigh. He hasn't said a word, keeps glancing at the clock on the wall, waiting.

Patiently.

Calmly, though I know there's a violent war raging inside him that he won't let me see.

He peeks at the clock again and grabs the handgun from his thigh, his finger dancing near the trigger. Arden is going to shoot me, and I'm not sure why. There's so much lingering in the crevices about this family that I can't reach. I can't say that

I'm not still curious about what they think I'm tied to. Their past somehow bleeds into everything they do. Someone wronged them, and I can't help but feel like it has to do with Preston's mom and his sister, Arden's wife and daughter.

Just because I slept with Preston doesn't give me a free pass to learn the things that mark their hearts. Those truths take time.

Now I may never find out.

A bang reverberating off the cold concrete walls has my eyes slamming shut. My scream is muffled behind the tape, my pulse accelerating to dangerous levels that could kill me alone.

The air shifts, more tension pulling at the already suffocating room. My eyes slowly peek open, landing on a pair of bourbon ones that inject a little warmth back into my limbs.

Preston's large frame is paused in the doorway. His frantic eyes lock onto mine. The bang was the metal door slamming into the concrete wall as he barged into the room.

He meets his father's gaze, Preston's voice raspy in that way that I usually love, but now it adds an extra dose of terror. "What are you doing with her?"

Arden's eyes keep me hostage. I fight to squirm. "I should ask you the same thing. Considering you've known this entire time that she's been our fucking mole."

Surprise transforms Preston's features, his dark brows furrowing. He shakes his head, a slight tremble to his usually stable tone. "She isn't."

"No?" Arden stands and reaches under his chair, grabs a manila folder, and tosses it at Preston's feet like a Frisbee.

Some of the papers inside fan out across the floor. My eyes dart between the two men.

"I didn't raise you to be this negligent. Or to lie for pussy." Preston's jaw flexes at his father's harsh words. "About a week ago, something about her seemed familiar. It stirred a memory." His fingers flex on the gun positioned at his side. "I remember seeing a girl's hiring paperwork over four months ago. Not for the medical center." His condescending laugh has me shivering. "I thought, what are the chances. But lo and behold, my gut was right. Kate Hannaford was already working for us. In the park." His lips lift in a sneer that has more goose-flesh covering my bare arms in my t-shirt. Luckily, I have leggings on.

Preston and I swallow simultaneously. We listen intently, too nervous to test what he would do if our focus wanders. He's commanding attention. Demanding it with his solid stance.

Arden swipes a hand over his jaw. "Kate was hired around the same time our first shipment went missing. Then, the other one came in this morning perfectly untouched, while she was protected on the estate. Why would she need to steal our product when she's on the inside, gathering intel that's much more valuable?" He tucks a hand in his pocket, keeping the other on the gun. For being in his fifties, he's dangerously handsome, even if he is unhinged and scaring the hell out of me.

"But that wouldn't explain the attack in Virginia." Preston treads lightly. "She wasn't living on the estate when that digital trail was left from inside our walls."

"The tunnels are on the same IP address as the estate," Arden sneers. "How do you know the night you found her in the tunnels was the first time she was down there?" Preston's shoulders tense. "Yeah. I got the security footage from Brody. That's the first time I've seen you weak."

Preston slowly stalks into the room, his attention not leaving his father.

Arden observes his movements. "You've known this entire time that she may be linked to everything that's happened. I'm shocked your knife didn't glide through her throat a month ago when you had her sitting in the very chair she's in now." I shiver at his words.

There is a conversation flowing between them through their stare-off that I don't understand. I'm missing part of the picture. I want to know why they think I was involved with the attack in Virginia.

Arden's dark chuckle seeps through my ears. "Not to mention she's been a ghost for the last year. No digital trail. Nothing. We pay her paycheck in cash, Preston! There are not enough discrepancies to save her—"

"It's not her! She's—"

"No," Arden spits, the one word laced with disdain.

He marches the few steps toward me. I flinch, eyes snapping shut, when a searing pain covers the lower half of my face. The sound of tearing fills the air as Arden rips the tape from my mouth. My shoulders drop, releasing the first real sob that escapes my lips in a rush of air.

Preston must move toward me, because when I look up, the gun is raised, its black body glinting in the fluorescent lights.

But it's not pointed at me.

Arden has the barrel steady between his son's eyes.

A blanket of white paints Preston's face.

As the boss, I've noticed that every time I've seen Arden, he's controlled in his movements.

Not now.

His eyes glisten from hurt, and there is a steady tremble in his hand with the gun. "It's not your excuse to make. If anyone's going to talk, it's going to be Kate. And if she cares for you like I think she does, she's going to tell me the truth before I pull this trigger."

"No, don't," I cry. Tears gush from my eyes now.

Preston's voice cracks, his hands raised. "Dad—"

"I said not another word! Luciano took them from us. Returned Lynn and Tayla's hearts in that fucking box! And she's fucking working for him!" He curses something I don't understand in Gaelic.

Acid sears my throat. My stomach's threatening to spill its contents all over the concrete before my feet. I'm sure this floor is acquainted with most bodily fluids by now.

Someone carved his wife's and daughter's hearts out of their chests and returned them in a box?

He somehow thinks I'm involved?

That means Preston thought I was, too, when he brought me here.

My heart splinters in my chest, some of the pieces skimming my throat as I bite down the urge to heave. My pulse sprints. The image of their bodies, with holes where their hearts should be, extracts all the oxygen out of the air, so that I can't inhale a full breath.

I'm hyperventilating.

Choking on my lungs.

I can't talk while my brain processes Arden's words, and I watch him hold the barrel steady on Preston's forehead. The man who I thought entered my life in the worst way, but has consumed me in the best way since then. It's painful to think about going a day without him around.

Like today, when I didn't get to see him.

The feeling churning in my chest and stabbing my heart like blades isn't just fearing that Arden might kill his own son. It's blended with something beautifully soul-consuming.

I gasp a tattered breath, my voice wobbling so bad I don't know if my words will make sense through the violent fog claiming Arden. "I-I'll tell you anything," I hiccup. "Just please don't hurt him."

Arden's fingers turn white around the gun. "Better hurry up. My fury is making my finger trigger hungry."

"Oh, God," I breathe, shaking—the movement causing the binds to dig into my skin further.

When I glance from Arden to Preston, Preston holds my

eyes. "It's okay. Tell him," Preston's voice trembles. It's the first time I've seen him shaken up.

I nod, my lip quivering, and let the shitshow that is my life spill across the room, giving Arden the name of the man who brought me here.

# THIRTY-THREE | PRESTON

Xander.

No last name yet.

I burn that name into my memory, engraving it into the place where it will soon be marked off, along with all the other people I eliminated who plagued this earth.

The moment she said his name, I planned to head straight to Brody with that information. But then I looked back into Kate's fearful and thankful eyes when my father finally lowered the gun he had positioned between my eyes, and my homicidal instinct shifted to caring for her in any way she needed me.

Arden's silence was deafening as he processed Kate's story. Maybe he could feel that she was being truthful. Or perhaps the thought of being at another dead end of finding who's infiltrating our walls had sent him into a spiral. His eyes were swirling with a heady blend of remorse and anger.

He had a gun pointed at his son's head.

I'm sure that will never sit well with him for the rest of his life, knowing how deeply he feels.

How deeply he cares.

How profoundly he hurts, even when he tries not to show it.

It's the only reason I could understand where he was coming from. I'm not validating his violence; he terrified the fuck out of me. But love makes you do eccentric things.

It manipulates you.

Haunts you when it's no longer physical, and only a memorial piece of it lingers out of reach.

Arden lost the love of his life too soon. Lost a daughter who had him wrapped around her finger since the day she was born.

A wife who was the sunshine in his life and a daughter who was the moon and the stars. Without them, he couldn't function, but he's been trying.

After Kate told him the truth, he shut down. He moved out of the room mechanically before briefly glancing over his shoulder and apologizing. Then he left us, not looking back. I haven't seen him since I brought Kate back to the estate and drew her a bath in my tub.

Honestly, I thought she would want to be alone after tonight, but I didn't want to leave her alone, and I get the sense she didn't want to do the same to me.

Tonight was brutal, and it tied us together in another way, though we have barely spoken.

The hot water envelops us, her head and back resting against my chest. There's a messy knot of dark blonde on her head, her fingers swirling the glass of Chardonnay I've filled twice since we got in. She lifts her arm out of the water to bring it to her lips. Suds drip off her elbow and back into the soapy water as she spits an ice cube back into the glass. I can't see her eyes, but with the way her body is tensed, her gaze is probably far off in thought.

The angry red slices on her wrists have me gritting my teeth when she reaches and places her wineglass on the rock ledge of the tub.

As if she can sense the tension pulling at my muscles, she murmurs, "Are you okay?"

Shock pulls at my features. "I should be asking you that."

"Your dad had his gun pointed at your head."

"And my dad had you drugged, bound, and sitting in that cold room for God knows how long."

She shifts uncomfortably, her soft ass gliding against my half-mast cock. Blood rushes to my groin as Kate's naked body molds perfectly to mine. Can you blame me?

I know now's not the time, so I ignore it as best I can.

"I'm sorry about all of this. He could've killed you because of me." I hear the tears strung with her tone.

As I move my body, I gently turn her around to sit sideways on my lap, so she can hear and feel my words. "Don't. Don't apologize. You are not responsible for my father's actions."

"I know I'm not the one who's involved with this war you're in, but I should've never found those tunnels. I feel like I've made things worse, and I understand if you want me to leave." Her lower lip trembles, and I want to stop it with my teeth.

The thought of what my life would be like if I didn't find her under the park makes me physically ill. I don't want to return to the darkness that once plagued my life. Sure, I might have been cautious about her, but in a way, I think I always knew she was telling the truth.

My eyes hold hers. "I immediately came to find you tonight when I got home. When I saw your chain on your nightstand, I thought you ran." Emotion is laced in my admission. "I was furious."

Her focus falls to her fingers gliding over the bubbles. "Because you still didn't trust me?"

I raise my hand out of the water, pressing my wet finger under her jaw to lift her gaze back to mine. "No, darling. Because I had a question." She waits with bated breath, those green orbs slicing between mine. "I was going to ask you to stay."

The soft column of her throat moves, the expanse of her chest looking empty without her chain. *I'll need to fix that.*

"Stay?" she repeats.

"Yes."

"Like...live here?"

My voice doesn't waver. "Yes."

"Oh." She nods, a thoughtful look pulling at her features when her lips twist to the side. "That's how you felt before everything happened tonight?"

My palm cups the side of her neck, droplets of water falling over her breasts like the sweetest temptation. "And how I feel now."

She blinks, a suppressed laugh escaping her lips. "Preston, I'm the reason your dad held a gun to your head."

"And it probably won't be the last. We are the mafia, darling. He may be my dad, but he's also my boss." Arden has never held a gun to my head, but I didn't expect him to pull the trigger, despite how scared I was. He knows exactly what moves to make to get the answers he wants. He made the right move. I was just a pawn in his game. "I lied to him about something that broke us both a long time ago. It's one of the reasons I brought you here. I should've told him about why I was keeping you here, but I knew how he would react. Tonight validated that."

I know Arden, and I need to have a conversation about it. Preferably over a scotch. Or two. But I know he needs space, and I know without a doubt he is going to give me mine.

She swallows, knowing what I'm talking about now. For some reason, I want to tell her the whole story about my past. About my mom and Tayla. A memory I've never spoken out loud to anyone because, even five years later, it still fucking hurts.

"Why are you validating his actions?" she says it so softly.

"I'm not. But he's a man in pain with nothing to numb it. I wasn't so different when you found me."

She suppresses a sad laugh that has my arms snaking around her back to pull her on top of me to straddle my legs. "I think it was the other way around, Captain. You found me."

My fingers glide around her waist, to the ridges in her back along her spine. "I don't believe that anymore."

She sucks in a breath as my fingertips lightly grace the swells of her ass. "You said you weren't so different. What do you mean by that?"

A corner of my mouth tugs upward. "It means that I felt lost until you, mo ghrá." She rolls those plush pink lips I want against mine. "Can you blame me for wanting to keep you?"

Her hands lift out of the water, gliding along my shoulders and down my pecs. Her fingertips play with the dark hair on my sternum.

Fuck, I'm addicted to the way she touches me.

My dick is fully awake now from her magic fingers.

Kate's body leans into mine, her arms snaking around my neck. Her perky nipples glide against my pecs. "We barely know each other.""We barely know each other."

"What's your middle name?"

Her brows dip. "Breanne. Why?"

I cup her ass, lifting her further onto my lap to draw her mouth closer to mine. I breathe across her lips. "Kate Breanne Hannaford, will you go on a date with me?"

Despite the warmth soaking us, she trembles in my arms.

I can be a gentleman.

For her, *only her*, I'll be a fucking great one.

# THIRTY-FOUR | KATE

I smooth my hands over the flowy fabric, unable to tear my eyes away from the dress that has emotion gripping my chest.

Back at my studio, I have the necessities: comfortable clothes, a few casual ones, and a few pairs of my work overalls. The only other thing I left back there are photos I've kept stashed in my wallet, along with all the money I have made from working at the park. I'm sure my landlord, Sindy, is worried sick, now that she knows I am running from someone. My rent was due the night after Arden drugged me at dinner and forced my secrets out. It's been four days since then, and she hasn't heard from me.

I may only have a few personal things and clothes, but my wardrobe definitely doesn't have a ten-thousand-dollar dress that appears to have been made for me.

Preston asked me to go out on a date with him in the bathtub, as if it were the most normal thing in the world. Like my mind wasn't whirling in a million different directions, recounting the night when I was bound to that chair, wondering if I would die, and then wondering if he would.

The whiplash happened so fast that it split my brain.

We both needed several days to recuperate and rest. And I'm thankful for that, considering there are still faint marks painted on both my wrists from the zip ties.

I haven't seen much of Arden. He's been avoiding Preston and me. The few times I have seen him, he's made uncomfortable eye contact with me from across the room with a vanquished look in his eyes. His mouth would faintly twist to the side, as if the remorse was oozing through the control he kept so well maintained all the time.

Then he'd give me a singular nod before disappearing.

The worst part? I don't hate him for what he did, and I know I should. I can't imagine the kind of trauma that comes with opening a box to see the hearts of two people you love.

The part of them that should keep the blood circulating through their body.

The part that feels.

That loves.

That keeps them alive.

I have so many questions I want to ask Preston tonight. Yet there's something sharp weaving between my ribs that tells me those answers might be figuratively written into the timeline tonight. He wants to know me, and I want to know him. The good things about the past and the worst. What the future could look like.

All our little ugly truths, no matter how unpleasant they may be.

I want all of it. All of him.

They are things I need to know if I'm going to answer the one question he hung over my head.

*"I was going to ask you to stay."*

It's not like I don't want to. I do. But when that request sliced through the air and then impaled my heart, my rationality somehow started kicking in. I barely know Preston.

What I do know about him, this life, is that it is equally composed of terrifying moments as it is of tender ones.

Like him.

I stare at my reflection in the floor-to-ceiling mirror in the closet, twisting and turning to admire myself from every angle.

The soft pink fabric highlights the tan notes to my skin. The sweetheart neckline with spaghetti straps dips low, pushing up my breasts enough that the light skims the swells. The flowy skirt with a high slit cuts up high on my thigh, leaving little to the imagination. All topped off with tan heels that I have to relearn how to walk in, and my long, curled hair tossed up into a slicked-back ponytail.

I've never felt this beautiful.

Preston plopped me in his office chair, gave me his card, and told me to order whatever I wanted to wear for our date.

Date.

It still doesn't feel real. Like any moment, I'll wake up from this dream and realize Xander and Preston are only a figment of my imagination.

Only one of those things I wish was a fantasy.

But without one, I wouldn't have the other.

I wouldn't be standing in a dress, waiting to go out on a date that I'm sure, knowing how extra Preston is, will blow all my expectations out of the water. If my collar were pure gold, I wouldn't be surprised if he had something overly extravagant planned.

My fingers drift to my collarbones. I kind of miss it.

Then he pressed his lips to my temple and told me to go crazy.

So, I did.

When I saw this dress from a boutique, I knew instantly it was what I wanted to wear. The best part is what is hidden under it; I'm wearing strapless lingerie that hugs my curves and comes with matching garters.

I feel like Marilyn Monroe with the flowy skirt, but I have a dirty secret underneath all the fabric. And I'm not just talking about the lingerie that I hope will end up on his floor at the end of the night. I also have my blade strapped to my thigh on the leg opposite the slit.

It's exhilarating.

A knock sounds at the door, and I walk out of the closet to see Gretta standing in my room. Her cheeks are painted a rosy pink, a smile dancing on her lips. She looks almost...proud. "Your date is outside."

Five minutes later, I'm standing in the circular driveway, my glossed lips parted in awe as I stare at the man leaning against a navy-blue Bugatti. Where the hell has he been keeping that beauty?

His short beard is neatly trimmed to perfection. One hand is tucked into the pockets of his charcoal gray suit, which I know perfectly hugs that firm ass. It stretches across the planes of his chest in that black button-down, my fingers already buzzing to pop those buttons and stroke his warm, strong body with my fingertips. Memorize every strain of muscle. His tendons that ripple when he moves. The veins that beg for the attention of my lips and my tongue, as if I can memorize the mapping of him.

My lace panties are damp on the spot. My pussy extracted all the moisture from my mouth. It's pooling at my core as my handsome devil tries to melt me with his presence alone.

And to make it worse, he's lethal, holding a bouquet of pink anemone flowers with the iconic black centers that pop against the pastel petals.

How he knows that's my favorite flower is beyond me. Then I remember this man's power is so unfathomable that I'm just scratching the surface of what he's truly capable of.

He probably knows my blood type, too.

I'm so engrossed in ogling him that I don't realize he's been slowly stalking toward me. The expanse of his throat moves, and those warm bourbon eyes fuse with mine.

"Goddamn. If looks could kill…" He shakes his head, his hoarse voice trembling in a way that makes me grin. I've never seen him this nervous before. Fire licks up my body as his eyes drop again, leisurely taking me in like he may not get another chance to. He holds out the bouquet. "These are for you."

I reach for the flowers, lifting them to my nose. The sweet, floral scent coaxes a smile to my lips. "You want to explain to me how you know what my favorite flower is?"

He smirks, holding a hand up between us. Placing my palm in his, he spins me around gently, pulling my back into his chest. "It'll ruin the magic, darling." Preston's hand brushes my hip. "For some reason, I want to keep impressing you."

His arm snakes around my side, a gold chain dangling from his fingertips in front of me. I inhale a sharp breath.

It's my collar.

I reach up, taking the gold jewelry in my hand. And I say jewelry, because there's no longer a lock on it with the tracking device anymore. Instead, there's a black gemstone that reflects the blue sky above us, and a clasp that allows me to take it off if I want.

He's giving me the choice, and that notion has butterfly wings fluttering in my stomach.

It's breathtaking.

Preston's hands cup my arms, his hot breath skimming across my neck before he plants a kiss on my shoulder. "Do you like it?"

I nod, trying to keep my emotions in check. "What about the tracking device?"

"I had it replaced with a black sapphire. I don't want you to have any doubts if you decide to stay. I want you to trust me."

I hold the chain in my palm. "Will you put it on me?"

With his arm wrapped around my front, his fingertips brush

against my hand to pick it up before he wraps it around my neck, securing the clasp. Clutching the bouquet to my chest, he moves the sapphire to rest on the dip between my collarbones.

Turning on my heels, I stare up at him, gliding my fingers over the metal. "Is it crazy to say I've missed wearing it?"

I follow the movement of his tongue wetting his bottom lip. "That's a dangerous thing to say to me, darling. It's putting images in my head of all the things I could give you to mark you as mine."

# THIRTY-FIVE | KATE

The fire dancing in the propane heater beside our table soaks into my skin. Somewhere above us, stars twinkle and dance. I may not be able to see them through the string lights weaving above us on the private rooftop of the restaurant Preston reserved for our date tonight, but I can feel them.

Every detail, down to letting me pick my dress, has made this the most magical night of my life.

Yet that imposter stirs deep down, reminding me I'm no longer protected behind the walls of the estate. Whereas it used to be potent and suffocating, it's dull now, knowing that my knife is strapped to my thigh and I have the control to put up a fight if a situation arises. Preston may be with me, along with several of his men who are guarding the door and outside the restaurant, yet I can't completely quell the anxiousness that pops in my veins like my blood is carbonated.

Inhaling a deep breath, I remind myself I'm okay. I'm content. I'm happy for the first time in a long time, and nobody —not even the thought of wondering where Xander is in the world—will keep me from this feeling.

The waiter pours a gentle amount of Merlot into Preston's glass, letting him taste it. Preston swirls it around his glass before taking a sip. He gives the waiter an approving nod. The young man fills both our glasses, sets the bottle on the table, and leaves us. Soft classical music plays over the speakers, filling the silence between us.

I grab my wine glass, taking a sip as the rich, fruity notes hit my taste buds. "So," I start. "I know you said I shouldn't ruin the magic, but you seem to know everything about me. How did you know I've been wanting to come to this restaurant since I moved to Lachlan Harbor?"

His lips arch. God, he is dashing and dangerous in that dark suit. "Just my luck, I guess. And I don't know everything about you. But I want to." I feel the sincerity in his tone.

He brought me to the fanciest, authentic Italian joint on Main Street. Apparently, the Lachlans are their lobster supplier, and Preston personally knows the executive chef. I'm not surprised, considering I've learned they cater to the entire town and most of the state, while their lobster business and Lachlan Park are a front for their true one.

I've walked past this place several times when I've been downtown. Kinda embarrassing to say I've peered through the windows like a child looking into a fish tank, taking in the sophisticated, dimly lit space with warm tones whenever I could—imagining what it must be like to have the money to eat at and afford a place like this. I've always run with enough money to stay afloat. Food and housing were the necessities.

This place would've cost almost every penny.

I'd say my nose print might still be on the glass, but this restaurant is impeccable. They probably wiped that off the second I left it.

My comfort level with him settles a little more. "What do you want to know?"

"You said you've been running for a year. What about your

parents and your sister? Have you talked to them?" I glare at him playfully. He takes a sip with a cunning expression, saying into his glass, "I said I don't know *everything*."

I give him a melancholy grin. "It's been about seven months since I've talked to them. I'd give anything to hear their voices — To let them know I'm okay. I ditched my phone when I ran, so I only contacted them from my motel rooms for a while, until I realized how dangerous it was. I don't expect Xander to hurt them, but he's crafty with finding me. I wouldn't put it past him to break into their house and look at the phone records."

His tone is strained. "They couldn't do anything about your situation?"

"They tried," I respond honestly. "Especially my older sister, Natalie. She went to law enforcement with me. Tried to help me press charges. But when that didn't work, she helped me get a restraining order. That only taunted him more. Was another piece of the game he found so thrilling."

Absentmindedly, I glance over my shoulder at the door that exits the rooftop and scan the space out of habit. Talking about it is making my skin crawl. I may feel a little more protected with my blade now, but as long as he's alive, a piece of him will be thriving inside me where I can't reach. That was what he wanted, for me to always feel like he's near, closing the distance.

I jolt in surprise, my gaze dropping to the large hand engulfing mine on the table. "He won't get you here. You're safe."

"You can't promise that." I swallow the lump in my throat.

I'm not sure where his mind goes when I say that, but I know I'm right when he releases my hand, dragging a palm over his face in exasperation. "What's his full name?"

My glare is threatening.

I'm not stupid. I know why he wants to know.

Preston's the kind of man who will stop at nothing to find

him. I was serious when I said he's a devil in a suit. He'd convict Alexander to his own hell under Lachlan Park and torture him for his sins—for hurting me.

But with this, his blood wouldn't only be on Preston's hands; it would be on mine.

Preston braces his arms on the table, leaning over them.

His hard eyes slice between mine before I let out a sigh. If Xander's death were on my hands, it isn't something I think I could live with. No matter what he's done to me.

When I don't answer his question, I observe the way Preston's fingers dig into his bicep enough to pierce through the suit jacket and draw blood to tarnish the pristine fabric.

"Are you going to kill him?"

"Yes."

His name is a warning on my tongue. "Preston…"

"Don't first-name me, darling. You know I will the moment you tell me. So put me out of my misery so I can finally put you out of yours by killing the fucker."

"You can't—"

"You better end that sentence with 'because I'm going to.' I'll stand by your side and get just as much satisfaction from you claiming his death when his corpse drops to its knees before I fall to mine willingly for you."

I can't withhold my nervous smile at that. It doesn't stop me from trying, as I pull my lip between my teeth.

The waiter pushes through the door, the sound making me jump. I haven't had time to review the menu fully, so Preston orders us the weekly special. According to him, I can't go wrong with anything on the menu. I'm thankful I didn't have to rush and choose, since my mind is thinking of all the ways Preston could carve out Xander's organs with his knife.

Over the next twenty minutes, we share stories about our childhoods. I talk about growing up in Oregon, and he shares his experiences of being raised in Ireland before Arden permanently moved their family to the estate in Maine when Preston was fourteen. Oh, and apparently his full name is Preston Thomas Lachlan Megalley. His great-grandparents, back in the day, thought naming a town after the mob was too suspicious and decided to use a double surname. Lachlan is from his great-grandmother, while Megalley is from his grandfather.

He doesn't mention his sister and mother much, but I don't press the issue. Preston's body has been pulled tight ever since he asked for Xander's name, and I wouldn't enlighten him.

Instead, I can't help but eagerly ask, "Will I get to see it?"

He lifts a brow as the waiter starts setting our food down in front of us. "See what?"

"The estate in Ireland. I've never left the country before."

He smirks. "I've never brought a girl home to meet my grandparents."

My eyes widen. "Your grandparents? They live in Ireland?"

He nods, removing the folded cloth napkin from beside his plate and spreading it across his lap. "My dad's parents." Damn. That means at one point, Preston's grandfather was the boss. I can't help but wonder what he's like after running a mafia empire his entire life. If Preston's father is this hard now, what is his grandfather like? "Gran gets attached easily. If I take you there, that would mean it's serious."

My face falls. "Oh. I get it. It's too soon." My stomach shouldn't be sinking like this. It's only our first date.

His eyes hold mine with an intensity that demands my body's attention. "I...like you, Kate. I'd take you next week if you'd let me. But I didn't want to say that and scare you off, especially since you said we barely know each other. I know how I feel, but I'm not going to rush how you do."

That admission has heat pooling in my belly.

For a man who forced me to stay at the estate so he could monitor me, he certainly makes it clear that I have a choice. That he wants me to feel safe. Cared for. Heard.

The collar without the tracking device spoke volumes. The same goes for when he asked me to stay, rather than demanding it.

God, I'd say I like him too, but for some reason it would feel like I'm lying. Because I really, really want him, in ways I can't explain. It's more than *like*, and closer to that L word that makes me wonder if I'm going insane. It makes me contemplate if I suffered a brain injury when Arden drugged me, because when I saw that barrel locked between Preston's eyes, I would've jumped in front of him if I weren't bound to that chair. The thought of going a day without him makes me physically sick.

I know that's love, but it seems too premature to say it, so I shift my focus to my pasta instead.

The scent of melted butter and sautéed garlic lingers in the air, the aroma so intoxicating and delicious that it's enough to make you salivate on the spot. I practically am as I shove a forkful of linguini into my mouth. The creamy seafood flavor blooms on my tongue.

Preston chuckles at my hum of satisfaction.

I groan, twisting more pasta noodles onto my fork.

I peek at his plate. His fork and knife are still perfectly in place beside his plate. I should feel self-conscious that he's watching me inhale mine like a vacuum, but I can't bring myself to care. On second thought, I should savor it more, considering I'd never be able to pay for this place on only a minimum wage salary.

My brows furrow. "Aren't you hungry?"

Shadows dance behind his eyes. "Your sweet noises and moans are making it hard for me to focus on my food. I have the urge to devour something else now, but that would involve your pussy trading places with my plate."

Heat crawls up my neck, flooding my cheeks. I like that I can make him unhinged like this. It makes me feel empowered. Bold. And those are two feelings I never thought I'd get back.

I place more pasta in my mouth, licking my fork up and down, chasing the power I wield. "Holy shit," I whimper. "This is the best thing I've ever tasted."

Preston lifts his red wine to his lips, his fingers pulsing into the glass. He raises an unconvinced brow. "You still haven't swallowed my cock yet."

"You're awfully confident," I tease. Dragging my finger through the sauce on my plate, my tongue darts out, licking the cream off my finger. I swirl my tongue around, releasing it with a pop.

I know I'm poking the devil with his own pitchfork, but I've never been this confident with my sexuality. I've never craved physical contact like this before—as if I may explode into a thousand pieces if I go too long without his touch.

"Darling," he warns, his gruff tone floating across my skin. "If you keep this up, I'm going to toss you on this table anyway, except my head won't be between your thighs. I'll hang yours off the table while I thrust my cock down that hot little throat, while my hand wraps around your neck, and I feel how perfectly you swallow every inch of me."

His words shake me. Dear lord. Thank God he reserved the rooftop for us privately.

"You wouldn't," I say with less confidence than I feel. "This is a public place."

He tosses his napkin on the table, making my muscles tense with both excitement and fear as he stands up and moves to stand beside me.

"Preston, what if they call the cops?" I mutter, flitting my eyes up to meet his.

He darkly laughs. "I think it's funny that you believe there isn't someone in this town that isn't wrapped around my finger."

# THIRTY-SIX | KATE

"I love it when you look up at me like this, looking so innocent," Preston growls.

He's looming over me with a ravenous look on his face, but I know it's not for the expensive meal spread out on the table before us.

"Your pupils get all dilated, and you do this thing where you wet your lips repeatedly, so they glisten. It's mean, Kate. You know why?" The lump in my throat expands, and I shake my head. The way he says my name shoots off like a cure through my bloodstream, fixing some of the broken things I'm still dealing with. His fingers lightly drift over my neck, and I shiver. "Because all I can think about is fucking this goddamn mouth and painting your lips with my cum instead."

I whimper, and he smugly grins in response. When I shift in my seat, I can feel the way my wet panties glide against my clit. And that's just because of his words. His filthy, erotic words that are just as authoritative over me as his body.

I'm staring at the man, with need written all over my features. My nipples pebble into peaks, my core throbbing with desire for him. It doesn't matter where we are. All I know is I want him to take me here on this rooftop like it might be the last time he touches me.

Taunting him, I lick my lips.

He groans, wrapping my ponytail around his hand forcefully to keep my eyes on him. "You're such a tease."

Reaching a hand out, I grasp onto the bulge in his pants near my face. "You're one to talk, standing here like this all hard and ready for me to take you in my mouth."

"Oh, shit," he hisses.

It's downright inspiring to see a man of his nature fold to some simple praises. Didn't stop the tremble in my tone when I said it, but I'll get better at it.

"Are you sure you're ready for this part? I don't want to rush you if you're uncomfortable." The way he breathes the words laced with apprehension almost makes him sound like he's in pain.

I never thought I'd feel confident enough to taunt a man, but the way he reacts to my words is enough to have me feeling comfortable. To explore a side of myself that I never got the chance to because sex was never about me. I was on the receiving end of the pain but never the pleasure. The way he asks for permission has me nodding with a smile. With Preston, I feel safe to rediscover my sexuality. Sure, he's dominant, but he responds to my body. Listens to my worries. He's mindful of my fears. And it all started that first night in my room when he let me take the lead and reclaim the control that had been stolen from me before I met him.

Pressing my palms into his thighs, I use my force to push him backward. He lets go of my hair, giving me enough space to slowly slip off the chair and sink to my knees on the outdoor rug. I should care about getting the fabric of my dress dirty or the waiter finding us, but the way his heated eyes take me in, I don't think he cares, and neither do I.

His muscular thighs are hard against my palms as I drag them upward toward his massive erection.

"Fuck. I knew you'd look gorgeous on your knees, desperate for my cock. But seeing you choke on my dick in the dress you chose just for me," he exhales, shaking his head.

His fingers fiddle with his belt before he unbuckles it and lets his cock spring free from its confinement.

I don't hesitate. My fingers wrap around the soft base, and he releases a harsh breath. He's been inside me already. I know how big he is. But he seems so much heavier in my hand like this, and bigger up close; the head nearly touches my lips.

I release a breath across his slit where that bead of precum glistens, waiting to melt on my tongue.

Placing my tongue on the underside of his shaft, I glide it up the vein bulging there. My eyes remain locked on his. "Shit, baby. I'm not going to last long if you keep looking at me like that."

"Like what?" My fingers tighten around him, and he hisses in pleasure. His skin is so velvety in my hand.

"Like you might be falling for me." His hand disappears from my ponytail, moving to bracket the side of my neck.

Flurries of desire and complete obsessiveness for this man send my body into a spiral. I hope he can feel my answer in the way my focus on him doesn't waver. I cup his balls and guide him into my mouth, relishing in how his muscles tense and his erection jolts in my mouth.

Pulling back, I swirl my tongue over his head and down his length before attempting to take him all the way. The head punches the back of my throat, but he still doesn't fit all the way. Mumbled curses fall from his lips as I gag around him, trying to breathe through my nose, attempting to take him deeper. He's so big, my lips will be stretched after this, but it will be worth it.

I release him with a pop. He moans, not taking his eyes off

his dick, wet from my saliva. I take some time, inhaling rapid breaths, gooseflesh peppering my skin when his fingers skim along my throat, hooking into my collar.

"Open," his command sends liquid heat rushing between my thighs.

I listen, letting my lips part.

He grips the chain around my neck, using it to draw my mouth back to his waiting cock. Preston thrusts his hips forward and pulls my collar simultaneously. He falls into a steady rhythm, filling the air with wet sounds from him ruthlessly fucking my mouth. My hands dart out to grip his thighs, my nails digging into the fabric to hold on while he uses me in a way that could make me come too.

His balls slap my chin, wet with my saliva. I moan around him, as tears start to fall from the corners of my eyes. My makeup is going to be smeared all over my face after this, like those abstract paintings all over the estate.

"Holy fuck. Do you like letting me use this eager little throat?"

My limbs are trembling below me.

With one hand still gripping my chain, he uses the pad of his thumb to drag it over my wet, flushed cheeks. "You didn't listen and provoked me. Look what I'm making of you now." What is he— Slipping his thumb between his lips, he cleans off my tears from his finger, keeping those burning brown irises on my watery ones. "But you listen so well when I'm fucking you. You're a whore for my cock, aren't you, baby? I bet that tight cunt is all soaked and ready for me."

I mumble in agreement around him. God, I wouldn't be surprised if I'm dripping on the carpet at this point.

Preston tosses his head back, groaning, "Your body is the closest to heaven I'll ever get."

He glances down at me and pulls out enough to let me swirl my tongue around him like he's the most delicious thing I've ever had in my mouth. The feel must set him off, because he mumbles "Fuck" as he grips my chain again to bury himself in my throat, keeping me steady for a heartbeat while I gag around him. His thrusts quicken, his movements somehow controlled and unruly at the same time. He's getting close. I feel it in the way his veins are throbbing against my tongue.

I peer up at him through wet lashes as my head bobs on his dick.

"*Shittt.* Open your mouth and stick out that tongue." I do so obediently, and the second I do, one of his hands darts to his cock. He hovers it over my tongue, watching in fascination as he coats my mouth and the back of my throat with salty streams of his release.

His chaotic grunts cut through the air, making my mouth tilt upward. He pumps himself a few times, carrying out his orgasm. "Don't you dare close that fucking mouth yet. I'm not done with you."

Preston catches me off guard when he swipes his thumb over my tongue, coating his finger with his cum before commanding, "Swallow every drop, darling."

My mouth closes, and I swallow, savoring the flavor of him. His thumb, glistening with his release, glides across my lips, painting them. A tattooed hand wraps around my throat, tugging me to my feet as he bends to kiss me sensually. My fingers dig into the lapels of his jacket for stability. Knowing he's tasting his flavor on my lips and in my mouth has electricity fizzling to every nerve ending.

The kiss is desperate. Heated in a way that has me aware of the sheen of moisture clinging to my skin. This dress suddenly feels like too much fabric. He's burning me with his mouth now as his tongue explores mine. Searing me through my flesh to the point he'll char my bone and leave permanent marks—physical signs of this undeniable fervor that flows between us.

My lungs are on fire, so I pull back, holding my hands

between us, worried he won't stop and continue trying to suck out my soul until I pass out.

Surprisingly, he leans forward, leaving a gentle kiss on my nose. "Now go eat your dinner. I'll be rewarding you later."

"You expect me to be able to focus on my food after that?" I whine.

He laughs. A genuine one that I want to savor. One that is so beautiful and lively that I want to draw it out more. "You distracted me from mine, darling. It's only fair. Plus, tonight's not over yet. There's one more thing I want to show you."

# THIRTY-SEVEN | PRESTON

The breeze brushes against my skin, the horizon a dark void beyond the harbor lights that dance on the surface of the water in the distance. A literal sea of stars that I've appreciated so many times.

Kate's hands are perched on the edge, her beautiful, big green eyes taking in the expanse of rainbow that stretches around us.

This view used to be one of my favorites. Despite what transpires below, I used to associate Lachlan Park with laughter and bright faces. Memories of Tayla and me running around here as children before we grew up and understood the role this front played in our operations.

In what feels like an instant, all the joyful recollections were replaced with carnage and blank, lifeless eyes. The joyful voices I heard as a kid were suddenly shattered into oblivion by the crack of gunshots slicing through the air. The breeze off the water rushing through the park transformed into the last gasps of breath from my men—from Luciano's—grazing against my skin and echoing in my ears as punishment for being fooled by the distraction that cost me the two people who were my world.

Through the years, plenty of massacres have happened in this park when the gates close. All those useless souls from men who broke our blood oath were sacrificed for our high-stakes training exercises, which aimed to train recruits and punish those who defied us. But that night five years ago, it became a battlefield. A piece of history that people walk on, unaware that once the concrete below their shoes was spoiled by blood and brain matter.

I could never bring myself back to this view.

Until tonight.

Even now, as I sit at the top of the Ferris wheel, pain and hurt are still dense in my gut. My muscles are clenched, a sweat breaking out on my forehead. It feels like gravity is trying to haul me back to the ground, like I was never meant to be back here without them. An inferno is raging in my lungs. Dropping my head and closing my eyes, I blow out a breath, folding my hands in my lap to stop them from shaking. The air isn't thinner up here, but it feels that way.

My body stills when soft skin envelops my hands balled on my lap. My head tilts, looking up at the striking girl beside me, her eyes transfixed on mine with a heady mix of wonder and worry. But she doesn't say anything as her body next to mine soaks up my trembling.

I'm the goddamn boss of a mob, and here I am quivering like I'm afraid of heights.

Kate doesn't say anything. She tenderly holds my hands in hers, her thumbs stroking soothing circles that start to chase away the darkness leaking in the corners of my vision.

I release a breath, the exhale carrying a little bit of the weight sitting on my chest. "Five years ago was the 90<sup>th</sup> anniversary of Lachlan Park."

Kate knows how violent my sister's and my mom's deaths were. A tidbit my father released when he had us in the interrogation room when she was bound to the chair. But she doesn't know why their hearts were in that box.

Why it happened.

Why they were killed.

Why I needed to watch her to make sure she wasn't involved.

Those green orbs bounce between mine, listening intently.

A bleak, breathy laugh leaves my lips. "We always used to throw this huge damn party where the entire town would show up. At the end of the night, after the park would close, my family would come up here—like you and I are now." My eyes dart around the black sky blanketing us, my heart smashing against my ribs. Recounting what happened is bringing it back in a violent wave. I push on. "Mom and Tayla made it on, but my father and I never did. We heard gunshots from deeper in the park and rushed there with Carter and our men, leaving my father's right-hand man to protect them. We thought they would've been," emotion clings to my tongue, "safe up here."

My gaze falls to the floor below our seat, while her eyes bore into my skull. Her fingers tighten around mine, giving me the strength to keep going.

"The Calco Cartel, an Italian mafia group, was looking to do business with us when it was under the leadership of Marco Giovanni. At one of our meetings with him, he was poisoned. His brother thinks we are the ones who killed him."

Kate sucks in an audible breath. Her voice is soft with caution. "Did you?"

My head shakes. "No. But that didn't stop him from wanting to get revenge. A sibling for a sibling."

One of her hands leaves mine, and I presume it's to cover her mouth in shock. "But your mom..."

The lump in my esophagus expands. I attempt to swallow it, but my stomach can't hold any more weight. Tears burn the corners of my eyes. Since they were together when they raided the park, he saw an opportunity and seized it.

"While we were face-to-face with him, thinking he was the threat, the real ones were taking out our men guarding my mom and my sister. The next thing we knew, the bodies of Calco Cartel soldiers and our men littered the ground." We should've taken out Luciano when we had the chance, but when we heard more gunshots coming from the direction of the Ferris wheel, protecting them was our priority.

A deep breath fills my lungs. "When we realized what was going on, we rushed back to them. But it was too late. Luciano, the new don, got away, and my mom and Tayla were gone." A tear falls, soaking into the arm of my jacket. My hands pulse into Kate's, searching for stability. "The next day, a box with their hearts and photos of their murders was waiting outside the gates of the estate."

A sob rushes out of Kate's mouth, brushing against my neck. "Oh, Preston—"

I shake my head. "My father and I were supposed to protect them. One distraction. One moment was all it took. In the blink of an eye, they were gone, and we've been punishing ourselves ever since, while Luciano has been creeping in to try and claim what's ours."

"That's why you brought me to the estate and wanted to watch me. That time you found me on the dock and in the tunnels. You thought I was working for him." Her voice breaks. It's not a question, because she knows she's right.

Using my arm sleeve, I wipe under my eyes before peeking up at her, nodding.

She rolls those plush lips. Her breaths are shallow now, matching mine. "Oh, God. That was the biggest massacre that happened in the park five years ago? The one that the employees at Lachlan Park spread rumors about. That's why I thought you sold organs to the black market when I met you."

What did she call it? The Evisceration Cellar?

I've heard the stories, no matter how hard I've tried to block them out. Like with every massacre or whenever there's bloodshed, getting rid of evidence is easy, but with as many gunshots as there were, someone was bound to hear them, even if it was contained inside the park.

"Several of Luciano's men were still alive that night when we left them to find my mom and my sister. We tortured them in the tunnels," I sigh. "But they stayed true to their oath with the Calco Cartel until their last breaths." We removed all their organs after my dad and I got the box, when it was solidified that they were never coming home. Nothing could've kept those screams of agony completely contained. I couldn't hear them over the void of rage and depression consuming me.

My blank stare is interrupted when a hand cups my cheek. I blink away the tears, letting my eyes clash with Kate's.

Her thumb drifts over my cheek. "It's not your fault. You were just dealt a fucking shitty hand," she breathes, throwing my words back at me that I said to her the night she showed me the marks lacerating her stomach. Her neck. "It doesn't matter what plagues your past. What things you've done in your lifetime. Nobody deserves to go through what you and your father have." I sink further into her warm touch, chasing the comfort. "We may come from different pasts, Preston, but I know how hard it is to forgive yourself for something you believe you should have been able to control. Alexander Brighton's actions weren't my fault, but it didn't stop me from blaming myself."

Swallowing, I clear my throat, my eyes darting to the side. "I don't think I can, Kate."

"Look at me, please," she whispers, cupping my neck. Reluctantly, my gaze finds hers again. "If there's anything I've learned over the last month, between you training me and helping me through my fears, it's that healing doesn't happen overnight. But slowly, being here with you, I've started. You've been here with me every step of the way as I work through it, and I'm damn well going to be here for you."

I exhale a shaky breath. My armor, I try to keep impenetrable, has slipped away, seeping through the cracks beneath my feet and to the ground somewhere below.

She asked me to, and now I am.

I'm fucking breaking for her.

"Your sister and your mom's final hours may have been tragic and painful." A tear falls onto my cheek, and she catches it with her thumb. "But they're probably at peace, wherever they are. And I'm willing to bet they're watching over you, hoping you find yours."

Kate had somehow buried below my skin the moment I saw her. Sitting here with her now, her words and kindness thread through my nervous system so tightly I don't think I'll ever be rid of her. I'm giving myself to Kate entirely, letting her implant herself so profoundly that she's the one I know I can reach for when I'm feeling empty—a gorgeous and strong woman who started out as a stranger. A girl who I thought had wrecked my world, but who has been the one helping me rebuild it. Injecting light back through the cracks.

The scars she lives with call to mine.

Both of our bodies carry stories from a past we'd rather forget, but they are memories that impact how we fight moving forward.

How we connect.

How we survive.

How we love.

I'm not afraid to admit it now.

I'm in love with Kate.

I'm in love with her heart. Her kindness. The way she can find something to love in a broken and hard man like me, but smooth my edges with her softness. I'm addicted to seeing her find her power. Want to bury myself in the warmth of her smile and curl up in the heat of her touch.

I want her in ways that are impossible.

I have blood on my hands. Lives that condemn my soul.

I'm a man people would consider pitch black and heartless for the lifestyle I was born into. But when she touches me with her caring hands, her words, parts of her soul that I know damn well she's never shown anyone else, I fall deeper. And in return, I've opened her up to the weakest parts of myself that she holds like it's her responsibility to take some of the pain away.

I should be the villain in her story. But as she scoots closer to me and brushes those addicting lips over mine, one thing is clear. Even black can't exist without a symphony of colors, and Kate Breanne Hannaford is one of mine.

## THIRTY-EIGHT | PRESTON

These fuzzy fucking feelings pulling at my chest feel foreign in a good way. In a way that makes me want to pick Kate up and carry her back to the seclusion of my room, where I can keep us tucked away in this bubble we've created tonight.

There's a fear deep down that if I expose her to this life, I could lose her as easily as Mom and Tayla. But suffering through a day without her if I let her go sounds just as painful.

The dominant beast inside may want to force her to stay now that I've acknowledged my fascination with her is more than that, but she needs to want to stay. After seeing her in that dress tonight with a smile that melts my world, I want her to keep it, even if I'm not the one she shows it to.

Kate deserves everything she wants in life.

Even if it destroys me, I can find a way to live without her, though it may take my whole damn life to pull myself out of love with her. But at least she'd be content. Thriving out there somewhere in the world because I helped her get a piece of herself back in the same way she helped me.

She clasps her hand in mine, threading our fingers, shooting me with a worried smile. "Are you okay?"

I lift our conjoined hands, pressing a soft kiss to her knuckles. "I will be, darling. I've got you now."

Kate stops, and I drop her hand, my eyes bouncing between hers as she turns to face me. With the way she's motionless in front of the Ferris wheel that's behind me, the pink and purple hues bathe her skin. She's glowing. Breathtaking. Looking like the color in my dark world.

I had the guards leave most of the lights on for us so I could show her a fragment of my soul I keep tucked away behind walls she's managed to collapse. Replaying the worst night of my life, knowing she can't make a sound decision without having all my pieces at her feet.

They should be turning them off soon, so I take my time memorizing the pink glow casting over her exposed skin in that pink dress she chose because she knew how fucking beautiful she'd look in it. How crazy it would drive me.

Damn, does she look like a dream.

*My dream.*

Those beautiful lips part, like she wants to say something, but then she swallows. A grin replaces it. "Thank you...for everything tonight. The dress, my collar, the dinner. This," she breathes. "It's too much."

I raise my arm, letting my palm cup her neck. "You deserve nothing less, Kate. I hope you know that."

The name she let slip on the Ferris wheel is eating a hole in my goddamn brain like a worm in an apple, but I pull her into me, not wasting another minute to claim her lips with mine. Her arms weave around my neck, her fingers threading into my hair. Her mouth parts, letting my tongue entangle with hers in a way that has blood flooding to my groin. Another reason I want to get her back to the estate is to see this dress on my floor. That's all I've thought about since she walked down the front steps. Doesn't matter if she's walking around in leggings and no makeup, scrubs, or a dress with a slit so high it tests my sanity, she's stunning.

Her body is flush against me, her touch searing through my suit to soak into my flesh.

I pull back, admiring her swollen lips, my mind briefly flashing with images of what I did to them at dinner. "Ready to go home?"

*Home.*

The estate hasn't felt like that in a long time, and damn does it feel good to say that.

"Yes." Kate may be in heels, but she still lifts to her toes to press a kiss to my cheek, her lips arching up into a smile against my skin, like she enjoys hearing that too. "But since we're here, can I go get some things from my locker and get my last paycheck?"

I groan, my chest pulling tight at the thought. But there's a place I need to visit first anyway, and it's better if she isn't there. "Fine, but make it quick and meet me in the interrogation room in the tunnels. I know you know how to get down there now."

She smirks, making my own mouth tilt. "That I do, Captain. And from what I remember, you said you'd reward me. You think I'd miss that?"

I should toss her over my shoulder right now and make good on my promise, but I don't. Instead, I slap her ass playfully, watching as she takes off in the direction of the mine ride, and I head off in the other direction to the next closest secret entrance to the tunnels.

It's midnight. The amusement park is nearly vacant, except for the few security guards on duty. So, I don't pass a soul as I enter one of the restrooms, use my master key, and walk into the cleaning closet, opening the secret doorway to the tunnels. My entire way to the tech room to see Brody, Kate's ex's name digs deeper until I'm bursting through the door with my fists clenched at my sides.

The anger is radiating off me in waves. They are big enough to knock Brody off his chair with the way he scrambles to attention when I enter the room. He quickly scurries to get his legs off the desk and puts them back on the floor where they belong.

He releases a sharp breath, his hands flying to his chest. "Fuck, you scared me!"

"Alexander Brighton," my deadly tone echoes through the room, not wasting any time. "I need you to look that up now."

Some of my other men, who Brody oversees, look at me inquisitively before returning to their work, their postures stiffer now that I'm in the room. There's something satisfying about carrying the kind of authority that can nearly break a man's back when you're in proximity.

Brody smugly crosses his arms over his chest, leaning back in the chair. The faint squeak from the hinges has the hairs on the back of my arms standing on end. "I'm going to need a little more information than that."

"That's Kate's ex," I clarify.

I want to punch him for the way his mouth lifts with a knowing grin. "You're gone for her, aren't you?"

I am.

Completely.

My eyes roll as I knit my arms over my sternum, trying to ignore the tight pull that's making me anxious. I just want to find this fucker and rid her life of him. Entirely.

"Shut up," I growl.

I may have to wait to destroy the bastard who ruined my life, but it doesn't mean I have to wait to kill the man who's tormenting her.

He clears his throat, typing away rapidly to match the pulse in my neck. "Arden hasn't come after my balls yet. I assume that's your doing?"

My eyes drift downward regarding him. I was the one lying to Arden. Brody kept his mouth shut about the reason Kate was here to save my ass while I watched her to see if she was involved with the Calco Cartel; it was only fair I saved his.

My father and I are slowly getting back to normal. We've always been close, and I hate that this has thrust an awkward space between us. He was shocked to see that I had brought him a bottle of his favorite Scotch a few nights ago—a fifteen-thousand-dollar bottle.

My visit was double-sided, though.

One, to apologize for lying and to tell him I forgive him. Arden may have held a gun to my head, but I was the reason it was there. Doesn't make it any better, but I had to own up to my actions, and in return, he owned up to his. The only time I've seen my father cry is at Tayla's and my mom's funerals, but as I sat in front of him in that office, he broke. His remorse was eating him alive. When he put the pieces together about Kate being at the estate, he was consumed by grief and overtaken by the demons whispering in his ear that Kate was working for the man who ripped my mother from him. His baby girl.

We just existed together for a while, like we have so many times when we're lost in that place inside our heads that seems impossible to escape.

He's all I have.

The man who taught me to perfect a shot with a handgun before I was in high school. The man who watched me gut a man with pride in his eyes instead of fear when I was sixteen. A father I look up to, knowing there's no line between choosing the mob and your family.

If he could love my mother, Tayla, and me endlessly through all the bloodshed strung through our world, there's no reason I shouldn't be able to do the same. The thought of having a family may terrify me, but imagining my future with Kate gives me something to live for. Something to fight for. One look at her was all it took for me to understand that a violent life can dance with a beautiful one.

The second reason for my visit with my father that night was to defend Brody. I was the one who asked him to lie for me, and the thought of him suffering at Arden's hand because of me had my gut spinning with guilt.

Clapping a hand on his back, I nod. "You did what I asked you to. Arden's wrath was mine to deal with. I owed you one."

He peeks over his shoulder, giving me an arrogant grin. "Damn. Was that an apology?"

I remove my hand from his shoulder, tucking it into the pocket of my suit. "Burn it into your memory. It won't be happening again."

His typing fills the space as he pulls up a string of code. "Any other details that might help me narrow the search for this guy?"

My head tilts. "He was a part of her life back in Oregon. She said he was a phlebotomist."

"Interest—" Brody's eyes expand. His fingers stay glued to the keyboard as his eyes take in the screen.

My eyes narrow on his still stature. "What?"

"That name is in our system."

"Well, yeah. I asked you to find him. It should be—"

"No, boss." Brody swallows, shaking his head. "I mean, *our* system... Like the Lachlan Park employee database."

I freeze, my sudden stiff posture forcing all the blood to my ears. "You better be goddamn fucking with me."

His hoarse voice is a dagger in my chest. "I'm not. Unless it's a coincidence and the new Lachlan Park security guard we hired a few weeks ago happens to share the same name."

That word is another blade to my sternum.

Coincidence.

His fingers fly across the keyboard as the blood rushing to my head starts to flood behind my eyes. The second a resume with a headshot fills the screen, the recognition is a metal rod to the backs of my knees.

I should've put two and two together when Kate finally let his name slip tonight. But I was too distracted.

The black-and-white image on the monitor confines me to my spot.

I'd know those eyes anywhere.

The last time I saw them, they were framed by a smearing of blood as they watched the life slip from Rowan's.

Alexander Brighton doesn't only go by Xander, he also goes by Lex.

# THIRTY-NINE | KATE

I almost said it, but the words sat heavy on my tongue. The way Preston's been making me feel all night nearly had me feeling light enough to tell him that I love him.

That I'm completely and utterly his.

The way he broke for me on that Ferris wheel, relaying the memories of that horrific night five years ago, had parts of myself reaching out to him like the roots of a plant somehow embedding themselves in the weakest parts of shattered concrete, like I could fill them.

Hold them together, though I'm not made up of the same matter.

Now, there's this hollow, regretful feeling churning in my stomach, knowing I could've said those words to him and didn't.

Tonight, when we get back to the estate, I'm going to.

I know he hasn't said them first, but I've felt them in all the details woven through tonight. Have recognized it in the way his eyes hold mine, like two magnets destined to fit. If love isn't a man offering to hunt down your demons to the end of the earth, even when he's haunted by his own, I don't know what is.

The silence in the break room is eerie as I open my locker, which contains an extra pair of clothes, my last paycheck, and a few other miscellaneous items. A cold draft pushes through the room, wrapping around me like freezing fingers clawing my skin. It sits on my arms and legs, making them prick with gooseflesh. My body is eager to return to the man who somehow injects heat into my bloodstream, even though he instills fear in others.

There's something oddly poetic and beautiful about that.

Knowing he's weak for me.

As if my body is aware, the hairs on my neck rise, feeling a presence in the small room behind me.

My teeth sink into my bottom lip as I suppress my smile. "Should've known you wouldn't be able to leave me alone for five minutes," I tease. A few heartbeats pass. The absence of a response has me shaking my head, as I rearrange the contents of my locker to make it easier to carry them down into the tunnel. "Luckily for you, I enjoy your possessiveness."

"Do you?"

My heart plummets into my stomach. The low timber of the voice has my fingers tightening on the handle of my locker. It's taking all my power to fight the tremors seizing every muscle. I must be hallucinating. The tone in my ears somehow shifts into one with the authority to have terror eating me from the inside out.

My feet feel as if they're buried in tar as I slowly turn, my entire body solidifying in fear.

Those dark eyes that appear in my nightmares arrest mine, breathing life into the petrifying dreams I've carried ever since I ran. "Because you know how much I love it when you run. But hiding from me?" he tsks. "Now that really pisses me off."

"Xander," I breathe, trying to ignore the way I feel like the scar on my neck is splitting open with his presence alone.

He takes a step forward, and I take one back, my back plastering against the cool metal of the lockers behind me. My palms flatten over the surface, trying to hold on while the ground I finally felt steady on is ripped out from below me.

"How...did you find me?" My lip quivers.

He blows out an entertained snicker laced with disdain. "I almost gave up. Thought you were gone for good. But finally, after months of looking for you—" His head shakes side to side in displeasure as he drags his hand over his dark, cropped hair. "You really outdid yourself this time. Fucking Maine."

It takes me a second to register what he's wearing. My gaze anxiously flits to the metal name plate on his security uniform. "Lex?" I mutter timidly.

He continues pacing toward me with that psychotic gleam in his eyes that paralyzes me on the spot. "Couldn't risk you running off if someone talked about me while I was going through the hiring process. Don't get me wrong, I was a little concerned that you had already run again since you seemed to be missing from work for a few weeks." His jaw flexes. "I assume *he* has something to do with that?" He clucks his tongue.

Preston.

Xander's hand whips out, wrapping around my throat. His rough fingers pulse into my flesh. I inhale a sharp breath, shaking below his burly frame. He may not be as big as Preston, but his body still swallows mine. I've always been something small for him to push around. To torture and flood with praise as if taking his violence is okay.

"You just said you like it when I'm possessive. So, consider me jealous, Kate. Do you know how fucking hard I am right now thinking about draining the blood from his body? You'll be a good girl for me and watch before I draw yours, won't you?"

I don't dare speak.

He doesn't know who he's messing with. If he did, he

wouldn't be attempting this. But again, he's always been a sociopath. I wouldn't put it past him to get off on his own pain.

The feeling of cool metal against my side causes a whimper to escape my lips.

His head tilts forward, his hot, repulsive mouth skimming the shell of my ear. I don't miss the hint of alcohol on his breath as it fans across my cheek and into my nose. "You know how much I love marking this hot little body with my knife. So, fucking sit down before I use this gun and ruin the game." With his hand clutching my neck painfully enough to leave a mark, he flings me forward. I stumble, my body slamming into the table in the center of the room. "We need to talk."

This man destroyed any confidence I had in his presence. Blasted it into tiny fragments that got caught in the wind, while only a few small shards landed at my feet. Now I'm collecting them. Clutching them in my hands like they'll be enough to give me the courage I need to end this.

"There's nothing to talk about. We're done," I seethe with my back turned to him.

A click emanates in the air, my body solidifying. I don't know much about firearms, but that faint sound of the safety clicking off somehow pulsates through the room, shooting through my nerves to have me shakily reaching for the chair to pull it away from the table.

I plop down, tears biting the corners of my eyes.

"Good," he praises, the one word causing acid to sear my throat.

The hairs on my arms stand on end. It feels like they follow his movement as he rounds the table slowly, his wicked gaze pinning me in place. The gun may be lowered, but it doesn't diminish the fear weaving around my frame, keeping me imprisoned in this chair like chains. He slams the gun on the table to trap it below his palm.

I jolt in place, inhaling to trap the sob that wants to be released.

"We're done when I say we're done, Kate. Does it look like I've given up?"

I shake my head, words escaping me.

"I've looked for you. I've chased you. I fucking moved across the country *for you*." His biting words should make me flinch, but they don't. Not like they used to. I may be terrified; however, they don't carry the same weight they possessed back then to hold me under. It feels different. While he continues talking, I try to gather any semblance of an idea to get out of this through the terrified haze fogging my brain. "I think you're forgetting the lengths I'd go through for you."

I've been running from you for a reason. "I haven't forgotten," I grit through clenched teeth.

Xander's head slants, his gaze dragging over the top half of my body. "You've changed. You're feistier than you used to be." His tongue darts out to wet his bottom lip. "I like it."

I ignore his comment, crossing my arms over my chest like they will somehow put a protective barrier between us. "How did you find me?"

He shrugs. "A facial recognition search gave me a lead—a picture of you in the background of a girl's social media post with a location tag. She made it easy for me." Xander's dark laugh bathes me in needles that pierce into my skin.

Shit.

Why didn't I think about Nicole? She's always taking pictures, or having Jeremy or me take them of her, and is obsessed with her image online. It never crossed my mind that I might be in the background of one of them. How negligent of me.

"So, you just decided to apply for a job here, as a security guard?"

A corner of his mouth tilts upward, making my stomach roll

violently. "It was easy. I guess I'm already up for a promotion," he adds. "They want to meet with me next week to discuss a new offer. But we'll be long gone before then. We'll be home."

"I am home." That effortless admission tumbling from my mouth hits my chest hard, nearly knocking the breath from my chest.

*Home.*

Xander ignores me, "I learned my lesson last time at that motel when I woke and you were gone. I was too impulsive. What better way to gather a plan than to watch you? To get a feel for the life you've settled into here." His gaze falls to the black-bodied handgun still trapped under his hand. "But like I said, you've been missing. And then, while I was on shift, doing my rounds and walking around the park, I saw you in the distance. With him," he utters through gritted teeth. His jaw flexes under the fluorescent lights. "So here I am again, having to be fucking impulsive before you vanish again. Luckily, he left you alone, and here we are." He scrubs a hand over his jaw. "You don't look at me the same way you look at him."

I nod. "I've moved on, and now I need you to."

"No," he drawls. "You've just forgotten what we had. Remember the first day we met at that blood drive?"

The mention of that memory has dread poisoning my gut.

When I don't answer, he does. "You were as obsessed with me as I was with you. Then you bled on my cock and have been mine ever since. Mine!"

I blow out a disbelieving laugh through the emotion clogging my throat. "It didn't stop there, Xander! You cut me open. You've given my body scars that will never fully heal. You've made me bleed over and over again because you have a blood fetish and like watching me break. I hated every minute of it, and I'm not going to let you hurt me anymore!"

His fingers drum on the table, his narrowed eyes a solid

void piercing into mine. "Don't give me that shit. The pain made you wet. You shattered on my dick. Every. Single. Time."

Yeah, so that it would be over.

Because you forced it out of my body like my pleasure was yours to take.

Tears streak down my fevered cheeks. I lick my salty lips, my voice quivering. "You need to leave. I'm not yours anymore. I never was."

Immediately, I know it's the wrong thing to say out loud as his fingers flex and he lifts the gun. Using the barrel, he motions the handgun toward the door carelessly. "Let's go."

"Please. Just let me go, Xander—" Tears fall from my eyes.

"No. I don't think I can do that, Kate. I win. I found you." He marches around toward my side, gripping my shoulder painfully to haul me to my feet. Pushing me, he shoves me around the table toward the door. "I'm not letting you go this time."

# FORTY | KATE

"**W**alk," Alexander shouts.

My eyes slam shut, tears falling from my lashes as I turn toward the exit. Xander digs the barrel into the middle of my spine, as if he's walking me to my execution. He pretty much is when he leads me down the long, bleak hallway.

The silence is overtaken by my thundering heartbeat, pulsating in my ears and masking my tattered and uneven breaths.

Shakily, I open the door. Not even the rush of the end-of-summer air blowing through the central area of the park can soothe me.

I frantically peer around, my heart squeezing through my throat, hoping someone will see me. Save me. But if he's in this uniform, it means he has authority and is an employee on the night shift, and I'm not sure how many they have on staff tonight. Usually, it's two or three; however, he said he was the one making the rounds. To anyone else on shift watching the security footage, it would look like he caught me doing something and is escorting me out of the park. I feel his chest so close to my body that I'm sure the gun would be hidden between us unless someone is looking closely.

I'd say I'm surprised Xander went through all the trouble to secure a job here, but I'm not. It's another challenge that adds to his high.

His obsession.

I could scream. Run.

Then I remember the cold tip of the barrel digging into my back, a constant reminder that he's in control and I'm not.

"Xander, you need to let me go." I slow my pace leisurely, hoping the extra seconds will buy me some time. "There are people here who you shouldn't underestimate."

"Shut the fuck up, Kate. Your excuses won't change this. I'm putting an end to this game. You won't be able to run from me anymore, sweetheart."

That nickname is a bucket of ice water over my head, making me tremble as I hook onto something he said. "What do you mean I won't be able to run anymore?"

His maniacal tone grinds through my ears. "Before I got that lead that gave me your whereabouts, I had time to plan our future. There's a nice, renovated basement in the bottom of the house I bought with your name on it." Nausea slams through me. "A place where you'll be safe."

*Safe.*

I know safe. This isn't it. And I would give everything for Preston to find me.

The thought of him has the straps on my thigh burning into my flesh like a reminder.

My blade.

My breath hitches.

I can't rely on someone else to save me.

That's what Preston's been teaching me, though I know if he were here, Xander's heart would already be a smattering behind his ribs from a bullet.

Xander continues his unhinged rambling. "It's a place where you can't escape. A place where I can play with you all I want, and nobody will hear your screams. Fuck!" I jump at the belted curse. "I love it when you scream for me. We'll be so happy there, Kate."

Needing to strip him of some of his control, I pause, hearing him growl in protest.

The words are bitter on my tongue, but I make them sound sweet. Innocent. "That sounds nice." Inhaling deeply, I turn to face him, my heart hammering wildly, trying to ignore the gun now aimed directly at my breastplate.

His eyes thin into slits, his head slanting hesitantly.

I nod, cautiously reaching for the uniform button-down hugging his chest. Touching him makes me want to cut off my hands. "You're right, I just forgot. Now you're here, and I need you to remind me why we were so good."

"Yeah?" He watches me inquisitively. The way his dark glare falls on my mouth makes me cringe, turning my blood sour. I'm damn near close to breaking down completely, but my determination to distract him straightens my spine.

Slowly, deliberately, I weave an arm around his neck, pulling my body closer to his while my other hand slowly snakes down to my skirt. It's like the universe was telling me to order a dress with a slit on the opposite side of where my knife is strapped to my leg so he wouldn't be able to see it.

"I've missed you," I lie with a whisper, letting my fingers dance across the hilt of my blade while my other hand glides across his neck.

I nearly give away my genuine fear of him when total nightfall envelopes us. All of Lachlan Park goes dark, but the panic that's flowing through my veins is white. Hot. Burning.

His forehead falls against mine, and I choke back my emotions, wanting to spill all over him. Tears drip down my chin and onto my chest as I slowly start to raise my elbow. "I'm sorry, Xander."

His alcohol-laced breath drifts across my face. "For running?"

"No," my voice shakes. His head lifts from being braced against mine, regarding me skeptically. "For this." My hand whips forward.

His choked gasp slices between us. He stumbles backward, his gaze locking on the scarlet liquid blooming in the side of his stomach, the dark gray shirt soaking into black before my eyes. Xander grits his teeth as a horrific roar tears through the quiet, slicing straight into my bones.

I don't waste another second, spinning with my blade, my legs carry me to the closest dark structure for cover. Gunshots hectically whip through the air, whizzing past me as Xander aims in my direction—his eyes failing to adjust to the new darkness that blankets the park.

I can barely see, but I don't stop.

My panic is so intoxicating that the agonizing, blistering pain in my leg starts splitting through the haze. I cry in pain, climbing onto the dark carousel, hoping someone will hear the shots and come running if the stab wound doesn't drop Xander to his knees first.

Sobs drift from my lips as I limp further onto the platform, ducking under one of the horses. I may be blanketed in the darkness now, but the stain soaking into my dress is somehow darker. With unsteady fingers, I part the slit in my dress open. A rogue bullet tore through the side of my thigh—streaks of crimson drenching my garters. The blood must have glided down my leg and calf while I was running, soaking into the straps of my heels and pooling below my foot to leave a sticky wet warmth.

My name is a curse. "Kate!"

I slap a hand over my mouth, attempting to keep my cries

from alerting him to where I am. Tears fall heavily now, wetting my fingers before an onslaught of rainbow lights has my eyes squinting. The repetitive carousel tune fills my ears over the roar of my heartbeat. The platform is spinning, the motion combining with the pain and fear, causing acid to swirl vehemently in my stomach.

*No. No. No!*

His voice is closer now. Lethal. "How do you think it made me feel to watch you shove your tongue down another man's throat, Kate?"

I try to train my ears, but I can't hear his footsteps on the metal platform over the music.

His growl penetrates the air. "That you let him taste what's *mine!*"

I'm quivering so badly, worried he'll sense the vibrations and find his way to me like a spider knows its prey is near.

"Did you let him touch you? Fuck you? Fall in love with you?"

The bombardment of questions has my heart shattering, thinking of leaving Preston, whether it's by Xander dragging me out by my hair or my heartbeat ceasing in the very park that ripped his family from him. It's a shame it took me this long, but there is too much I need to fight for now.

The life I'd never thought I'd have.

My peace.

*Preston's peace.*

"I know what it feels like to kill a man now," he adds when I don't speak. A weep escapes through my tightened fingers, but I keep both hands clutched to my mouth. "It gives me the same high I get when you're squirming beneath me, pretending you don't like it when I make you bleed for me. Well, now I'm bleeding for you," he shouts through clenched teeth, sounding like a horror movie coming to life. "Is that what you wanted?"

Another gunshot reverberates in the air, the proximity

making me jump and slam my head against the underside of the metal horse I'm crouched under. In an instant, my blade, my security, falls from my fingers as black and white dots pepper my vision.

The bile in my stomach crawls up my throat, my heartbeat now thrashing against my skull, buzzing in my ears. He's a blur in my vision, but his uniform is unmistakable.

Xander's fingers wrap around my ankles, forcefully dragging me out from my hiding place. I fall to my back on the floor, my head bouncing off the metal plate below me with every tug. The endless void is trying to pull me under.

Xander swings a leg over my body, straddling my thighs. He tightens his knees around my legs to try and keep me still, the searing pain in my thigh shooting through my muscles. I surely have a concussion now, combined with being shot, but I'm not giving in to him.

I won't make it easy for him.

That Kate is long gone.

The rainbow lights reflect off the body of the gun in his hand. "You know the only solution for this, don't you?"

I scream, my hands pounding at his chest, his stomach, my brain forcing my exhausted, hysterical physique to relinquish any energy I have left, trying to keep myself alive. I try to use a variety of self-defense moves Preston taught me in case I ever found myself with a heavy mass on top of me. My legs kick to try and gain any purchase, but my body is surrendering to the pain, to the throbbing in my head.

I force another scream from my lungs before a bloodied fist whips out, clenching my throat to rob the air from my lungs. "God, we would've had so much more fun if you had always put up a fight like this."

My arms slap at his forearms as he draws painful whimpers up my throat as he clutches harder. My vision continues to blur. I fight for breath, but it's no use.

"If I can't have you, Kate, nobody's going to. You understand that, don't you? Such a shame to waste a pretty thing like you, but you're giving me no choice, sweetheart." His hard, bulky body folds over mine to keep me from smashing his sternum with my fists.

Tears pour from my eyes, my lungs an inferno raging for the oxygen he's denying me of. His nails dig into my skin, my hands flailing to the side, frantically searching on the floor for the thing that's marked me permanently forever.

Now, it's the only thing that can save me.

Our lives are on the line.

It's him or me.

The brief flash of a cool object brushing my thumb has my fingers dancing with the edge of the hilt.

I choose mine.

Something animalistic floods through my veins and chases back the panic as I grip onto the handle and slice the blade through the air without remorse. Hot spray peppers my face, and onto my lips, at the same time, a gunshot obliterates my ears.

# FORTY-ONE | PRESTON

Another gunshot rings, the shock through the air shaking the concrete, making my pace quicken as dark park buildings pass me by in a blur of gray and black.

The tech and security room, located beneath the park, is situated at the opposite end of the park. When we finally located Kate and Lex on the monitors, they were in the center of the walkway between the maze ride and the carousel.

Then the park was shrouded in darkness.

I was running to her before the cameras switched to night vision, which instantly happens when all the lights are shut off. Locating the nearest secret exit, I flew up the stairs as the first gunshot rang out through the park, followed by four more that had my knees damn near gravitating to the ground.

I didn't let them.

I couldn't trust myself to navigate the maze of tunnels when my heart was somehow sucked into my head. Her name has been a constant, roaring pulse against my skull, making me wonder if I'm losing her.

If I've already lost her.

I urged myself through the crippling panic and fear, hoping that my other men, positioned around the park's perimeters, would reach her first.

I'll lay my life down at Lex's feet with no hesitation if it saves her soul. Every fiber of my being wants to save her, but that's of no importance.

All that matters is that *someone* gets to her.

Anyone.

Briny sea air floods my lungs like poison, its vigorous fingers piercing through my ribs and chest like it's reaching out for any sign that Kate's still alive.

The soft hum of music from the carousel glides through the pounding of blood in my ringing ears. I pump my legs faster, my suit clinging to my sweaty frame. Rainbow lights start to spill across the concrete, my eyes drawn to a figure in the distance, sprinting toward me. For a brief second, through the panic and blurry vision, it feels like I'm somehow peering through a mirror, watching myself run to her.

But it's not me.

And I'm too far to recognize who it is, but the uniform tells me it's one of my men.

The figure stops in the center of the walkway, their arms lifting to raise the gun. They hesitate momentarily, but their aim is steady.

Fuck, why are they hesitating?

The blast cracks through the air. The shot wasn't aimed at me, but for some reason, it feels like it is.

Because Kate is a part of me now in ways I'll never comprehend, and I know damn well that shot was aimed at her, but meant for the man trying to steal what's mine.

Eerie silence consumes the park, but it can't drown out the cacophony of sounds as my body threatens to break.

"Kate," I bellow.

The face comes into focus now. Vincent doesn't waste a

second to pay me any mind as he takes off running toward the twirling carousel. He must have had to wait to get a shot. I didn't think I was capable of running any faster, but I prove myself wrong.

For an older man, Vincent launches himself onto the rotating platform with the fucking agility of a ninja. I'm right behind him. The metallic stench of the bloodbath is overpowering now. The colorful lights are damn near blinding me as I follow him, frantically weaving through the benches and animals.

My world shakes when my eyes land on the bloody pile of entangled limbs on the floor. But it's the squirming of the body underneath in a pool of pink fabric tainted with scarlet that has Vincent and me lunging for the mass of carnage on top of Kate. Vincent manages to get Alexander rolled over onto the ground, his eyes now a void while his blood continues to pool below him.

A dead look I should be savoring.

But my focus is entirely transfixed on the frantic green ones, rimmed with red, darting around the space. They have me sinking to my knees. It takes a moment, but Kate releases a sob that should have rage injecting into my veins, yet it's a sign of life that has my fingertips gently reaching for her.

One stroke of my thumb against her reddened cheeks, flushed from crying, has the crimson splatter streaking across her face. I pray to God it isn't hers.

Her eyes magnetize to mine, the recognition appearing through the shock. My name is a breath. "Preston?"

Kate scrambles, her arms weaving around my neck as I timidly pull her flush against my large frame and rest against the center of the ride—the reflective wall at my back.

"I'm right here, baby," I croon, cupping her sweaty face with my hand.

Vincent's commanding tone adds to the strain in my

muscles, his voice ordering someone on the phone to get here immediately. It must be Imogen on the other end.

A rapid breath escapes her lungs in a whoosh, my gaze dropping to the pool of dark blood soaking her dress near her abdomen. Dropping my hand from her face, I scan her body desperately with frantic fingers.

Kate shakes her head, her voice hoarse from the purple and pink bruises already painting her neck. "That blood isn't mine," she tries to assure me.

My voice struggles to emerge through the fear clogging my throat. "Are you sure?" I rush out, still touching her as she rests against my chest while I search for proof.

The crimson trailing down her calf in stripes has me opening the slit in her dress. In the leg opposite her sheath, the torn muscle in her thigh spills fresh, bright-red blood.

Acid sears my throat. "Shit," I hiss. My shaky hands hover above the wound. She's caked in blood from head to toe.

Hers.

His.

I've seen every type of wound imaginable, and just like seeing those hearts in that box, I want to release everything in my stomach.

Tears fall from her bottom lashes. Besides the blood, her mascara is streaked all over her overly pigmented cheeks.

"Baby, I need you to tell me everywhere he hurt you." I swallow, tears burning the corners of my eyes.

Her arms drop from my neck, one of her palms resting over my thundering, rapid heartbeat, as if it will bring her some comfort. "Just my neck and my leg."

"I need you to be okay," I mumble, my sweaty forehead falling against hers.

She lifts her hand, her soft touch stroking warmth over my skin as she says the exact words I said to her earlier tonight. Her voice is raspy and broken from him choking her. "I will be. I've got you now."

Vincent hastily steps toward us. "Imogen will be here in five. Hang in there, Kate."

Her head lifts from mine, those watery eyes landing on Vincent in astonishment.

I give him a curt nod, meaning every word. "Thank you. I owe you one." If it wasn't for him, Kate might be dead.

He places his phone into his pocket, scrubbing a hand over his jaw. "I got a shot off at the same moment I watched her slit his throat." My brows furrow, following his eyes as they gravitate to the motionless body near us. The gnarly gash across his neck is dripping dark blood, her knife lying off to the side, coated in a thick sheen of crimson. "She might not have needed me. We'll never know if it was that or the bullet that killed him first." His gaze finds Kate, and his mouth lifts into a grin. I don't see it often, but when I do, it means he's proud. "You've got a fighter there. Should've known you'd be nosy enough to find your way into the tunnels."

She lets out a breathy chuckle, the sound quickly shifting into a groan of pain. Her head lolls against my chest. "I should've known that you weren't just a cleaning man."

He smirks, shoving his hands into his pockets. "I'll go wait for Imogen and call our team to come get this cleaned up." Then, he leaves us.

My heart still won't slow. Not until I know she's going to be okay. It feels like the weight of my entire life is sitting heavily on my chest, but then I realize, it is.

Gently, I press my thumb into her chin, lifting those beautiful, glassy eyes to mine. "I should've said something to you earlier, but I was too afraid to. But nothing scares me more than seeing you like this, so I need to tell you now."

"Preston, I'm going to be fine—"

"I love you." She inhales a sharp breath at my words, swallowing. "I'm so helplessly, fucking in love with you, Kate. I have been for a while."

Her eyes bounce between mine.

"I'm not saying this to convince you to stay, because that's still your decision, and I can't always promise you a safe life with me," my jaw flexes, "but I can't go another moment without saying it." Not when tonight could've ended differently. "I'll regret it for the rest of my life if I don't, and you never get the chance to hear how much you've changed my perspective on life since you've flooded my house with your warmth. Your kindness. Granted, I forced you to stay, but whether you decided to stay with me or leave," I shake my head. "I just need you to know that I love you," I whisper.

Another tear falls from her bottom lashes, and I catch it with my thumb.

She licks her tear-soaked lips. "I'm not going anywhere, Preston." Those irises hold mine as she says six words that obliterate the breath from my lungs. "I'm in love with you, too. Making sure you heard those words was what kept me fighting. I know you can't promise me a safe life, I don't expect you to. But I'd rather love you for as long as life lets me than never having had a piece of you at all."

I angle her face up to mine tenderly, trying to be cautious about her neck, but not caring about the crimson splattering her face. "Are you saying you'll stay?" I breathe across her lips.

There's zero hesitation as she draws her mouth to mine in answer, letting me claim her lips with a gentle intensity that has my future sparking before my eyes. Her soft tongue brushes against mine, her fingers drifting across the nape of my neck and threading into my hair, deepening the kiss.

I lay there with my legs spread out, the girl who's my world braced against me like she's my stability.

My anchor.

And I'm starting to think I'm hers.

# FORTY-TWO | KATE

I killed someone.
*He shot me.*
I murdered a man.
*He was going to kill me.*
He's dead now.
*But you aren't.*

Those thoughts and excuses have been running through my head on a constant loop. A record player stuck in a cycle.

Yet every time my gut starts to churn, carrying that twinge of guilt, I remind myself that if it hadn't been Xander's life that drained onto the floor of the carousel in a pool of blood, it would've been mine.

Some people don't deserve second chances.

I realize that now, as I rewrap the bandage on my thigh protecting the bullet wound that Imogen stitched the night I thought I was going to die. I shouldn't have missed the first time my blade penetrated his abdomen. But I was still holding onto that sliver of innocence I thought I had left until I realized he stole it from me a long time ago.

I'd say I'm not that same girl who let herself be a slave to a blade and a violent man, but I am. I'm just stronger now. I know how to fight for the life I deserve, even if it means taking someone else's who was hell-bent on stealing mine.

It's been two weeks since our date. The night when running for my life turned into fighting to keep the breath in my lungs and the heartbeat in my chest thriving. The night Preston held me to his chest, speaking beautiful words that made me feel more alive than the adrenaline and panic that was coursing through my veins.

Words he's said to me every day for the last two weeks without fail.

Preston's been here, taking care of me, as a part of myself scabs over to turn into another scar that I'll carry around.

Metaphorically and physically.

It's a reminder that sometimes the only thing that can save us is ourselves. A part of me wishes I could have learned that sooner. But I wouldn't have found myself here. Wouldn't have sought shelter in a cute, small town and found a job at an amusement park.

I've realized that Lachlan Harbor and I share something in common, because pretty things that seem harmless on the outside can be just as dangerous.

I killed someone.

But I've never felt more power and strength.

I murdered someone.

But I've never felt this kind of peace.

Xander's dead now.

And I can finally live.

Life around the estate feels somewhat normal now. Maybe that's because I've slayed my demon, but Preston has yet to conquer his. But I'll be by his side when he does.

He's still pulled into countless meetings, works most of the day, and has just returned from a short trip to New York with

Carter and Arden, where they delivered a shipment that arrived at the harbor last week.

He hated leaving me, but at the end of the day, he still has an empire to run. Knowing what happened in Virginia, I was a nervous wreck the entire time he was gone, especially since Imogen had put me on leave from the medical center.

Preston told me I don't need to work, but I like being a part of it and working with Imogen and the team. Keeps me busy. It has helped me find that other part of myself that I lost. Now I get to help protect the place I thought I'd never escape from. I found a home here—a family, though I'm craving to see my own. In time, once I've healed completely. They don't need to see me limping around and find out I was shot.

Preston surprised me last week by saying that he plans for us to head to Ireland next month to see the estate. But the surprise didn't stop there. He managed to get my dad's contact information and has arranged for my family to join us for a few weeks. I'm not sure what story we plan to tell them about where Preston gets his money, or how we'll address their questions about the guards with guns, but we'll work that out when we come to it. The important part is that he knew how important seeing them was to me after running for so long—that a part of me has a hole without them to fill it. Preston understands that more than anyone. I cried so hard in appreciation and gripped him so tightly that I thought I would suffocate him.

Just because I had to wait three weeks to see my family didn't mean I couldn't call. It was a phone call filled with tears and "Oh my God, you're okay!" When they asked about Xander, I went quiet. Heartbeats passed between us, somehow louder than words.

Still, I said, "He won't be a problem anymore."

Then my father's voice calmed the twinge of guilt and shame that was stirring, making me feel lighter. "All that matters is that you're safe now."

My family's voices have added a new sense of contentment, keeping me grateful to live life on my own terms now, rather than submit to it.

I can't say the same for Preston and Arden, though.

They're still in a war.

Playing a game they don't understand while they wait to finally make their move.

I found Arden in the garden one evening last week, sitting in the same spot we met. He apologized for using Preston against me, and I felt every word, seeing it in the glaze of his eyes. Then, something inside me cracked for the man, and I asked about her. Lynn, Preston's mother, was apparently as beautiful as her soul was, and Tayla, his daughter, took after her, whereas Preston is like him. He told me stories through the tears clogging his throat, telling me that they plan to end it— get their revenge—at Luciano's fiftieth birthday celebration in April.

As for the mole, they're still lurking out there somewhere. The last few shipments have been untouched. Haven't been missing product like the few others before.

One would think they've given up, but we know that's far from the truth. They're just in the shadows, waiting for orders.

Preston and Arden's revenge plan is set in stone to take down the leader of the Calco Cartel, but that's still seven months from now.

I tighten the straps of my garters, giving myself a once-over in the dim light of the en suite bathroom mirror. Moonlight is starting to peek through the window, spilling across the floor like silver paint. There may still be faint bruises on my neck and a healing bullet wound in my thigh, but I've never admired myself as much as I am now. The baby-pink strapless lingerie from our first date and that night at the park has been stripped of bloodstains thanks to Gretta.

I never got to show it to him since it was under my dress,

and it finally feels like the right time. I miss the heat of his touch. Don't get me wrong, he keeps me tucked into his side every night and peppers me with kisses when his tongue isn't in my mouth, but that's the extent of our physical contact. Last week, I kept trying to push it further since his hot, nearly naked body is pressed against mine every night, but he just growls my name. A warning because he knows I'm still physically healing. But I'm out of the weeds with my concussion and only have these damn stitches still in my leg.

But I can't take it anymore.

Is wearing this a form of manipulation? Probably.

Something tells me once he sees me in this, he'll lose his control. I'm his one weakness, and I'm learning not to take it for granted now.

I do one last check, taking in the way the stockings crawl up my long legs and how the silk-and-mesh body of the fabric hugs my curves. There's an ugly bandage around my thigh, but I don't care. Because I know he won't. He finds beauty in my scars, just as I see the beauty in his.

Running my fingers through my long, curled hair, I blow out a breath and exit the bathroom. The soft light of the bedside lamp cascades across the hard planes of his tattooed chest, which my fingertips yearn to trace and memorize more.

Every line. Every vein. Every stroke of ink.

Preston's bourbon eyes lift from the laptop on his lap, his eyes expanding when they land on me stalking toward him. I ignore the slight limp in my leg as a blush creeps up his chest and floods into his cheeks. He lifts a hand to his bearded jaw, taking me in and taking his time like he always does.

"Fuck," he exhales, the one word covering me from head to toe in goosebumps. "You're really testing my control here, darling."

My tone is sweet. "Then let it go." I toss my hair over my shoulder, stopping in front of the bed.

His hand drifts further up his face as he rubs his eyes. When he drops his arm, I see the cracked web in his resolve. He's hanging on by a thread, and I want him to shatter. "I don't want to hurt you. Your leg is still healing."

My fingertips drift over my collarbones and down my stomach, tauntingly. "I don't care. I want you. I want to feel everything." I place a knee on the bed, crawling to him slowly. "That's why I'm wearing the same lingerie that was under my dress that got ruined the night of our date."

He curses under his breath, placing the laptop on the bedside table, hungrily observing the way I carefully crawl on top of him. Luckily, he's propped on top of the comforter, so I have a view of how badly he wants me. His massive cock is straining against his boxers. A low thrum circulates in my belly, drifting to my clit as I settle on top of him.

"Goddamn, Kate. You're stunning, looking all ready for me."

I bite my lip, nodding as my hands fondle my breasts in the strapless top that gives them enough lift to drive him mad. "Are you going to break for me now and fuck me the way I want you to?"

"Holy fuck. That dirty mouth is begging for my cock, too, isn't it?"

Another nod. "*Mhmm.*"

He sits up, wrapping his arms around me to tenderly pull my center flush against his erection and his warm, hard chest. There's way too much fabric between us as his lips slam against mine. His tongue demands entrance, and I part them for him to let his flavor invade my senses and drive me wild.

My pulse is hammering as he gently picks me up, flipping me onto my back so he's on top. Keeping my eyes on him, I slowly part my legs, letting him see the mess I'm already making of my lace panties.

His fingers press into my center, rubbing circles on my clit. I whimper, pleasure wracking through me. Our gazes hold firm, his fingers pulling me closer to an edge I want to fall over with him.

His husky voice floods through my ears, making me wetter. "Fucking hell, you are soaked for me. We're about to see just how much this tight cunt missed me."

My heart drops into my stomach, a bomb making the wings take flight when he shoves my panties to the side, making me shiver. Our desperation for each other is evident when he doesn't waste time taking my lingerie off. He reaches into his boxers, pulling out his rock-hard cock. Preparing himself, he pumps it from base to tip a few times. His thumb swipes over the bead of precum on his tip before he aligns himself with my entrance. Catching me off guard, he takes that thumb, pressing it between my lips at the exact moment he slips every inch of himself inside of me like it's where he belongs.

He does.

He was meant to consume me.

I moan around his finger and swirl my tongue around, clenching around his cock when he tosses his head back and groans, rocking into me. He removes his finger from my mouth to push down the fabric containing my breasts and releases them. His expert fingers twist my nipples, releasing tingling flurries that dance across my skin and pool in my belly as my pleasure builds. My pussy tightens around him.

"You're such a greedy little whore for my cock, darling."

"Oh, Preston," I breathe.

"When I saw those soaked panties, I knew you'd make a mess on my cock."

"You feel like—"

His thumb finds my clit, making me cry out. "Like what, *mo ghrá*?"

Heat floods my neck. My chest. My cheeks and all the way down to where my pussy is being filled. "Like you were made for me," the admission is effortless.

Preston thrusts in and out, his focus falling to where we're connected. "*Shittt*," he hisses in an exhale. "I was. As you were for me."

My hands reach out, gliding along his abdomen as his hips slam into me. I'm breathless as I ask, "Preston?"

"*Hmm?*"

"What does *mo ghrá mean?*"

"It means, *my love*, baby."

Oh shit. My breath is shallower now, the oxygen feeling weak as I draw in air. My orgasm is swirling, his words carrying me closer to euphoria. Stars are starting to dance in my vision. Little white lights vibrating, making me shake below him from the pleasure.

Draping his massive body over mine like a security blanket, his clammy skin plasters to mine. His thrusts are controlled, his dick now going so deep that he's hitting that sensitive spot over and over again.

My question is a whimper. "But you said that to me when you caught me in the garden?"

His mouth falls to my shoulder, his teeth gently nipping at the skin there as he pounds into me. He soothes it with his tongue, his words lathering over my skin. "I know. I've loved you since you stabbed me with your knife. You told me to ruin you, but that was the moment you completely ruined me." A desperate sound escapes my throat. His lips lift against my skin. "Fuck, your pussy is squeezing me so tight. You like hearing me admit that, baby?"

"Preston, I'm going to come." My arms knit over the hard planes of muscle in his back.

"Come on my cock, *mo ghrá*. Let go for me so I can fill this tight cunt and make a mess out of you like you've made of me."

The stars burst. Bright white light floods behind my eyelids as I orgasm at the same time he does. I feel like I'm floating.

Warmth coats my walls, the sensation of him filling me, making me want never to come down from the heavens.

But I always will, because here is where he is, and I was almost torn from Preston once.

I have blood on my hands now, too.

And I'd cover them again if it means I can always come home.

# FORTY-THREE | PRESTON

Lounging back against the couch, I soak in the warmth from the tabletop fire pit in front of me and the beautiful woman tucked into my side with her hand draped on my chest. Night blankets us, the reminder making me want to take Kate to bed and make love to her again like I have tried to every night since she walked out of my bathroom in that lingerie that nearly gave me a heart attack.

Kate tugs at my t-shirt with her fingers, her head resting against my shoulder as she watches the flames dance into the air. Her soft, even breaths soothe me, along with the nip in the air that brushes across the patio. The kind of chill in the air that hints at the approaching season of fall.

All I want is more time with Kate. Although the park may be slowing now that school has started again and summer vacation is over, we are still head-fucking-deep in this war with the Calco Cartel that I'm determined to end.

Life may feel a little more peaceful now with Kate by my side, but I won't let my guard down until my blade plunges into Luciano's heart and both carotid arteries in his neck. I've never been into throat slitting; it's too quick, but my darling inspired me.

I twirl the scotch in my glass, taking a sip. The spiced flavors bloom on my tongue and slip down my throat. My father lounges in one of the outdoor patio furniture chairs across from me, Carter in the matching one, while Kate and I are on the loveseat. I'm grateful that we've found small moments like this to exist together now that Kate and my father are on speaking terms.

I've started noticing he has a soft spot for her. I think it's especially therapeutic for him when he can talk to her about my mother and Tayla. When he can speak about their memories in the way they deserve, since we've bottled it up for so long. I'm grateful Kate can give him something I can't. It's still too hard to mention them sometimes, but I'm getting better.

She sometimes sits with him in the garden, knowing he feels closer to my mom there, since it was her favorite place on the estate.

Besides dealing with our revenge plan to destroy Luciano, my dad seems lighter, and I can't help feeling that part of it is because I am.

Maybe it's because he's seeing me carry on with a luxury in life he never thought I'd experience after seeing love ripped away from him.

It makes me want to fight harder to keep her.

Protect her.

To not take Kate for granted.

If I can somehow find love, why can't he?

I know he said finding one soulmate is rare enough, but I have this feeling in my gut that it doesn't end there for him. It can't. Our empire may be brutal, but he is not. Arden deserves more. He may have given up on himself, but I'll hold on to enough hope for the both of us.

I peek down at Kate, reminding myself she's there, and she smiles up at me with those beautiful, big green eyes. Her fingers drift down my abdomen suggestively, but slowly enough that nobody else will notice.

Which was shit thinking on my part when Carter lifts his tumbler to his lips, muttering, "You guys are disgusting."

My father hides his dark laugh with the rim of his glass.

"Oh, fuck off." I can't help my evil grin. "You're just jealous."

Something that feels like a warning flash behind his eyes when they slice to mine.

Carter's another one I have hope for.

I don't think he's fucked anyone for six years. Not that I expect him to tell me if he did, but he's been extra moody lately, and his lack of dick wetting might be why. Not that I have room to judge, since Kate was the first woman I slept with since Mom and Tayla died.

Now that I think about it, he has been temperamental for the last few months, since I brought Kate to the estate.

Deciding not to rub my happiness in his face, I reach out and set my tumbler on the fire table, letting Kate sink into the couch beside me.

"How was the wedding?" I ask him.

"Hmm?" He lowers his glass from his lips.

"Your sister's wedding."

"Oh." He shakes his head, as if clearing the fog that's been looming over him. I wonder how many glasses of liquor he's had. His fingers pulse into his glass. "It was good. Glad to be back at work, though. My family was asking too many questions about my tech job."

I know he hates that part—lying to them after he's been trying to gain back their trust after they cut ties when he was an addict. But he's trying. He made up a story about working at a tech company here in Maine, so they don't know that he's a right-hand man for the Irish mafia.

My father sits forward, bracing his elbows on his knees with an inquisitive look. "Can we see some pictures?"

Carter drags his hand over his black hair and exhales, sinking back into the chair. "I don't have any. Didn't want to have any physical ties to put them in danger."

I nod at him curiously. I can understand that, but there's something potent about that comment that's stinging my gut. Not the words, the look in his eye. His mannerisms.

"You want to know what's crazy?" Kate speaks up beside me, drawing my attention. "That morning you found me at the end of the dock; I thought it was going to be Carter who caught me when I saw him getting off the boat with that duffel bag."

That stops me short, and I swear I feel the air shift in the way Carter's muscles tense.

"Is that so?" I deadpan.

Kate's brows furrow at the same time my hand reaches for the Glock at my hip. With quick precision, I have it aimed.

"Oh my God, Preston. What are you doing?" Kate tosses her hands up like I'm pointing the gun at her.

But it's not. It's on my best friend.

"What does it look like?" My tone is bitter. Deadly. "I found our fucking mole."

Kate gasps at the same time my father's eyes shoot to me. His voice is worried. "I know this feeling, son. You won't be able to take it back if you're wrong."

Arden stands hesitantly, but I don't move. "Just put the gun down," my father encourages.

My tone is sharp. "I'm not wrong. Am I, Carter?"

Carter's eyes are firm on mine as he slowly moves to stand, my barrel locked between those wrinkles between his eyes. My heart thunders, but I contain the shake that wants to take over my limbs.

Carter swallows. "No." Arden curses under his breath before the first excuse comes. "But it's not for what you think."

"So, you aren't a fucking traitor working for the bastard who took everything from us? Who took *them* from us?" I shout. "All this fucking time it was you stealing those shipments. That's why the one when you went to Chicago was accounted for." If he were even in fucking Chicago, the lying cunt.

Arden's hand drifts to his Glock now, but he doesn't pull it. My father snarls. "Is this true, Carter?"

It doesn't faze him. His hands slowly raise in front of him. "Preston, I need you and Arden to listen to what I'm going to tell you."

"This is bullshit! You can't talk yourself out of this. You dug your fucking grave, and I'm going to be the one to bury you in it!" I click the safety off, so Carter hears it. I'm not fucking around. It's loaded, and I'm ready to put a hole in his goddamn skull. "We fucking trusted you! You were the reason we lost our territory and men in Virginia. Your brothers!" His family.

He shakes his head. "I wasn't sure at first when I saw it, but I had to be sure."

"Stop fucking mumbling and speak," I shout, re-aiming the gun so he knows I have zero patience.

"Fuck," he mutters, inhaling a deep breath. "Did you ever thoroughly look at that anonymously sent invitation that came in the mail?"

My father is the one who speaks in a dark tone. "For Luciano's fiftieth?"

Carter's unhurried nod has chills piercing my spine. "There was something off about it. And then I looked closer at the inconsistency in the letters."

My father reaches into his suit pants pocket hurriedly and takes out his phone, his fingers flying across the screen. My eyes dart between his and Carter, blood whirring in my ears. When my dad pulls up a picture of the invitation that we have in our digital files, he looks back up at Carter frantically.

"You wouldn't have survived it if I were wrong." The tremble in Carter's voice has my hair standing to attention. "I didn't say anything because I had to be sure. I had to do *everything* to be sure. Needed to get in and prove it with my own two eyes."

My father approaches me, holding the phone out. Our eyes fall to the screen displaying the image of the invitation, and I zoom in, scanning the letters with a newfound focus.

Then I see it—the discrepancies in the capital letters.

**Time to celebrate. A *new era is beginning. You must show this invite at the gate to join us for Luciano's 50<sup>th</sup> birthday party on April 12<sup>th</sup> @ 7 p.m.***

"We were never supposed to get this invitation, Preston. It's barely noticeable, but she was hoping we'd find the clue," Carter treads carefully.

My heart fucking stops when I realize they make a word.

A name.

My gaze snaps to Arden.

Tears form in the corner of my father's eyes. The hopefulness lingering there is blinding.

"That's why I did what I did." Carter's voice is rough. "Why I'm getting him to trust me."

"Are you sure? That's my baby girl, Carter. It's been five years. We saw the pictures." Arden's voice breaks.

Carter nods, his voice a whisper. "I've seen her."

"Who?" Kate breathes cautiously from behind me, as if she's worried she'll scare me.

I am scared. But for a completely different reason.

I turn to look at her, the reality settling in like a bullet to my chest. It's a breath out of my lungs. "Tayla's alive."

Kate gasps. Her hand reaches for mine, her warmth a

reminder of why finding redemption is worth the wait sometimes.

Why I should keep fighting.

Because sometimes, when it feels like something is ending, it's because something new is beginning.


THE END

# ACKNOWLEDGMENTS

It finally happened! I published a book, and it's out in the world, finding its place. First and foremost, I need to thank my husband for inspiring the *Lachlan Park Trilogy*. Not only do you listen to my crazy book ideas, but you've pushed me to chase my dream of becoming an author. I knit a piece of you into every one of my MMCs.

To my readers, your eagerness to have my stories in your hands is uplifting and inspires me to push the boundaries with my plots. You've helped me find new readers, and even though this one ended on a MASSIVE cliffhanger, I hope you loved Kate and Preston's story and are as immersed in this world as I am.

To my agent, Angie, thank you for letting me veer off course and publish this book as my debut. Your excitement for my ideas and your dedication to your craft inspire me. Forever grateful for everything you do to give my books their best chance.

To my editor, proofreader, and beta readers, Melissa and Clair, you helped me refine this story. Because of you, I feel completely confident sending this book out into the world.

I could thank so many people, but last (and by far not least) has to be my family. I know I told you that you aren't allowed to read my books, but you support me anyway and never fail to ask how my author journey is going. You're always there, and I know how incredibly lucky I am.

# ABOUT THE AUTHOR

Cassidy Cole is known for her dark and fiery romance novels. From a young age, she was fascinated by the vivid dreams and unconventional thoughts that played out in her mind. Now, she brings them to life, weaving these ideas into her books.

Cassidy embraces the seclusion of her writing space, where coffee keeps her grounded by day, and wine or beer fuels the night. She lives with her husband and two dogs, finding peace in the shadows where her stories take shape.

Connect with her on her social media or her newsletter (The CassCult) for the latest updates on books, teasers, events, and more.

Instagram & TikTok: @cassidycoleauthor
Website: www.cassidycoleauthor.com